Fireworks

Jill Wellington

and

Edna Mae Holm

Stargate Press, Inc., Michigan

This book is lovingly dedicated to our husbands

Mark & Bob

For their endless support.

And much love and thanks to

Fred, Daisy, Carlos & the gang.

For further information, contact the authors at:

Stargate Press
P.O. Box 6535
Saginaw, MI 48603
Jill@stargatepress.com
Edna@stargatepress.com

Book design by:
The Floating Gallery
331 West 57th Street, #465, New York, NY 10019
877-822-2500   www.thefloatinggallery.com

PRINTED IN CANADA

Jill Wellington and Edna Mae Holm
Fireworks
1. Author 2. Title

Library of Congress Control Number 2002107682
ISBN 0-9721783-0-9

Acknowledgments

Our sincerest gratitude to the many friends who read our book and kept us on the right path throughout the writing of this novel. Love and appreciation to our editor Brian Smart who has incredible focus and vision. Many kudos to Jill's brother-in-law, Joe Schmidt, who masterminded the electrical details of the explosion scene. Special thanks to Sergeant Greg Price a former Detective with the Saginaw Police Department, whose expertise was invaluable with the police logistics in *Fireworks*. And, also to Dan Erdlejohn with Rozzi's Famous Fireworks in Cincinnati, Ohio who provided the accurate information that puts the sparkle in all fireworks.

FOREWORD

When I was growing up in the Midwest, I loved hearing the fascinating stories about the psychic lineage in my mother's family. Mom told how back in the depression years her Aunt Ruth read the cards and predicted the future. Of course, this was hush-hush back in the 1930's.

My grandmother, too, could foresee the future through vivid dreams. Grandma envisioned the deaths of both her brother and sister.

The family psychic gene seemed to fall to the females as my mother and sister inherited the amazing ability. I wanted so much to be like them, but never seemed to have any premonitions.

In my teen years, Mom brought home books written by Ruth Montgomery, a talented journalist who discovered her gift for automatic writing. The author would sit at her typewriter and spirit guides would supposedly dictate fascinating information from the spirit realm. I would devour these books and felt a powerful sense that I could do automatic writing, too. Yet Montgomery firmly warned about playing around with this medium. She frightened me out of trying.

After struggling through college with dyslexia, I finally found my niche in broadcast journalism. Through a series of amazing coincidences, I ended up as a news reporter at WNEM

TV-5 in Saginaw, Michigan. On the job, while my eyes mixed up words, my ears heard them clearly.

The moment I arrived at a news event, the story would start writing in my mind. I would actually *hear* the first line of the story dictated word for word. Eventually the entire story would pour into my brain in perfect order.

I was compelled to find the correct people to interview for my stories, and the best video to match the dictated text. Even more amazing, those people would be right there. I was certain that if I needed to interview a three-eyed pygmy goat, one would surely stroll by!

My co-workers dubbed it Wellington Luck. I thought I simply had the reporting knack. I totally trusted this *creativity* and it rarely let me down. Eventually I wrote a newspaper column. It, too, poured into my brain word for word, line by line. Mom wrote a weekly column for her local paper in Cincinnati, Ohio, and also swore it wrote itself.

Seventeen years into my journalism career, Mom completed her first novel, a sweeping historical epic. I recognized and envied her talent for fiction. After that, she felt a strong urge to write a mystery, and coaxed me into writing it with her. Though I couldn't imagine writing fiction, the plot line started gushing into both of our minds. The writing process was so easy and fun, I gave up my journalism career after eighteen years to write fiction.

Without full time reporting, I finally had more time on my hands. A former co-worker begged me to attend a meeting of her psychic/spiritual group. I dragged Mom along with me. Of course, I was fascinated, but knew I didn't have any ability myself. One group member conducted a meditation to meet our spirit guides. "Huh? What's that?" I thought. Yet, I was thoroughly intrigued.

Shockingly, during this meditation I heard the name Fred loud and clear. Then I felt an itching sensation on my neck. Mom heard Daisy. The group member told us we both have the gift of automatic writing and should begin journaling with Fred and Daisy every day.

Immediately I remembered the Ruth Montgomery books, and every night I would curl my fingers over the keyboard of my computer waiting for this Fred spirit to take over my hands and write something. To my great disappointment, it never happened.

One day I was trying to think of a gift to buy a friend who was moving. A candle? A book? Suddenly I heard these words loud and clear: "Write a letter." Instantly, the letter began to dictate in my mind word for word. At that moment I realized my truth and burst into tears. I was guided by the spirit world my entire life and never knew it! My news stories, that column, those endless lines of text were put into my mind by God and my spirit guides.

This discovery changed both our lives. Mom and I began to write questions for Fred and Daisy on the computer and would hear the answers just like those news scripts. We were overwhelmed with the information they provided and soon realized we must introduce a spirit guide into our second novel.

Always fascinated by pyrotechnics Mom wanted to write a story around the fireworks industry, where things blow up. We set aside our first mystery novel and the story of *Fireworks* poured out of our collective brains in mere months.

Though the mystery part came quickly, the spiritual messages came painfully slow. Mom and I were forced to learn them through first-hand experience. We were launched on an odyssey of amazing coincidences and synchronicities, a discovery process that we transferred to the main character in this book, Police Detective Webb Hannis.

Fireworks is more than a mystery. Mom and I truly hope it is the catalyst that opens your eyes to your innate spiritual gifts and ignites the fireworks in your life.

Jill Wellington

Fireworks

CHAPTER 1

"IT'S TIME you start noticing me," Samuel said as he strolled beside detective Webb Hannis. Samuel was hard to miss. His dark brown jacket, more than a size too large and rolled up at the cuffs, was certainly eccentric in the July heat. His sideways gait through the holiday crowd, one leg absentmindedly crossing over the other, also commanded attention. Unlike Hannis, Samuel didn't weave through the pillar-like obstacles of people. The crowd, necks craned to watch the fireworks exploding above the Detroit Riverfront, unconsciously shifted or stepped aside for him.

Yet Hannis, edgy and withdrawn, didn't even glance his way. The giant officer peered through the mass of people as if searching for something he didn't even realize was lost. What the hell am I doing here on my off day? he wondered. He hated crowds, yet a nagging urge led him to come.

Samuel knew why Webb was here, but he wasn't going to tell. The officer beside him, dressed in beige chinos and a yellow, ribbed, crew neck top, was searching for the addictive joy of the chase. Even the dazzling Lazare Fireworks company's

Fourth of July extravaganza that boomed and crackled above them failed to tantalize Hannis.

Webb was, after all, an addict. His years as a detective saw to that. While the crowd oohed and aahed over the artillery-like fireworks exploding overhead, the detective was left wanting. He craved a challenging crime to satisfy his addiction.

"Tonight you'll get your stress hormone hit, Bud," Samuel vowed with amusement. "It'll get your adrenaline pumping again."

Webb frowned and strode ahead. A veteran detective in Cincinnati for twenty-four of his forty-six years, Webb had recently transferred to the Detroit Police Department. It was an unusual move; senior detectives simply didn't sacrifice the intimate knowledge, resources, and snitches of their home turf to start over somewhere else.

Samuel grinned. Webb still thinks the Detroit Police Chief somehow suckered him into the move. The big guy has no idea that I was the true force behind it.

"There are no coincidences in life, kiddo." Samuel said the words aloud, knowing Webb would simply ignore him again.

Webb never realized he and Chief Gallister were supposed to meet as rookies at the Cincinnati Police Academy. In fact, Samuel carefully orchestrated the friendship. The greenhorns just seemed to hit it off immediately. After both joined the Cincinnati police force, they merged into an incredible team. They thrived on solving bizarre and intriguing murder cases, the more convoluted the better.

Fred Gallister was the charismatic leader of the duo. His people skills persuaded many a murderer to confess to the crime, and his logical mind was adept at analyzing the most minute details of an investigation.

But it was an unspoken understanding between them that Webb Hannis was the eerie force behind the pair's successes. He possessed the real gift of cop instincts. So precise were his gut feelings that it awed Gallister and irked many of the other senior detectives. Together, the pair amassed an incredible record; few of their cases left unsolved.

Eventually the team split up. Gallister, with his people skills and understanding of department politics, was offered the Police chief position in Detroit. Fred pleaded for Webb to join him, but the giant officer declined. He wanted to remain in the field, working homicide cases instead of sitting behind a desk. His kick was in the hunches, the hunt. Without it, he felt stymied.

Finally Fred convinced him to bail out and join the Detroit Force. Actually it was the new chief in Cincinnati that clinched Webb's decision. What an asshole. Damn guy blew into town and tried to tell *me* how to solve a murder. Nobody could leash Webb Hannis.

Gallister called him the very weekend he was contemplating his resignation. What luck, huh? Damn right he'd join Fred in Detroit, if Gallister understood Webb needed free reign. The chief hired him on the spot.

Ready for fresh excitement, Webb soon discovered a new can of squirmy worms. His fellow officers expected Gallister to promote from within the department. Who was this cocky bastard from Cincinnati?

He traded one set of problems for another. Now Webb bristled, suddenly angry. He focused his anger on the fireworks, the crowd stoking the negative emotion.

"Relax, Bud, we're here for fun. You're right where you're supposed to be," Samuel declared as he caught Webb glaring at the throng along the water's edge. As if to distract the detective, Samuel turned a perfect cartwheel on the soft grass.

A young child, his neck encircled with a glowing neon necklace, giggled. Samuel pulled the delighted young boy to his feet and danced with him. The child kicked his small legs in a frolicking jig before finally falling back onto the family blanket in a fit of laughter.

"You're having a good time tonight," the boy's mother teased as she caught him up into her arms.

Webb didn't notice the child's magical smile. He also missed the sky erupting in flashy red and gold above him, each explosion synchronized with music blaring from the loudspeakers. Instead, Webb's trained eyes spotted the occasional brown bag nestled among the picnic baskets. He shook his head and muttered, "Lots of boozing going on here."

Samuel was aware that a crowd this large might pull Webb's trigger. Hannis lived his job. It ended his first marriage. Too many hours spent tracking premonitions, following hunches. Webb's dogged impatience with a case would smolder, then combust into fury until finally it was better for both he and his wife that he went back to work. She finally accepted his compulsive nature, and released him from the marriage.

I'm surprised he let me drag him down here tonight, Samuel thought. He never likes fun things. Not enough action for him. Just a distraction from his real mission.

Off duty, Webb didn't need the gun buried in the waistband of his chinos. Yet, without the weapon, Samuel knew the detective felt naked.

Webb shook his head, a dark curl flopping over his damp forehead to match the curved mustache above his upper lip. Crow's feet around his eyes intensified as he focused on the bumper barge anchored on the river. Why did the barge bother him?

Perhaps it was his cop's instinct that caused him to interrupt his daily jog along the river yesterday. One glance at the men loading fireworks onto the docked barge triggered an alarm in his mind. His badge, always with him, got him onto the restricted barge, but his pestering questions to the Lazare Fireworks crew yielded nothing to explain the sensation of danger that plagued him. Then the newspaper and television crews, polished and perky, barged on the scene for background interviews, snapping photos and impeding the meticulous fireworks set up.

Webb knew the media was a double-edged tool. Sometimes they were useful, but most of the time they just got in the way.

At the moment he didn't know what he was looking for or why. He only wished he could grill everyone on the barge. The news crew's sideshow only fueled his frustration. Finally he left and completed his run, hunches left hanging.

Impatience always ignited a heated rage in Webb Hannis. Now, knowing there was a television crew out on the barge, caused his anger to flare again.

Samuel watched the detective's face, following his gaze across the water. His voice was almost a whisper. "You'll learn, Webb. I can help if you will only listen."

*   *   *

On the barge, television news reporter Max Anglim lolled in a canvas lawn chair. He chatted into a live microphone, narrating from notes on his pad. "The finale alone has ten thousand shells, including several twelve-inch bombs that cost seven hundred dollars apiece."

The camera, poised on the grandeur overhead, captured the glittering fireworks that feasted the eye and the thunder that drummed Max's muscular body. He shoved crisp shirtsleeves over brown arms that glistened like burnished mahogany in the summer humidity. Standing just five-foot-eight, Max, an African-American, exercised relentlessly to appear larger on TV. He was still peeved at the local newspaper — a rag in his opinion — because of the article describing him as stocky.

Reciting verbatim from his notes, Max announced, "The Lazares put on one hundred fireworks shows every Fourth of July, but they always save the best finale for their hometown, Detroit." Off-camera, he rolled his eyes. *How many Fourth of Julys have I said those exact words? I gotta get some new material.*

He slapped at a nagging mosquito and peeked at his watch. Almost eleven o'clock. *Hopefully the surprise segment that the Lazares had hyped for the past month would be something* unique. He had used up all of his adjectives to describe the colorful poufs.

As the show increased in intensity, gathering momentum toward the grand finale, the director back at the station switched to a second camera onshore among the crowd. The sky blazed with color, one shot after another followed by multiple booms.

Photographer Glen Gerard clicked on two glaring lights, Max's signal the camera would soon focus on him. He jumped up, shrugged into the summer jacket shed previously because of the heat, smoothed his shirt and tie, and checked his close-cropped black hair in the camera lens.

The photographer framed him with the launch panel over his left shoulder. "Pull down your coat around the collar," he shouted just before cueing the reporter.

Puffing out his chest, his shoulders high, Max spoke into the camera. "The French have been creating sensational fireworks since Napoleon, and Detroit's own Lazare family continues that tradition. The show's not over yet. You haven't seen the incredible new spectacle the Lazares have been bragging about for weeks. Tonight's debut is a first in all of fireworks history."

*   *   *

Onshore, Webb never heard Anglim's words. The sky blackened with a lull in the fireworks. A hush fell over the crowd as it waited. Webb kicked a stone into the grass.

It's time to get Hannis's attention, Samuel mused. He'll think it's an accident. I wonder when he'll learn there's no such thing? Samuel stood at full attention. Now I need your total concentration, Bud.

Samuel spotted a man hurrying through the crowd. He smiled. There he is. Right on schedule. With agility, Samuel leaped up behind the fellow and shoved him directly into Webb Hannis.

"Hey, watch it, Mack!" Webb automatically felt for his gun with one hand as he shoved the man back with the other. That guy's moving too fast, Webb thought. Wonder whose purse he nabbed.

A stocky man, dressed in baggy wrinkled pants and an oversized T-shirt, glared at the detective.

Something about him was familiar. Webb never forgot a face. He cleared his throat and stared at the fellow. "You're one of the Lazare brothers. I saw you on the barge yesterday."

The man's neck was so squatty his head appeared to sit right on his shoulders. He avoided eye contact, muttering something under his breath as he tried to scoot around Hannis.

"Not so fast," Webb said, grabbing the fellow's shoulder. "What's your hurry? I thought you ruled the show."

A distant boom of artillery sounded from the river barge. Lazare backed away and tilted his head toward the cosmos, pointing upward. "This is it...the best damn thing in the show."

Instinctively Webb's eyes riveted on the sky. There was a popping sound and then purple florescent jewels splattered like raindrops against the black velvet night. The heavens twinkled with rich shades of violet and magenta erupting in perfect harmony with the strains of Prince's *Purple Rain.*

With his eyes fixated on the transient masterpiece, Webb finally felt the addicting surge he craved. He stood mesmerized. Hypnotized. The colors filled him with exhilaration, grabbed his very soul. "Holy shit!"

He stood, transfixed. Time passed without conscious thought until he was jolted from his trance by a vivacious patriotic ballad. A collage of colors pummeled the sky. When he looked back down, Lazare had disappeared into the crowd.

Webb glanced at his watch. The finale was beginning, but he had no interest in watching it. Webb shook himself to attention and headed for the parking lot. "No way am I getting caught in the madhouse after this is over."

He wasn't the only one who wanted to get ahead of the traffic. Even with his behemoth six-foot-seven stride, the first wave stampeding to the parking lot swallowed him.

The heavens erupted in a continuous wave of explosions and light. The parking area was as chaotic as the electric sky; tempers flared as drivers jockeyed for the exits. Webb began directing traffic, feeling like he was caught in the madness of a war zone. A set of glaring headlights raced toward him, horn blasting. He dodged out of the way and watched the car roar toward the main street.

"Damn! What am I doing? I'm not on duty." His heart pounded, adrenaline racing through him at the close call. Fear flipped to anger in a heartbeat. He stormed to his car and hopped in, determined to escape the pandemonium. He wasn't alone.

He slapped the steering wheel. "Come on! Move it, people!"

A tiny gap appeared between two vans in the line beside him. Webb gunned the engine and swerved, forcing the nose of his car into the space. The driver of the rear van slammed on his brakes, honked, and slowly inched his vehicle forward until the bumper was almost pressing against Webb's car door.

In front of him a small grassy incline separated him from the main street. He was tempted to just drive over the lawn and get out of the mess, but Webb pictured the result. Like cattle, once his car stepped off the beaten path, others would stampede to the same escape.

The guy in the van laid on the horn and switched his headlights from low to high beam. Between the raucous blare and glaring lights, Hannis could barely think. He began rolling down his window, ready to tell the other driver to back off.

The driver stretched a balled fist out the window, the middle finger pointed upward.

"That's it!" Webb's temper ignited and he tromped on the gas pedal. His car surged forward, gaining speed as it climbed the slight embankment. It shot into the street, directly into the path of an oncoming Suburban.

* * *

On the shoreline behind him, the crowd went wild. The remnants of the finale spiraled in the night sky. They crackled and sizzled, slowly fading into darkness. The show was over.

Cheers reverberated off the calm river, adoration emanating toward the barges. Max Anglim closed his eyes and smiled, basking in the adulation as if it were directed at him. The final sparks hissed on the water as smoke settled on the barges.

Glen snapped his fingers for Max to open his eyes and face the camera.

Max breathed deeply and sighed.

"Prima donna," Glen muttered to himself.

Finally Max woke from his reverie and motioned for Glen to ready the camera. He watched the cameraman count down with his fingers. Through his beatific smile he began speaking.

"You just witnessed the most spectacular and expensive finale ever produced by the famous Lazare family." Max gazed toward the darkened sky. "The Lazares are the largest supplier of fireworks in the United States, and their plant is right here in Detroit. Those of us at Channel Three, along with our friends at Lazare Fireworks, are proud to celebrate the birth of our nation with you. This is Max Anglim, live at the Riverfront."

Max held the smile on his face until Glen lowered the camera. With the broadcast concluded, he yanked the tie away from his throat. Beads of sweat trickled down his back like a thousand spider legs as he wiped his face with a fast food napkin. "Thank God that's over."

"What the hell's your problem, Anglim?" Glen asked, bending his bulging waist to coil a light cable. "You're always anxious to cover the fireworks."

"I'm here for the danger," Max said. "Channel Three has sponsored this show forever. You'd think, at least, they'd have a fire onboard some year so we could get exclusive video." He snickered.

Glen, his yellow T-shirt soused in sweat, pulled the camera from the tripod and placed it in the stand-up case. "I doubt that will ever happen. The Lazares are experts. Don't they do like six hundred shows a year? I've never heard of a big accident."

"Take your time, Glen." Max settled into his chair, gazing toward the shoreline and the traffic jam behind it as his cameraman worked. "I'm really not in the mood to do 'on the scene reporting' of some fender-bender. I just wish something big would happen, that's all."

* * *

With a sickening screech of brakes, the Suburban plowed into Webb's van. The detective's head crashed into the window beside him, pellets of glass peppering his hair, face, and shoulders, his car hurling sideways. The world spun once, twice, then stopped.

"Call 911!" Frantic voices sounded around him. Webb opened his eyes and tried to focus. Everything appeared murky, but the voices were clear. "Is he dead?"

I'm alive! Webb wanted to shout, but his lips refused to cooperate. I hear you.

A man leaned through the broken window. "Stay cool, Bud. Don't move. You did a real number on your head."

Webb struggled to respond.

The man reached in and grasped Webb's shoulder. "I'm here. Help's comin'."

"Thanks," Webb mouthed. He studied the stranger's face…tan, with clear blue eyes that vied for recognition with his long pointed nose. Straggly long hair, a nondescript dark color, was pulled back into a makeshift ponytail. Yet his presence comforted Webb before he sank into oblivion.

* * *

Back on the barge, loud cheering roused Max Anglim. The hundred or so volunteer pyrotechnics who swarmed to Detroit each

Fourth of July smacked each other on the back, sharing congratulatory hugs.

"Damn if I'd work my ass off in this heat without pay," Max chided from his chair. "Those guys must be morons."

"I guess they have a primal need to blow things up," Glen said, laughing. "Must get a euphoric rush from the cheering crowds."

"I know that feeling well," Max said.

The reporter watched as the Lazare crew scattered about the barges to make sure all the guns had fired. He was stripping down to a white T-shirt when loud shouting caught his trained ear. He jumped from the chair. "Glen, grab the camera. Something's happening."

As the photographer gathered equipment, Max scrambled over sandbags onto the launching site. Floodlights bathed the area with a midday glow illuminating crewmembers huddled between two rows of gun racks.

Someone shouted, "Call the Coast Guard!"

Tall cylinders and hills of sand safety pits blocked Max's view, but the voices were loud. Desperate. From a distance, the radiating panic drubbed Max's heart. He waited for Glen to catch up. "Stay back so they don't notice us," Max warned, stepping behind his trusty photographer.

Glenn's camera rolled.

"Zoom in, zoom in." Max tugged on Glen's T-shirt. "Somebody's down. Keep shooting."

With tape rolling, Glen moved forward. Closer. Closer.

A body was sprawled on the ground.

"Get the paramedics."

Max recognized Conrad Lazare.

Conrad turned his face away from the horrid scene. "Good God!"

Checking the camera's VU meter, Max noticed the red needle bouncing too low. "Turn your sound up," he whispered to Glen.

Max studied Conrad Lazare. He'd interviewed him many times over the years. Chiseled features, tall and slender…probably

in his mid to late thirties now. The dark hair must've been pro-
fessionally styled; not a strand out of place. The navy Polo shirt
looked ironed, the tan slacks tailored. He looked out of place
among the grimy crew.

"Grab a shot of Lazare," Max whispered to Glen.

The photographer tilted the camera to capture a frantic
Conrad.

Anglim's eyes now focused on the man kneeling beside the
body. Even with the figure's back turned, he recognized the
shaggy hair of Harry Strickland, the show manager.

Strickland turned his head. "He's in bad shape." His eyes
widened and he stood, pointing toward the camera.

Conrad Lazare spied the reporter. "Get those news people
away from here!"

Two burly pyrotechnics stepped in front of Max. Another
blocked the camera lens with his hand and pushed, forcing Glen
to lower the camera. His voice shook with confusion and anger.
"This is an emergency, buddy. Stay outta the way."

The news crew stepped back. Max hoped Glen was still
rolling. They could do wonders with sound bites, even if the
video only showed the barge deck. It could be what Max was
waiting for…the chance to get noticed by the national networks.

It was obvious from the crew's stunned silence that the man
was dead. This story would make national coverage, and it was
all his.

A strident voice called from behind them. "Make a hole!"

Everyone stepped aside as two paramedics with white
crosses on the backs of their T-shirts rushed past.

Max nudged Glen. They stepped forward, following the
medics to the body.

Attention was focused on the medics as they knelt beside
the corpse.

Max found himself standing next to the tall, spaghetti-thin
Harry Strickland. Vile odor assailed Anglim's nostrils. It was
then he noticed the glaring metal hook jutting from the grimy

cuff of Strickland's purple sweatshirt. God, that always grosses me out.

"Looks like he leaned over one of the guns and it went off," Strickland said slowly, "Part of his head is blown off."

Conrad Lazare stared at the corpse, his face pale.

One of the paramedics turned, looked up at the show manager and shook his head. "He's gone."

Conrad slowly nodded to Strickland, his voice low and empty as if reciting cold procedure from a contingency plan. "Better get the Fire Marshal. Coast Guard too, and notify the Detroit Police. Everybody, go back to what you were doing until the authorities get here. And get that news crew out of here!"

Max backed away and checked his watch. Eleven-thirty-five. He tugged on Glen's sleeve. "Maybe the station can break into programming." They both stepped away from the circle of men and hurried back toward the boxes of camera equipment.

Max flushed with excitement. I could win an Emmy for this.

* * *

Miles away in Royal Oak, Detective Daisy Farrell welcomed the hum of the air conditioner as she entered her apartment. She was glad to be home from her family's annual holiday barbecue. Being single, she always volunteered to be on-call at work during holidays, and this was the first time the cell phone and pager never buzzed. No overtime on her next check, but celebrating with her family more than made up for it.

She tossed her baseball cap onto a chair, dropped her cell phone and pager on the dining room table, and headed for the bathroom. A soak in the tub would feel wonderful and wash off the scent of barbecue grill smoke and sweat. That would be tempting fate for sure. The phone would definitely ring then.

Umber hair was pulled into a high ponytail as she slathered cleansing cream onto her face. She picked up a toothbrush and went to work on her teeth, her full lips foaming. Spit and rinse,

brush again, then a final spit and rinse. She grabbed a washcloth, dipping it into warm water, and rinsed off the cleansing
cream.

Almond-shaped brown eyes looked back at her from the
mirror. They were unique, startling eyes, rarely noticed by others. Usually she hid them behind dark framed glasses. Like the
lustrous auburn hair she concealed in a ponytail or bun every
day, she deliberately disguised anything that could be considered attractive.

Daisy was, first and foremost, a detective. Anything which
interfered with that was pushed away, hidden, or disguised. She
spent years honing her skills, and insisted her sharp mind com-
mand other's attention.

The ringing phone startled her. "Here we go," Daisy said.
She glanced at her watch. It was almost midnight. She rushed to
the closest phone and lifted the receiver, her voice businesslike
and professional. "Detective Farrell."

"This is Detroit Receiving Hospital, Detective."

Daisy sucked in air. It was never good when the evening
started with a call from the hospital. That usually meant she'd
be up all night, bouncing from hospital to crime scene. "What's
happened?"

"We have Detective Webb Hannis here. He was in an accident."

"What?" She balanced the phone on her shoulder, rebuttoned
her blouse and grabbed her glasses off the dresser. "Is he okay?
What happened?"

"His car was hit at the fireworks downtown. He's dazed but
stable," the nurse said, and chuckled. "He's very adamant that we
inform someone at the department that he may be late tomorrow."

"Head injury?"

"Yes ma'am."

"Uncooperative?"

The nurse chuckled again. "Just stubborn. He says you work
with him and asked us to call."

"I'll be right there," Daisy said and hung up abruptly. On her way to the garage, she pulled out the ponytail, hair cascading over her shoulders. "Webb probably doesn't have anyone else to call," she theorized as she pulled from the parking lot. "It's not like he has any friends except Chief Gallister in the division."

Red-brown hair bounced as she nodded to herself. "I suppose with all the heat Gallister has taken for hiring Webb, calling him would be the worst thing to do."

Daisy reached for the cell phone in her purse. Her fingers searched blindly in the leather bag as she sped down side streets and onto the entrance ramp for Route 696. That was when she remembered placing the on-call cell phone and pager on her dining table. She laughed.

"Looks like Jake Rubel's the backup detective now. Hope he isn't already in bed if the phone rings." She tore down the highway and onto I-75 South. A sea of glaring headlights nearly blinded her. "The fireworks. Damn, the traffic is still a mess."

Detective Farrell took the exit to the hospital, screeched to a stop in the parking lot and dashed into the emergency room. She spoke to the desk clerk, who motioned down the hallway and directed her to room three.

Webb was propped up on a gurney when she entered the room. He smiled sheepishly, his dark curls matted on top of his head.

Daisy leaned against the wall to catch her breath. "What's going on, big guy?"

"Don't ask me how it happened," he groaned, struggling to sit up. "My memory is shit. Can't even remember waking up this morning."

"I hear you hit your head." It was a facetious question. The bandage on his forehead told the tale. What she really wanted to know was if Webb was aware of his surroundings.

"Yeah. Needed a few stitches. I'm whirlin' around all over the place." He tried to laugh, but one eye scrunched up in pain.

"You look terrible," Daisy teased.

A doctor yanked back the curtain. He jotted something on a clipboard and tucked it under his arm. "You're a lucky man, Mr. Hannis. The X-ray ruled out any broken bones, and the CAT scan is negative for skull fractures or internal hemorrhaging. You did suffer a concussion. I'm going to keep you overnight for observation, just to be on the safe side."

"I'm fine," Webb argued and struggled to stand up. His knees buckled and he fell back onto the gurney.

"Better not try that just yet," the doctor advised with a generic smile. "The painkillers and sedative may make it difficult. Lie back and I'll have you admitted."

"My legs aren't following orders," Webb said, squeezing his eyes shut.

"Just sit still," Daisy said. "Keep your eyes open, though. Otherwise the room will start to spin."

Webb focused on the doorway. "Daiz, I need to thank that guy."

She turned to follow his gaze. "What guy? The doctor?"

"No, *that* guy. Right there in the hall. The guy with the ponytail and the crummy brown jacket."

Daisy glanced out the door. "Nobody like that out there, Webb."

Hannis cupped his head in his hands and shut his eyes, then quickly popped them open again. He lowered his hands and focused on them, as if willing the world to stop spinning. "He was at the scene when I got hit and he stayed until the paramedics arrived. Then he rode along to the hospital. I don't even know his name."

"You probably just dreamed that, Webb. They said you were out like a light when they picked you up."

"No, it was real. I can still see his eyes." The detective's words began to slur. "He looked kinda…different. But I gotta admit, I was glad he was there."

He carefully laid down on the gurney, his legs curling up

against his chest as he settled into a fetal position. "I'm so tired."

Daisy watched his eyelids roll down like window shades. He began breathing evenly, his face relaxing in sleep.

An aberrant thought hit Detective Farrell. Webb Hannis is a handsome man.

A stout nurse in a stiff white dress whisked into the room breaking that thought.

"We're moving Mr. Hannis to room three-twenty," the nurse announced. "Looks like he's out for the night. You can visit him after eight tomorrow morning."

Daisy patted him on the shoulder. "I'll be back, Webb. You're not alone."

She smiled at the nurse as she stepped toward the door, then turned back. "Can I use your phone? Police business. I need to check in."

"Pay phones are right down the hall and to your right, dearie. You can't miss 'em."

Daisy frowned and left the room without responding. She needed to let the dispatcher know that two of the three on-call detectives were out of the loop, at least until she got home. She just hoped Detroit was quiet. Otherwise Detective Rubel, the third on-call officer, would have a fit.

*   *   *

On the barge in the Detroit River, Jake Rubel was running other invectives through his mind. He was angry at Daisy Farrell for not answering her beeper, and why didn't they call that jerk Hannis?

This case would be a cinch. He knew his investigation and questions would be purely academic. The Coast Guard Lieutenant and the Fire Marshal standing beside him already discounted foul play and were ready — in the spirit of "interagency cooperation" — to hand the case over to the Detroit

Police Department. In other words, they had come to Rubel's same conclusion and were washing their hands of the paperwork problem. It was a freak accident, nothing more. "How did this guy get out here during the show?"

"Dunno," a grimy man next to him replied. "Sometimes a wire gets detached, and we gotta go out and fix it. But my crew's well trained. Ain't nobody gonna stick his face over a gun."

Rubel turned to eye the Lazare employee. "What's your name?"

"Harry Strickland. Everyone calls me Purp. I manage the show." In his mid-fifties, Strickland's graying, unruly mop of hair hung to his shoulders.

Then Jake saw the silver hook. God! That thing looks murderous.

"I guess this guy didn't know the rules," the detective quipped. He grinned at his own joke and was surprised at the angry frowns from the other men circling him. Jake turned back to the body and raised his camera. He snapped various pictures of the partial head with facial features blown away, the ravaged chest, and red oozing arms. He pulled out a tape measure, carefully stretching it near the gun rack, and jotted measurements in his notebook.

Rubel rolled the body onto its side. He hated this part of the job. The victim's white shirt was soaked in blood. He pulled a wallet from the back pocket of the corpse's slacks and fished out a driver's license.

"Marc Lazare," Jake read aloud. He heard a sharp intake of breath, almost a sob, from behind him. Turning, he saw a man in a dark blue Polo shirt and tan pants stepping toward the starboard railing. The detective rose and started toward him.

Purp Strickland blocked his way, hook hand raised as he shook his head. "Give him a minute, detective."

Rubel glanced down at the license in his hand and repeated the name. "Marc Lazare. One of the brothers?"

Strickland stiffened. "He's the company president."

"Well," Jake said, snapping shut his notebook. "Looks like an accident. The coroner can make a positive ID on the guy. Thank you for your cooperation gentlemen. I have everything I need."

The detective pulled out his cell phone and called for an ambulance to meet the Coast Guard boat.

CHAPTER 2

CONRAD LAZARE STRAINED to read his watch in the moonlit hallway of his parents' home. Almost two o'clock. The master bedroom door was his shield from the horror he was about to wreak inside. Should I wait until morning? he wondered. He paused, his heart throbbing in his temples.

Head bowed, Conrad silently shook his head in the shadows. No. Father will be enraged if I don't tell him tonight. He freaks when I take charge.

He thought of his mother, frail bodied yet soul-strong since his father's recent stroke. Conrad's horrific message would destroy her. I can't wake her, he vowed. Father first. He'll know how to tell Mother.

His hand quaked as he gripped the doorknob, turning it slowly, slowly…don't make a sound. He stole into the room, disoriented in the darkness. Waiting for his eyes to adjust, he pictured the room's layout in his mind. The double bed, his parents' marriage bed from years ago, was to the left. Conrad pictured the four posters stabbing within a foot of the ceiling.

Edging toward it, he felt with his foot for the bedspread his mother always folded and placed on the floor at night. He remembered waking as a child frightened of the dark, scurrying into his parents' room and snuggling into the bedspread. He knew not to awaken them. If he did, his father would rant on about how boys needed to face their fears if they wanted to grow into real men. Oh, how he longed for his parents to take him into their warm bed and keep him safe.

No safety tonight. He stopped to listen. Rhythmic breathing from his mother's side of the bed. His eyes, now adjusted to the dimness, stared at the darkened bump of his father's body. The older man was lying on his side, breathing labored.

"Father," he whispered directly into the man's ear. He gave the aged shoulder a slight nudge. "Father."

"Huh?" The old man sat up straight.

Conrad stumbled backwards in shock. "It's me, Conrad."

"Wha…who's here? What's wrong?"

Conrad sat on the bed next to Pierre Lazare, the family patriarch. "Please…Father, I…I need to speak with you."

He gripped his father's arm and was appalled at the emaciated condition…bony, the muscles shriveled. Carefully, he pulled him up from the bed, wrapping him in the bedspread.

Pierre threw it aside. "What are you doing here?" He coughed violently. "Don't wake your mother. I'll meet you in the study."

Conrad nodded and quietly stepped from the room, leaving his father in darkness. He sighed heavily as he closed the bedroom door, and then made his way down the winding staircase to the study.

He began pacing the worn carpet. God, how he hated this room with its green leather chair facing the fireplace. It was from here, Pierre would sit and preach about family tradition.

The old childhood memories rose inside him once again. "Damn, I don't need this." He kicked the chair leg. But the memories were as fresh as a seeping wound. So much to live up to, that strapping man on his mighty throne. He wanted perfection.

Conrad's loafers scuffed the carpet. Where were his brothers? Last he saw of Marc, his oldest brother was being zipped into a black bag like somebody's leftovers. Luc refused to come with him, walking away in disgust when Conrad suggested that he tell their father. He was undoubtedly off in a bar somewhere, pausing only long enough from his drinking to piss away more responsibility and beer.

The grandfather clock in the foyer chimed twice. Conrad knew the late hour would only make things worse. Pierre would question and blame about not summoning him immediately. The fact that he drove around the city because he needed to think wouldn't matter.

"Dammit, I'm doing my best—"

Conrad was still confused. *What should I say? How do you tell your father his oldest son is dead?*

Flipping on a table lamp, the light glared off the etched glass door of his father's gun cabinet. It was open. He stepped to the rich cherry wood wall unit and quietly closed the door.

"Conrad!" Pierre Lazare stood in the doorway.

"Yes, Father?" It was Conrad's automatic reply from childhood.

"Do you know what time it is? Why ever are you here at this hour?"

Conrad sucked in a sharp breath, pausing to look at his father. He didn't seem so commanding now. His body was shrunken, skinny even. Slack muscles from the stroke made one side of the old man's face appear melted.

Conrad felt a tinge of pity. "Father, I —"

Pierre Lazare snorted, then turned his back as he limped toward the liquor cabinet. "Sit down. I'll be with you in a minute." His right leg dragged behind him.

Conrad remained standing.

"This better not be about your raise again," Pierre said as he poured whisky over ice. "You and Jade will have to learn to exist on your more than adequate salary."

He turned around. Eyes narrowed as he saw his son still standing. "Sit down, Conrad."

"Marc's dead."

The glass paused on its way to Pierre's lips. "What did you say?"

Conrad struggled to find his voice. "It…it was an accident, Father. He got too close to a mortar tube last night and—"

Glass exploded against the fireplace. Pierre gazed down at the alcohol pooling among crystal shards on the hearth. Slowly he raised his head to stare blankly at his son, his voice hollow. "What?"

Conrad watched emptiness seep into the older man's eyes. It was as if part of the soul had fallen into a deep chasm, never to be retrieved again. "He can't be." Pierre shook his head slowly. "No! No!"

Conrad stepped toward the older man, arms raised as if to catch him. "Marc was too close to one of the bombs on the launch barge."

Conrad pulled his father toward him.

Pierre collapsed into his embrace.

"It was an accident, Father. We didn't find him until after the show. It was too late. There was nothing we could do."

The squeeze lasted for several precious heartbeats until muscles tightened across Pierre Lazare's shoulders and he forced himself to stand tall. He raised his hands and pushed his son away. "I need my chair."

Shock and hurt scarred Conrad's face. "I'm only —"

"I'm not an invalid." Pierre slumped into his green leather chair. Liquid eyes stared into the fireplace. "Does Laura know? We must call Teddy home. Where's Luc?"

"I don't know."

"Find him. He can help with arrangements."

"I can do that. You know I'm a better organizer than Luc."

Pierre snapped his fingers without looking at Conrad. "Come now, Conrad. Luc is the oldest son now. I need him."

Oh yes, Conrad thought wryly. Tradition. Over the years he learned the one acceptable response. "Yes, Father." He suppressed his anger and turned away.

The third Lazare son strode from the study and through the foyer. Before he reached the front door he heard the harsh sobs.

The air was thick and muggy as Conrad hurried to his car. He yanked open the door and slid behind the wheel. Letting out a prolonged sigh, he pounded the steering wheel. "Damn, that man will never change!" he said aloud, "Thank, God, that's over." But his night would drag on. He had one more onerous stop to make.

*   *   *

Webb Hannis slowly stirred from his black abyss, the dreamless state where the mind runs to escape physical pain. With awareness came misery; he groaned, his bruised brain throbbing. Forcing his eyelids open he struggled to get his bearings. The room was dark except for the dim light seeping through the windows.

"Don't pull any of your macho stunts, Bud," a low-pitched voice said. A figure leaned over him. "You'll be okay if you follow doctor's orders."

Webb squinted at the outline of the man's head as he struggled to sit up. "You're the guy who was there when I got hit. How come you're still here?"

"Lie back."

His head hurt too much to protest. Webb slowly eased back onto the pillow. "You don't have to stay here all night."

The low voice chuckled. "I'm here to see that you behave."

The rebellious response was automatic. "Who in the hell are you, telling me what to do?" He winced in agony at the pain caused by the outburst.

"I'm Samuel." As if that explained everything, the silhouette plopped into a chair next to the window. He draped one leg over the padded arm and bounced his foot in the air.

At that moment, a nurse burst through the door carrying a small tray. "You're awake, Mr. Hannis," she said and switched on a dim light.

Webb scrunched his eyes closed in distress.

"It's three o'clock. You can have more pain medication now." She handed him a tiny cup with two white pills, poured ice water into a foam cup and gave it to him. "You'll feel much better when this takes effect."

Webb popped the medicine into his dry mouth and eagerly sipped the water. He felt the cold liquid ease down his throat. The instant it hit his stomach, he felt nauseated. "I'm going to be sick."

The nurse grabbed a vomit pan and held it under Webb's chin.

It was too humiliating. He swallowed heavily, forcing the bile to settle. "I'm okay now. Just leave me alone."

The nurse chuckled as she placed the vomit pan on the stand beside the bed. "Okay, tough guy. It's there if you need it. I'll check on you again in an hour."

She retrieved her tray, flipped off the light, and left the room.

Webb sighed heavily.

Samuel was back at his bedside in an instant. "Sleep tight, dream right," he whispered.

*　　*　　*

Conrad pulled his car onto Harrison Drive. The dashboard clock glared three-thirty. This was Marc's street. The grand houses, magnificent by day, appeared murky in the soft streetlights.

The neighborhood was asleep. Conrad stretched taut muscles wishing he, too, was in bed. Enough tension for one night. Though he was relieved to be out of his father's house, the night dragged on.

He hated to wake Marc's wife Laura with the devastating news, but knew it would be all over the television in the morning.

He turned into the driveway at Marc's house, surprised to see lights in the living-room window.

"Don't tell me she already knows. Who got to her?"

He turned off the ignition and settled back in the leather seat. His entire body ached. Better to get this over with and maybe grab some sleep. Tomorrow, with all its worries and obligations, loomed before him. He forced himself out of the car.

Conrad crossed the lawn and hopped up the front porch steps. He rapped on the door. Movement sounded from inside. Sure enough, Laura, swathed in a peach nightgown and matching robe, opened the door. She hesitated when she saw Conrad.

A commanding force at five-foot-ten, natural ringlets of Titian hair fell over her shoulders. "Conrad." A quizzical frown wrinkled her freckled forehead. "I…I thought you were Marc."

"Actually, that's why I'm here, Laura," he said with confidence he didn't feel. "May I come in?"

Laura nervously coiled one of her long red ringlets around her finger. "Of course, please do."

She opened the door, led him into the living room, and motioned for him to sit down. She grabbed the cell phone off the couch and set aside her address book. Slowly she sank onto the sofa and eyed her brother-in-law. "I'm sorry, Conrad. Marc isn't home yet. Fourth of July is always a long night, but he's never this late." She crossed lanky arms over her flat abdomen.

Conrad's heart pounded. God, why did he have to be the one to break this to her? Where in the hell is Luc? He cleared his throat, leaned forward in the chair and placed a consoling hand on her knee. "I don't know how to tell you this, Laura."

The regal woman withdrew from his touch. Her back pressed against the sofa, body tensing. Her voice sounded hurt and bitter. "So, the family sent you to tell me?"

Conrad turned his head, looking away. His gaze fell on the picture resting on the table beside him. It was Marc and Laura.

Between them was their three year old son, Austin. God, how he hated to do this. "I'm afraid so. Father would've come, but he's…he's not taking this too well."

"So everybody knows?"

"No." Conrad forced himself to turn and face the commanding woman. "I told Father, and Luc was at the show. I'll call Teddy at college tomorrow."

"What?" Laura's eyes flooded with fear. "Slow down. I don't want the whole world to know my business."

"Teddy is Marc's brother. Of course he has to know." Conrad shook his head.

The slender redhead turned away, avoiding Conrad's gaze. "It's my fault. I never should've—"

"It's nobody's fault," Conrad corrected softly. He patted her knee. "It was an accident."

Laura turned back, her green eyes wide with confusion. "Accident? What are you talking about, Conrad?"

"The accident. At the show tonight. I thought you heard."

Slowly she shook her head. "There was an accident? Was anybody hurt?"

Conrad lowered his gaze to stare at the floor.

"Marc is hurt?" Her voice quaked.

The memory of Marc during the company celebration picnic, after the fireworks last year, holding Austin in the air and laughing with his son…carefree, innocent laughter… flashed through Conrad's mind. It was such a rare thing to hear his burdened older brother laugh…and now, it was impossible.

"Conrad?"

The tender hand that touched him on the shoulder unnerved him. Conrad pushed down his grief and raised his head, unaware of the tears streaming down his face. He had to be strong. Family required it. "I'm so sorry, Laura."

"What is it, Conrad? What are you saying?"

"A bomb misfired during the show. Marc is dead."

"What? Marc…no, not Marc. He's always so careful."

Conrad forced himself to look directly into her green eyes. He nodded slowly. "It's tragic."

Laura stood and turned away from him. Clapping her hand over her mouth she muffled a sob. "No!" She glared at Conrad. "How could this happen? I don't believe it."

Conrad rose and wrapped his arms around her. "I'm so sorry. But it's true. We have no idea why he was out by the mortar tubes. One hit him." He laid his head on her shoulder. "Laura, we're all devastated."

Laura pulled away from him, wiping her tear-streaked face. "Oh, Conrad, this can't be true. I know I was angry, but I never meant to—"

"You can't blame yourself, Laura."

Collapsing onto the couch, she bit her lip, her breathing shallow. "Yes," she whispered. "Yes, I can."

She looked off into the distance with glazed eyes.

*   *   *

On Wednesday, July fifth, Webb awoke at nine o'clock to a sun-filled room. He cursed his aching head. "God, I need more pain pills."

Daisy Farrell leaned toward him from the chair where the stranger had kept his all-night vigil.

Webb looked at her through a haze. "Did that guy finally go home?"

"What guy?"

"The dude I told you about last night. The one who helped me at the accident scene. He was here all night."

"I've been here since eight o'clock, Webb. Haven't seen anyone except the nurse."

Hannis struggled to pull his giant frame into a sitting position. "What're you doing here, Farrell? Come to get the scoop on what happened so you can pass it around the squad room?"

Daisy laughed. "Complete paranoia, eh, Detective?"

Webb wasn't quite sure what to make of the detective sitting across from him. He only knew there was something unique about her. Her slanted brown eyes seemed to sparkle with merriment and life. Gradually his mouth shifted into an apologetic grin. "Did it again, didn't I? Sorry. I'm not very good with people."

"I noticed. If you only stayed in charm school, Webb…just think where you could be now. To answer your question, I'm here because a fellow officer is hurt. And also because I'm curious."

The brawny detective rolled his eyes and glanced toward the doorway. "There's that guy again. Out in the hall. Hey dude, why are you hangin' around?"

As Daisy turned to look, the nurse walked into the room. "The patient was just asking for more painkillers, Nurse," Daisy said with an evil grin. "Do you have any that require needles? Really dull, rusty needles will work quite nicely, I think."

The nurse chuckled as she placed a medicine tray on the table beside the bed. "I see Mr. Hannis is awake again. I'm sorry, but we're fresh out of rusty needles. Would a cold bedpan do instead?" The nurse tidied the bedside table. "How are you feeling this morning, Mr. Hannis?"

"I feel lousy, but the medication worked last night. Do you have anything that won't make me drowsy?"

"All the good stuff makes you drowsy," the nurse teased. "With your injury, you really need a narcotic."

"I'm leaving, and I want my wits about me," Webb said.

The nurse perused his chart. "You had a good night. If the doctor approves your release, you can be out of here by ten. I'll get you something milder for the pain." She scurried out of the room.

"Really, Webb, you should stay an extra day," Daisy said.

"You heard the nurse. I had a good night. I'm going to work."

"Don't be crazy. You can crash at my place. At least you'll have someone to wait on you."

"I can't afford to take time off," he said. "The entire patrol squad wants my job."

"Oh, Webb, you know how it is. They just hoped the chief would hire a detective from within the department. You work your butt off trying to better your rank, and then a new guy comes in and nabs the most desirable spot."

"Yeah, I guess so," Webb said. "It was the same in Cincinnati."

"Why did you leave Cincinnati where you had so much seniority?"

"I needed a change of scenery, but now I wonder if this move was a bad idea."

The nurse breezed back into the room and handed Webb two pills in a cup.

He swallowed the medicine and washed it down with water.

"You're too ill to work," Daisy said.

A doctor in a white jacket entered the room, picked up Webb's chart and flipped through. "Looks like you survived the night."

"Your drugs work wonders."

The doctor smiled and jotted something on his chart. "You're free to go, but take it easy this week. I'll sign for your discharge. Call me if you have any other symptoms such as nausea or double vision."

After the doctor left the room, Webb pointed toward the hall. "Damn it. Samuel's still here."

Daisy whirled around. "Where?"

"Right there eyeing us," Webb said, exasperated. "Tell him to hit the road."

"I think you're hallucinating. I'll take you home."

"No, Daiz. I'm serious. I'm going to work if I have to call a cab."

* * *

At exactly fifteen seconds before nine-thirty in the morning, Jake Rubel walked straight to the county coroner's office door.

Sure, his coworkers called him anal retentive, but he liked control. He relished painstaking precision with things like schedules and appointments. He glanced at his watch, waiting until the second hand touched the top of the dial before knocking sharply on the door.

The middle-aged detective's hair stood in jagged peaks where he ran fingers through it during the night. Unshaven, his clothes were wrinkled and spotted with coffee stains.

His report, however, was meticulous…all seventeen pages of it. He spent the rest of the night putting it together. The only item missing from the folder under his arm was the autopsy report. Once he had that, he could hand everything to Chief Gallister with a smug smile. It would embarrass both the Chief and that new guy, Hannis. After all, Rubel — who was third down on the backup squad — only got the case because neither Hannis nor Farrell was available. Why?

"You're outta here, Hannis," Jake muttered as he turned the doorknob. "I'll see to it personally."

The office was empty. Doctor Lee Homigouchi would be in the morgue. Rubel made his way down the long hall.

"Morning, Doc!" the detective bellowed at the morgue door. The doctor, unfazed by the abrupt greeting, simply raised a hand in reply.

"Sure you want to watch this, Rubel?" Homigouchi's words were barely loud enough to hear over the bone saw. "I remember way back, when you puked all over my lab trying to be a macho man."

Lee Homigouchi was highly respected among police and court officials for his thorough expertise. The detectives appreciated his easy humor during autopsies. They called him Doctor Homi, short for homicide.

Jake Rubel walked to the foot of the gurney. He was a bit pale as he watched the squat Japanese coroner — straight blue-black hair stabbing out on the sides of his head — do his thing.

The detective remembered the first time observing an autopsy. He was a rookie cop back then, answering a domestic violence call where the ex-husband bludgeoned the victim to death. Jake's supervisor insisted he sit in on the autopsy.

Although he had viewed the battered woman at the scene, Jake gagged at the sight of her bloody naked body lying on its back without dignity on the cold examination table. He lost his lunch.

Doctor Homi saved him that day by pointing to the victim's rounded breasts standing at attention like two perfect little cupcakes. He poked them with a pen. "Maybe the ex didn't like the boob job. These are fake, you know. Real ones spread flat as fried eggs when you lay them on their backs."

Jake Rubel learned that if he was to remain in police work, he must lighten up to the horror. Now, he looked over at the man who taught him that necessary lesson.

"Here, hold this." Homigouchi extended a small white bowl toward the detective. He waited until wide eyes told him the detective recognized the corpse's skull on the table. He chuckled as he used a scalpel to slice through pulpy brain.

Rubel swallowed hard.

"Ah, we don't have to go far to find the cause of death," Doctor Homi said.

Rubel moved next to the coroner. "Yeah, his brains were blown to hell. Right?"

"Yes, but here's a nice little bullet nestled in the right hemisphere." The coroner studied the wound with magnifying glasses. "The point of entry is under the chin. I see some spackling there. I'd say it was close range. Did you find the gun?"

"Nope," Rubel said, his excitement growing. "Looks like we have a homicide."

"Could be." The coroner used tweezers to remove the copper bullet. "Maybe you'll get to work with that new detective, what's his name. Hannis? The Cincinnati medical examiner speaks highly of him."

Jake's eyes frosted over. "Yeah, they always say wonderful things when bums move somewhere else."

"No, really," the doctor replied. "The M.E. made a point of calling me. A courtesy of sorts. Wanted to warn me bizarre murders seem to follow Webb Hannis. Said he hopes I have a strong constitution because the corpses can be pretty messy."

"Doesn't matter." The chill entered Rubel's voice. "This is my case. I'm handling it alone."

The doctor dropped the copper bullet into a small plastic vial. He screwed on the cap and scribbled a notation on the container. With a hint of amusement he extended the vial toward the detective. "Hannis' first case was a serial killer. Bodies were in the Ohio River for a week. Catfish had their fill, I bet. Eyeballs missing, bloated corpses...I hear Hannis didn't even turn green, much less hurl all over the bodies. Unlike—"

Rubel grabbed the vial and stuffed it into an evidence envelope. "This is my murder case, Doctor. *Mine.* I don't need some has-been like Hannis in my way."

Jake Rubel turned abruptly and stormed from the room. He had things to do, a murder to solve. But first he had to call headquarters. No way was Chief Gallister going to saddle him with a partner on this case...especially that brown-noser Hannis.

*   *   *

Finally got that oddball Samuel off my back, Webb thought as he made his unsteady way through the ingratiating din of the police station. He sighed as he entered the quieter peace of the detective division.

Shaking his aching head, he walked to the safety and solitude of his own cube and slowly lowered himself into his chair.

A newspaper rested on his computer keyboard. Webb picked it up and opened it, his eyes crossing dizzily as he saw the small type. The morning edition of the Detroit paper flashed a headline about a death at the fireworks show. The caption said the accompanying photograph was taken on the launch barge the day before the show.

Webb sucked in a long breath, released it slowly, and focused on the picture. A shaggy-haired fellow with a hook for a hand knelt beside two men behind a row of metal tubes. The caption named the guy with the hook as the show manager, Harry 'Purp' Strickland. The other two were Marc and Conrad Lazare.

To his complete surprise, Webb saw himself standing in the background. He stared at the picture for a moment longer, trying to determine its significance. Then he began reading the article.

He gave up after five minutes of struggling through letters that swam in and out of the first two paragraphs. "I don't get it," he said to himself. "What am I supposed to see here?"

A picture flashed in Webb's brain. It was a duplicate of the one on the newspaper page, with one exception. The head of one of the Lazare brothers was illuminated, and Webb knew in an instant that the dead brother had a bullet in his brain. He dropped the paper. "Whoa, what was that?"

"What was what?" a voice behind him asked.

Hannis swiveled in his chair to face the man in the oversized brown jacket. "Samuel, right? How did you get in here?"

The thin man leaned against the cubicle wall. "I'm here to give you a hand, Webb."

"Oh, really?" The detective leaned back in his chair. "A hand with what? I don't have any active cases right now, and I only handle homicides. Did you witness a murder, Samuel?"

"I've witnessed a few in my time, but that's not why I'm here." The oddly dressed man pointed toward the newspaper resting on the officer's desk. "You'll have an active case soon."

"Goddamnit! What the hell are you talking about? Do you know something about this death on the fireworks barge?"

"I have lots of information to share with you, Webb Hannis. However," Samuel said. "I don't like excessive profanity. Now, if you'll excuse me." With that, the man turned and left the cubicle.

Webb jumped from his chair to follow. Sledgehammers pounded inside his skull, and for a moment he thought he might vomit.

A slamming door boomed, magnifying the pain. Webb grabbed his head and peered around the corner. Samuel was gone, but a fuming Jake Rubel raced toward him.

"Hannis!" the irate detective bellowed as he stormed toward the cubicle. "I know you pulled shit to get on the Detroit force…I'm telling you now, this is my case and you better not get in my goddamn way!"

Webb held up a hand. "Keep it down, willya? You're splitting my skull."

"I see. Hung one on last night? No wonder you didn't answer your damn phone." Rubel shook a file folder in Webb's face. "You were home sleeping it off when you should've been working this case. That's your loss, you worthless drunk. I don't give a damn that Gallister assigned you as my partner on this. It's my case, understand me?"

"Partner?" A cold fury rose within Webb. "What are you talking about? I don't take partners, and I sure as hell wouldn't work with a twerp like you. Calm your ass down before I do it for you!"

Daisy Farrell appeared in the doorway. "Now boys," she said with a smirk, "Why don't you take your testosterone moment outside? Some of us are trying to work here. Crimes to solve, bad guys to catch. You know, real police stuff?"

At the sound of Daisy's voice, Webb's anger vanished. Suddenly he found Rubel's grimaced face, narrow head, long pointed chin and big ears hilarious. The man reminded him of an angry little leprechaun whose scrawny body still hadn't filled out at the age of thirty-six.

Rubel slapped the file folder against Webb's chest and released it. The contents scattered across the floor. "That's your copy of the case file, Hannis. Now you're up to speed. I set up an appointment at Pierre Lazare's home to interview the family at one thirty. If you can sober up enough to get there, maybe I'll let you ask a question or two. Do you know why, Hannis?"

Webb couldn't resist. He grinned as he said, "Because you think you're in charge?"

Rubel's face purpled. "Goddammit, I *am* in charge! I have more seniority here, and don't you forget that!"

Hannis smiled and rose to his full height, towering over the spindly man.

Rubel quickly turned, a smug grin on his face as he bolted toward the department door.

Once Rubel was out of sight, Hannis slowly knelt and began gathering up the loose pages. A slender hand crossed his field of vision. He looked up and found himself gazing into startling brown eyes.

"That certainly went well," Daisy said with a grin. She took the pages from his hands, stuffed them back into the folder, and handed them to him.

"Thanks, Daiz," Webb cleared his throat audibly. "I need to see the Chief."

Webb wove unsteadily through the mass of cubicles until he reached the Chief's door. Without bothering to knock, he opened it and stepped into the hardwood paneled office.

Gallister looked up from his desk, peering over the rim of his glasses. The Chief frowned. "Where were you last night?"

"At the fireworks, Fred. I got clobbered pulling out of the parking lot. The doc said I have a slight concussion."

"Are you okay?"

"Lousy headache, but I'm fine."

"Good." Gallister motioned toward the chair centered in front of his desk. "Sit down, Webb. We need to talk."

Hannis grinned. "Firing me already, Fred?"

"No, you jerk." The burly Chief — a little larger around the waist since their partner years — pointed toward a chair. "I don't want you denting my floor when you fall down. Sit, please."

Webb took a few moments to settle into the chair. His head hammered in time with his pulse. Finally it all calmed to a monotonous throb. "We had a deal, Fred. No partners."

Gallister nodded and made a dismissing motion with his hands. "Yes and no, Webb. You wanted autonomy, remember? Free to handle cases as you see fit? That's what we agreed to, and I'm holding to that promise."

Webb frowned.

"That doesn't mean you can't have a partner," the Chief said. "Rubel is a good worker. As I remember, you loathe paperwork." Fred leaned forward in his chair. "Webb, the prosecutor is leaning on me to solve this case. Our record here isn't too swift. It's the main reason I need you." Gallister ran his fingers through silver hair. "Rubel is meticulous on details, but he lacks your cop instincts. Believe me, you need him."

"Damn that Rubel. He's already bragging he has seniority over me. You can forget it, Fred."

"Actually, no. The city picked up your contract and pension from Cincinnati. Twenty-four years experience on the books makes you the senior detective. You answer directly to me."

The leather chair squeaked as the Chief leaned forward. "I need the old magic, Webb. Get cracking on this Lazare case. The coroner has the body, and–"

"Bullet in the head, right?"

Gallister nodded. "So you already read Rubel's report."

"Not yet. That just popped into my mind."

"That's what I'm talking about, partner. The old magic. I'm hoping it rubs off on the other detectives. I need you to teach them how it works."

Webb Hannis, his hand grasping the edge of the desk for balance, slowly stood and walked out of the office. Weird request, Webb thought. How can I teach it when I have no idea how it works myself?

CHAPTER 3

WEBB HANNIS maneuvered the unmarked police car north on Lake Shore Road toward Grosse Pointe, his window open just to get a breeze moving. Instead of cool comfort, a steamy blast spewed from the air conditioner. "Damn, why don't they fix these things?" He pounded on the dashboard.

Yanking on his noose of a tie, he loosened it enough to wipe his clammy neck with a handkerchief. Gallister's rigid dress code tortured Webb. He soured at the sight of his navy blue suit coat tossed over the back of the passenger seat. "No way am I wearing that in this heat and humidity."

The beauty of Lake St. Clair on his right was the only thing keeping him from going ballistic. The subtle blue waves oddly calmed him. Lake St. Clair was a pond compared to the Great Lakes. But to Webb, accustomed to the muddy Ohio River in Cincinnati, Lake St. Clair was a dazzling ocean. He understood why the wealthy chose to settle near its peaceful shoreline.

Daisy Farrell's voice sounded from the tiny recorder on the seat beside him, summarizing Rubel's tedious report. He grinned at the memory of her waving him away from her desk as she dictated onto the tape. Daisy presented the completed tape fifteen minutes later, along with driving directions printed off the Internet. Then she pointed to the clock and told him to hit the road if he wanted to reach the Lazare home before Rubel arrived.

The clock on the dash read one-fifteen. Webb turned left according to Daisy's driving instructions, crossing over the four-lane road and onto a side street. Majestic beech trees, white oaks and sugar maples lined both sides of the lane. Some were probably older than the multi-million dollar mansions tucked behind the privacy of their green boughs.

The detective noted the faded house numbers stenciled on the curb at the end of each driveway. They were barely legible. He slowed the car to a crawl as he tried to find the right address.

"Sure would be nice to know where I'm going," he muttered.

Motion in the passenger side mirror caught his eye. He pulled toward the curb and waved out the window for the car behind him to go around.

A silver Mercedes, with an angry blare of the horn, screeched past him.

The detective glanced at the rearview mirror to check for other cars. Suddenly, he slammed on the brakes. Twisting in the seat, he stared out the back window gaping in disbelief. "What the hell?"

A midnight-black stallion reared in the middle of the street, fore hooves lashing angrily at the muggy air. The rider on its back raised a massive sword, brandishing it wildly before slashing it downward as he loosened the reins.

Steel-shod hooves crashed onto the concrete street. The harness jingled as the horse cantered toward the police car in an odd three-beat rhythm.

The rider's bright blue silk shirt, full-length sleeves ballooning in the air, commanded Webb's attention. The front of the shirt hid behind a shiny steel breastplate. He wore a hat of matching blue, the left side of the brim pinned up and plumed with thick white feathers. A long gray cape caught the wind behind him as he kneed the horse's flanks.

Canter perked to gallop as the stallion charged toward the car. The rider thrust his sword forward in the age-old signal of a cavalry charge. At the last minute he touched the reins and the giant horse veered to the left, sweeping past the police officer's window.

Webb caught a brief glimpse of the rider's face and shook his head, bewildered. "Samuel?"

Horse and rider continued to the end of the street where the stallion reared again as Samuel pointed his sword toward a three-story brown and red brick mansion. Tan stone outlined the six-foot bay windows on each side of the house. Numerous chimneys broke the roofline.

Then, as if acknowledging that Webb was looking at the right house, the rider cued his steed to drop back down to the ground. With a flick of the reins, the black war-horse sprang forward and leapt the row of bushes lining the sidewalk in front of the house.

"Okay, buddy, enough games! Are you some kind of wacko?"

The detective whipped the car into the circle drive and slammed on the brakes, barely missing the rear bumper of the silver Mercedes. He threw the gear into park, jumped out of the car, and dashed to where the swordsman stood beside the giant horse. "Hold it!"

The flamboyant creature slipped the large broadsword into its scabbard and smiled innocently at the giant policeman. "Och, wha hae we here? 'Tis Laird Hannis!"

The Scottish accent stopped Webb cold. "Huh?"

"Come now, laddie. Willnae ye enter yon hoose an tak' the varlets?"

"What?"

The colorful character pointed toward Webb's forehead. "'Tis the knot on yer 'ead, a'right. Cannae e'en un'erstan the King's tongue?"

Webb held up his right hand. "What in the hell? I don't understand a word you're saying!"

"An it please ye, m'laird. In this form, Samuel Graeme, loyal cavalier ta 'is majesty King Charles."

"Samuel the nutcase!"

"Aye, m'laird."

Webb pressed a palm against his aching head. "The same Samuel at the accident last night and the precinct this morning?"

"Aye."

"What are you doing here? And what's with the crazy get-up?"

"Dinnae ye oonerstan, Laird Hannis? I be catchin' yer attention."

"You want my attention? For what?"

"So you will finally start listening to me, Bud," the man replied. Now he spoke perfect English without any accent. "I thought that was obvious. Hmm, not quite a believer yet, I see…and seeing is believing, as they say."

Samuel wrapped his arms around the black stallion's neck in an affectionate hug. He whispered into its ear, then swatted the horse on the rump. It bolted toward the tall row of privacy bushes lining the side yard, easily jumped over the six-foot barrier…and vanished in midair.

"Do I have your attention now, Bud?" asked Samuel in a gentle tone.

The detective stared where the horse disappeared, his jaw hanging. "What the…what the hell just happened?"

"I sent Ahearn home. I needed him for only a little while. Next question?"

"I'm hallucinating. Right? You're not real…it's the accident. You're some wild fantasy my battered mind is imagining."

Samuel pushed down on the hilt of his sword and stepped back. The tip of the scabbard pressed against the doorbell. A chime sounded from within the house. "Can a hallucination do that, Webb? Don't worry, they can't see me."

The detective shook his head. "I'm losing it. That's what it is. I'm completely and totally bonkers."

"Really?" Samuel grinned. "Well, I suggest you pull yourself together because someone is going to answer the bell right...now."

The front door opened. An elderly gentleman, pink scalp glowing through wispy white hair, glared at Webb. "Yes? What is it?"

"Detective Webb Hannis with the Detroit Police Department. I have a one-thirty appointment with Pierre Lazare."

"I'm Pierre Lazare," the man announced. Wrinkled skin pillowed beneath red rimmed eyes. Despite his height, withered shoulders curled forward like a falling wave.

Webb pointed to Samuel. "And this is—"

"*He can't see me, Bud,*" Samuel interrupted. The cavalier removed his plumed hat and brushed away bits of lint. "*Don't embarrass yourself.*"

The officer shook his head in frustration. "Uh, this is...certainly a hot day."

"Yes, Detective, it is." The older man spoke as though the right side of his face was frozen. "Will you come inside?"

Webb, light blue shirtsleeves rolled to the elbow, nodded and stepped into the house. The door closed behind him and cold air immediately embraced his large frame. He mopped sweat from his brow as he glanced around the entryway. The two men were alone in the elegant foyer. An elaborate winding staircase with a hand-carved newel post swept up to the second floor. Flowered wallpaper, straight out of the fifties, needed updating.

"We need to begin," the detective said and nodded toward the living room.

Webb heard a voice from above. He looked up with wide eyes.

Samuel stood on the landing, left hand resting on the rail. The detective watched in bafflement as the Cavalier leapt onto the banister. With sword dangling over the edge and gray cloak beneath him, he slid sideways down the handrail.

Samuel jumped off at the last moment before reaching the newel post. He removed his plumed hat and bowed.

Webb quickly looked away. This guy is not really here, he assured himself.

"Come into the living room, Detective," Pierre said and walked slowly toward the doorway on the right.

Webb shook his head and followed Lazare. He noticed the elderly man's right wrist curved back, the hand balled into a fist. The stooped figure dragged his right leg. All definite indicators of a stroke.

Sofas and occasional pieces, covered in gold brocades and brown velvets, were scattered about the large room. The fabric on one chair was faded, while the velvet settee exposed thinning nap.

A petite woman, stunning waves of white hair framing her genteel face, offered a strained smile from across the room. She was dressed in a peach blouse and white linen skirt. A rope of pearls surrounded her wrinkled neck and spilled down over her bosom.

"Detective Hannis, this is my wife Katherine," Lazare said, and gestured toward a young man standing beside the fireplace. "Our son, Conrad. He's manning the office for now."

"Running the business," Conrad said through clenched teeth. "And cleaning up the sloppy bookkeeping," he muttered under his breath.

Webb studied the son. He remembered seeing him on the fireworks barge two days ago, but now he could really focus on Pierre's third son. Dark, wavy hair expertly cut and styled, sculpted cheekbones under tanned skin, too pretty for a man. Preppy in khaki slacks and a white polo shirt, he was a younger version of his father. Webb guessed him in his mid-thirties.

Katherine gestured for Webb to sit down. "Would you care for coffee?" she asked, her demeanor morose.

Webb saw it many times before. The family, gripped by grief, denied their loved one's death by engrossing in ritual. Offering coffee was the most common. Hands moved while the mind idled in denial.

"Yes, coffee." He watched the grateful smile cross her face as she turned and walked toward the kitchen.

Pierre Lazare carefully lowered himself into a winged-back chair, bracing his back against a pillow. He sighed heavily, but spoke with authority. "What is this all about, Detective?"

Webb watched with apprehension as Samuel moved about the room, examining the bric-a-brac on various tables. The cavalier's sword seemed to move of its own volition, rising or falling in time to barely miss the expensive knickknacks.

He forced himself to turn away from the fanciful mirage and focused on Pierre Lazare. "Let's get started."

"Yes, yes," Pierre said, motioning impatiently with his left hand. "I expect you have some questions about the accident."

Webb pulled a small notebook and pen from his shirt pocket. "Did Marc have any enemies?"

"Of course not. Everyone loved him."

He turned to Conrad. "When did you last see Marc?"

"I don't remember. Things were awfully busy, you know." Conrad shifted his eyes away from the detective. He stood with head bowed beside the fireplace, slowly twisting a ring around his finger. He grabbed an ashtray off the mantle and began turning it over and over in his hands.

An expert at body language, Webb watched him closely. This guy isn't mourning. He's nervous about something. "I see Marc was president of Lazare Fireworks. Did he have business problems?"

"Marc ran a tight ship," Pierre said. "Business is the best in years and we have a new innovation ready for release this fall. Sales will boom."

Webb heard someone clear his throat near the fireplace. He turned to Conrad. Samuel stood opposite the sharply dressed man, right elbow cradled in his left hand as he stroked his clean-shaven chin.

"That's not quite right, Father," Conrad stated. "The records are in shambles, just as I suspected."

Pierre heaved a deep breath. "I don't understand."

Conrad focused his gaze on the detective, ignoring his father. "I checked the books this morning. More than half our customers have outstanding bills. Some are a year overdue."

Pierre rested his chin on his hand. "I'm surprised to hear that. Marc never mentioned it to me."

Conrad scowled at Pierre. "It appears he doctored some figures to make it look like the company has more cash flow, too. I told you, Father, Red wasn't a businessman and he hated handling customers. Oh, he was good with chemicals...but you should've let me run the business end from the beginning."

Webb's head pounded from the rising anger in Conrad's voice. "Red?"

Conrad leaned against the fireplace. "We called Marc 'Red' because he used to manage the bunker that produced red fireworks. We also have workers named Pinky, Purp, Blue Boy, and Goldie."

"I can't believe Marc would do anything to jeopardize our business," Pierre said, his voice shaky.

"Marc was great at fireworks, Father," Conrad argued. "He just didn't know how to solve the business problems. Don't you see he was losing it? Maybe he was so ashamed, he committed suicide."

Pierre struggled up from his seat, nearly losing his balance, and waved his fist in the air. "How can you say that about your brother?"

"Because there's three quarters of a million in past-due payables, Father. And a million dollars in last year's receivables that Marc didn't bother to collect!" Conrad slammed his fist against the mantle. "He sat on the invoices so damn long, we'll probably have to write off most of them!"

"I trusted Marc with the family business," Pierre said, a haunted tinge in his eyes as he grasped the meaning of Conrad's words. "My grandfather created Lazare Fireworks almost one hundred years ago. Do you mean now we could lose everything?"

Conrad stretched a hand toward his patriarch, his voice both accusing and pleading. "Well, Father, you trusted the wrong son. Give me some time and I'll get the business back in order."

"Your brother Luc is next in line to run the business." Pierre's voice was heavy iron. "I will honor family tradition."

Bitter pain and fury whipped across Conrad's face. He dropped his hand to his side, fingers clenched. The two men locked glares for several moments before Conrad turned away. He crossed in front of his father and walked right through Samuel.

Webb sucked in a shocked and disbelieving breath.

Conrad slammed the front door with such force it echoed throughout the room. Webb's eyes and thoughts were on the strange Cavalier who casually moseyed over to the fireplace.

Unfazed, Samuel simply crossed one ankle over the other and folded his arms. He grinned at Webb, and winked. The picture of contentment.

The detective turned away, swallowing heavily. I'm definitely cracking up.

Across from him, Pierre Lazare covered his face with his hands. His back bowed, as if in defeat. "Oh, Conrad," he mumbled through his fingers, "tradition is what makes us family. Can't you see that?"

"How do you like your coffee, Detective?" Katherine asked from the doorway. She held a silver serving tray in her hands, the china cups and silverware rattling as she trembled. Her head turned slowly in confusion. "What happened to Conrad?"

"Guess he had to leave," Webb said. "Black coffee for me." He glanced up and noticed Samuel pointing toward the foyer.

The doorbell rang.

Pierre Lazare, with little enthusiasm, excused himself to answer it. A few seconds later, a familiar voice sounded from the foyer.

"Sorry I'm late. I hate being late," Jake Rubel blared. "Damn road construction. I left the station on time, but I was stuck in a traffic jam on the way. You must be Pierre Lazare. Detective Rubel, Detroit PD. Let's get started."

Webb ignored the scrawny dwarf as he entered the living room.

Rubel's eyes shot daggers at Webb. "How long have you been here? You better not have started without me."

Webb glanced at his wristwatch. "You said one-thirty, right? That was twenty minutes ago."

"Well, I'm taking it from here." Rubel settled onto the couch. "You just sit back and shut up," he muttered under his breath.

Pierre resumed his seat. "Why does an accident require two detectives?"

Rubel leaned forward in his seat. "It wasn't an accident," he pronounced bluntly. "We found a bullet in the victim's brain. Your son was murdered."

Katherine Lazare gasped, rose on unsteady legs, and went to sit close to her husband. Fingering her pearls with one hand, she unconsciously patted Pierre's arm with the other. "Murdered? My child murdered? Who would kill our son?"

"It wasn't suicide," Rubel stated. "We didn't find a gun at the scene, and his body was over the mortar tube."

"I can't believe this," Pierre said, his voice quivering. He wiped his eyes and pulled himself up straight. "I thought one of the bombs misfired. Everyone admired Marc."

"We need to start working the case immediately while the evidence is fresh," Webb said. "Who was the last to see Marc the night of the show?"

"He usually worked in the office," Pierre replied. "The others handled the actual launch."

Rubel jotted furiously in his notebook.

Webb continued. "Was he with the crew that night, maybe helping set up?"

Katherine grabbed a tissue and wiped her eyes. "I can't believe Marc is gone," she cried. "Murdered."

Webb watched Samuel step from his position at the fireplace and move behind Katherine. The gray-caped figure wrapped his arms around the grieving mother and held her tenderly as she sobbed.

"Gentlemen, can we finish this another time?" Pierre's eyes painfully pleaded as he stroked Katherine's arm. "This is too much for my wife."

"Not yet," Jake replied. "I have several more questions. Who do you think wanted to kill —"

"Mrs. Lazare," Webb interrupted firmly. "What can you tell us about Marc?"

Rubel scowled at him and continued writing in his notebook.

Samuel supported Katherine by the arms and helped her rise. The elderly lady stepped toward the fireplace.

"Our Marc was the kindest, most decent human being on this earth." As Katherine spoke, Samuel placed his hand beneath hers and guided it to a photograph on the mantel. "His family was everything to him."

Katherine carried the picture to Webb, holding it out gingerly toward him. "Here he is with his wife Laura. Such a lovely couple," she sighed. "And that's their precious three year old son Austin. Marc adored the child."

Marc, dapper in a navy suit and dark tie, bore a close resemblance to Conrad. So, how did this supposedly nice guy get a bullet in his brain? Webb wondered. He focused on the woman in the picture. Laura Lazare was earthy with long curly red hair and tan freckles sprinkled across the bridge of her nose. She appeared self-assured and poised.

Rubel grabbed the frame from Webb's hand. "Yeah, that's nice," Rubel said, glancing briefly at the picture before directing his attention back to Pierre. "As I was saying, do you know anyone —"

The front door slammed, interrupting the younger detective. A fellow, dressed in a T-shirt and camouflage pants bloused in black combat boots, strode into the room. Without so much as a nod to anyone, he threw himself into a chair and propped his boots on the coffee table.

"Luc. You should've been here an hour ago." Pierre waved a hand toward his son. "Detectives, this is my second son, Luc."

"Luc is a genius at pyrotechnics, just like Marc and his father," Katherine announced proudly. "You haven't met Teddy, our youngest, yet. He'll be home soon. He's at college, studying to take his place in the business with his brothers."

Luc was shorter yet heavy compared to the other Lazare men. Acne scars pocked fleshy cheeks. He spotted Webb and tossed his head. Long dark hair lay in greasy strings over his eyes. He looked away quickly.

Webb frowned as a sense of déjà vu struck him. "Do I know you?"

Rubel snapped to attention.

Luc looked bored. "No."

Searching his aching brain, Webb tried to recall the previous night's events. The pounding in his head muddled the picture. "Did I see you at the Fourth of July show?"

"I was on the barge all night," Luc said without looking at Webb.

Webb eyed Luc. "So you handled the bombs?"

"Yeah, I set off a few guns. We have a crew to man the show."

"Why would anyone be out near the guns during a show?"

"Usually no one is allowed beyond the barriers. Only the technicians are permitted out there after the show starts. But Marc could go anywhere he damn well pleased. He was the pres-i-dent." Luc drew out the word in emphasis.

"Sounds like you hated that," Rubel declared, "Unhappy enough to kill him, maybe?"

Pierre Lazare stiffened. He pushed himself up from the chair, trembling with weakness and anger. "That's all, gentlemen. You will leave my house now."

"This is a police investigation," Hannis stated. "If you want to know who killed your son, you must cooperate with us."

"From now on, all information comes though my attorney. Good day, detectives."

"I need your lawyer's name and phone number," Webb declared. "We also need a list of the addresses and phone numbers for all employees at Lazare Fireworks."

"Leave your card, Detective Hannis," Pierre said. "I'll see that you get a list."

Webb, stretching almost a foot taller than the shrunken Lazare, extended the card to the older man.

Rubel stood, red faced. "I'm not finished yet. Where were you last night, Mr. Lazare?"

Pierre glared at the detective's narrow face. He raised one shaky arm and pointed toward the door. "I'm telling you to leave my home now. I know my rights. Contact our attorney."

Webb was already halfway to his car before Rubel stepped out of the house.

*　　*　　*

"Okay, Father, I won't tell them anything," Conrad said into his car phone. He turned into his driveway, relieved to be home. Clicking off the phone, he steered the car into the garage and turned off the ignition. Exhausted, he rested his head against the seat. "At least Father is keeping the cops at arm's length," he sighed.

As Conrad stepped through the interior garage door and into the kitchen, his wife Jade called out from the family room. "Darling, come and see what Tristan chose for the new house."

Just hearing the name made Conrad Lazare bristle. Jutting his long jaw forward, as he always did when his wife used her high-toned lilt, he dragged himself through the kitchen, stopping in the doorway to the family room to leaf through the mail.

"Conrad," Jade said tersely. "Tristan's time is precious."

Conrad looked up to see his wife, her slender body outlined in a manila pants set, seated next to an effeminate creature. Tristan's most striking feature was his hair, moussed into a curly pyramid on top of his perfumed head. Goddamn fag. Conrad gritted his teeth.

His wife's long golden hair sparkled, illuminated by the skylight Tristan insisted they install last year. Like we needed a skylight in this place when we were already planning to build a new house, Conrad thought.

"Come sit and look at these samples." Jade patted the creamy sofa.

Instead, Conrad carried the mail to the caned rocker across the room.

"Isn't this color yummy?" Tristan drooled in a conjured British accent, holding up a peachy fabric. "Jade will positively glow surrounded by this warm hue. Note how the fabric drapes."

Conrad felt his stomach turn as the fellow pleated the silky material adoringly across his chest.

"Tristan's doing color in the new house," Jade said. "He's bored with the monochromatic beige he did in this one."

Conrad's eyes darted up from the mail. "Damn it, Jade. My brother died last night and I had to tell my father his precious first-born was a coward. I don't need this decorating shit today."

Jumping up from the couch, Jade rushed to her husband's side, kneeling down next to the rocker. "I know you're upset about Marc, sweetheart, but we can't just drop the house plans. I'll handle the decorating, but I want you to be excited too."

The decorator adjusted his funky glasses and flipped through a leather notebook. "Jade, darling, I'm completely booked through Christmas next year. I'm fitting you in because

I love you, and I want to work with your new hair color. You will radiate with the peach tones."

Conrad wanted to grab the fellow by his skinny neck and squeeze.

"Honey, you know Tristan's a legend in Detroit," Jade pleaded with him. "People beg for his time. Just look at these colors."

"I don't want this crap in my life right now," Conrad said as he pushed up from the chair.

Tristan drew his mouth into a fluted circle.

Jade hurried to him. "Tristan, darling. I love the peach." She whispered something in his ear.

Conrad loosened his tie and left the room, retreating up the cream carpeted stairs.

So the police suspect Marc was murdered, he thought as he pulled off his starched shirt, tossing it in the dry cleaning bin. Jade was too busy keeping up with the jet set to iron his shirts.

Ten minutes later Jade bounded into the room, removed her jeweled strap sandals and dropped on the bed. She rested her chin on her hands.

Oh, no, the pout. He steeled himself. Conrad looked into his wife's eyes, florescent from the green contacts Tristan suggested, to match her name. A beauty, Jade was the kind of woman any man would want on his arm.

"Gillian and Richard joined the country club," she said, etching doodles with her finger on the spread.

Conrad pulled on a pair of Dockers. "Good for them," he said.

"We really need to join," she said in that little girl tone that irritated him. "If I want to take golf lessons from that fabulous pro, I have to be a member."

"We don't have the money right now," he snapped. "And you can forget about Trisket—"

"It's Tristan, Dear."

Conrad, buttoning a shirt, turned to her. She looked so sexy with those long tanned arms and rounded derriere. He felt a wave of arousal. "The house is this year. Maybe we can join the club next summer."

Jade rolled onto her back, staring at the ceiling. "All my new friends belong to the club."

Conrad dove onto the bed, nuzzling next to her. "We're on our way, honey. The house plans are set, and I'm president of Lazare Fireworks now."

"Oh? Did your dad make it official?"

"Official or not, who else could run it? Luc? He can't even organize his wardrobe." He kissed her shoulder tenderly. "Soon money will pour in."

Jade laughed and tugged at Conrad's zipper.

He grabbed her hand. "I promised Laura I'd be there in fifteen minutes to help with last minute arrangements. The funeral is tomorrow."

Jade straddled his waist. "Laura can wait. I can't."

* * *

Teddy, the youngest Lazare brother, gently rapped on Laura's front door. Half hoping nobody would answer, his pulse quickened. He longed to flee. This was a house of death, and a place filled with memories. Was he ready to face the truth? Marc, his big brother, was gone.

The door opened and Rosa Perez, Laura's hired girl appeared. Her eyes were misty. Beside her a cherubic face with dazzling Lazare brown eyes beamed at him. "Hi, Unca Teddy."

Teddy reached out and pulled the little boy into his arms. "Austin! Is your Mommy home?" He stepped into the front entry and looked about.

"Mrs. Lazare is upstairs," Rosa said and headed back to the kitchen.

The little boy wriggled free. Austin, dressed in denim shorts and a red shirt that set off his dark features, scrambled up the carpeted steps.

Teddy hesitated, peering into the cluttered living room. Clothes littered the sofa and chairs, boots and shoes tossed about on the floor. This wasn't like Laura, the meticulous housewife.

"Austin, who was at the door?"

Teddy stiffened when he heard Laura's voice from upstairs.

"Unca' Teddy," the young boy bubbled.

Teddy studied the clothes in the living room. They belonged to Marc. Suits, jackets, shoes, a few scarves and hats were all that was left of his brother. He reached down and fingered a leather glove. The sight sickened him.

A hand touched his back. He whirled around. Laura stood there.

"I'm surprised to see you here," she said wryly.

"Come on. I'm not a total oaf. My brother died." He pointed to the clothes. "What's going on here?"

"His things remind me of him," Laura said, picking up a jacket. "I want them out of the house. They'll go to Goodwill after the funeral. You can go through them, and if you want anything—"

"Laura." He cleared his throat. "You're moving too fast."

Laura threw the jacket onto a chair. "I'm the one who has to live with the memories. This part of my life is over."

"Damn it, Laura." Teddy grabbed his sister-in-law by the shoulders. "He was a human being. He lived on this earth for thirty-eight years. You can't wipe away his existence."

"Aren't you the loving brother." Laura pulled away from him and headed up the stairs.

Teddy followed her. The spacious hallway led to the master bedroom where more of Marc's clothing was piled on the bed. Austin jumped onto the spread and tossed Polo shirts into the air. Teddy caught him around the waist, lifting him down to the floor. "Don't mess up your daddy's things."

"Where's my daddy?" Austin said.

Teddy cuddled the three-year-old, placing him on his lap and smoothing the silky dark hair. Poor kid.

Laura pulled men's socks and underwear from a drawer and stuffed them into a corrugated box. "Austin, run downstairs to Rosa. She just made cookies."

Tumbling from Teddy's arms, the child charged out of the room and pounded down the stairs.

Laura wadded up white tube socks. "Can you believe all this? Pierre called. The police found a damn bullet in Marc's brain."

"I'm so confused," Teddy said. He watched Laura bend over the bureau. "Why is this happening?"

"God, Teddy. He was so devastated that afternoon. I feel guilty about that, but I didn't want him dead."

"Somebody obviously did."

"Austin is oblivious. He thinks Marc is on a trip."

"A three year old doesn't understand the finality of death," Teddy said. "I feel guilty too. I should've stayed here to help after Dad's stroke. Marc was a gentle soul. Never hurt anybody."

"He was milk toast," Laura declared, pulling dress shirts from hangers. "Everyone walked all over him."

"I won't let you talk like that about my brother," Teddy bristled. He darted across the room and dumped the box of Marc's socks on the bed. "Put these things back in the drawers and mourn like a normal wife. This isn't fair to my family."

He stormed down the stairs and out of the house.

*   *   *

Webb winced at the sharp explosion of pain as the door slammed. He sat at his desk, hands cradling his aching head. A muffled, angry voice — Rubel's, of course — sounded from the Chief's office. The little runt wasted no time voicing his opinion, Webb had to give him that. Gallister's response was brief and terse, followed by momentary silence. The office door banged open again a few minutes later. Muttered cursing faded slowly as Rubel stormed through the department.

Webb grabbed the orange medicine vial off the desk and leaned back in his chair. He wanted to call it a day. His head throbbed from the steamy drive back to the precinct, Rubel's door-clanging tantrum, and the glaring sunlight that stabbed through his window.

It took several seconds — and a hand over one eye — before he could focus on the prescription that cautioned him not to operate heavy machinery. A grunt was the closest he could get to laugh off the warning.

Suddenly Samuel appeared with a bouquet of flowers in his hand. Webb watched the Cavalier sniff the fragrant roses.

"Nice, huh?' Samuel said. "Divine gifts." He turned and held the blooms toward the detective. "Plants are loaded with spiritual energy. Want some?"

The officer swiveled his chair to face the blue-clad figure in the gray cape. "No, I don't need any flowers and I don't need you!"

"Oh, really?"

"Okay, I'm sick of talking to a loony illusion," Webb snapped. "What do you want?"

Samuel smiled innocently, as if to a child. "What do *you* want?"

"I want to get on with my life without you tagging along. It's nuts to deal with a sword-wielding ghost in rusty armor. God, you probably stink in that thing."

"God probably stinks?"

"No!" Webb tugged his hair. "That's not what I said!"

"You said, 'God, you probably stink.'"

"God! I was talking about you!"

"You said it again."

Webb let out a throaty growl. "I don't have all day to play word games with you." He turned away. "You don't even exist!"

"Think before you speak, Bud. Spoken words are strong." In a flash, Samuel's archaic wardrobe disappeared and was replaced by his brown jacket and jeans. "Since you don't like this outfit, I might as well be comfortable."

"You're playing games again."

Samuel began arranging the bouquet of flowers into a vase on the windowsill. "I'm just following what you said. I asked what you want. Just be careful what you ask for."

"What does that mean?"

"Thoughts are things, Bud. You create your own reality with your thoughts."

"Oh, yeah?" Webb stood. "Then I'll think about getting you out of my life!"

"No chance, Bud. I'm your spirit guide. We have a pact. I've always been here. You couldn't see me before, but you were pretty good at following my guidance. You know, those brainstorms you call hunches?"

"Spirit guide? Guidance? You're not even the hell really here."

Samuel nodded. "It's always hard for earthlings to accept at first. Your ego is telling you to ignore me."

"Ego? Dammit, Samuel, what are you talking about?" Webb groaned and looked at the floor. "I'm out of my mind. I'm talking to a mirage that doesn't even exist!"

Samuel tsked. "Language, Bud, you really must watch your language. You're a tough guy, but you came to earth with an agenda. Time to start working on it."

"What in the hell do you mean?"

Samuel began rolling the sleeves on his brown jacket. "You'll understand eventually."

Daisy Farrell stood at the doorway. She paused, eyebrows furrowed in deep concern as she scanned Webb's face. "Are you okay? You look like a coronary candidate."

"Yeah." Webb focused on the vial in his hand. The cap still wouldn't budge. He longed to throw it against the wall, but Daisy stood in the way. "Can't get this damn thing open."

She extended her hand. "From what I saw from you and Rubel today, I'm not surprised. It's childproof, you know."

Reluctantly he placed the vial in the slender outstretched hand. "Don't start, Daiz. It's been one helluva day."

Daisy glanced at the label, then shook her head. "Must've been, if you're going to take these. That chair doesn't look like the most comfortable bed...this will put you out like a light."

"I have to do something. This headache is killing me!"

"*Oh, my*," said Samuel. "*Better treat it before it kills you. Watch your words, Bud.*"

Webb moaned.

Daisy smoothed her free hand over Webb's shoulder. "Let me take you home. Gallister will understand."

"Can't." The brawny detective started to shake his head, then stopped. Even that simple motion was painful.

"*You should listen to her, Bud*," Samuel's voice sounded from the windowsill behind him.

Hannis scrunched his eyes shut and slammed his hand against the arm of his chair. "I told you before to shut up!"

Daisy's eyes widened.

Samuel smiled.

"You're starting to scare me, Webb." Daisy backed toward the hallway. "I offered to help you. I don't need your rage."

He raised his head and opened his eyes.

Daisy's brow narrowed.

"I'm okay, really. It's just.... You'll think I'm nuts, Daiz. Hell, *I* think I'm nuts, but there's someone else in this room."

"You're not nuts," her voice softened. "You have a concussion, that's all. Aggressive outbursts are perfectly normal. Just to be safe, let me call a cab. Okay?"

Webb opened his mouth to reply, then chuckled instead. "You don't need to talk down to me, Detective. I still have my wits. It's just that my head feels like it's splitting, and I'm...."

"Hearing voices?"

He wagged his head. "Just one. You remember that guy I told you about? The one who was in here earlier today?"

Slowly she nodded. "The same one you saw at the hospital. Samuel, right?"

"Right." The detective pointed a thumb over his shoulder. "He's standing by the window."

Daisy glanced that way, and smiled. "Oh, really?" She curtsied. "I'm sorry, Samuel. I'd really like to see you. Anyway it's a pleasure to meet you."

"*A pleasure to meet you, Detective Farrell,*" Samuel responded courteously.

Daisy tried to suppress a smile. "So, what did the invisible man say?"

"He's pleased to meet you," Webb said gruffly. "Of course, you didn't hear it because he isn't really there. Right? He's just a figment of my bruised brain."

"*There are more things in heaven and earth, Bud,*" Samuel said as he chuckled from the windowsill, "*than are dreamt of in your philosophy. I borrowed that from an incredible writer who listened to his spirit guide. You might've heard of him...William Shakespeare?*"

"Oh, God," Webb moaned. His eyebrows furrowed as he glared at Daisy. "Now you did it. He's quoting Shakespeare. Or my brain is quoting him. But I don't know shit about Shakespeare. Ah, the hell with it. I'm going home."

"Good idea ," Daisy hastened to say. "If you're quoting Shakespeare, there's definitely something wrong."

His frown darkened. "Go ahead, Farrell. Laugh all you want, I don't give a crap."

"I apologize. It's just...I picture you more as the brain-dead action-adventure movie type."

"My life *is* an action-adventure movie," Webb retorted. Fury flared at the thought of her mocking him. He stood rigidly, then grabbed his forehead and groaned. Waves of dizziness crashed over him as the pounding in his temples doubled.

Soft, firm hands steadied him, and guided him back to the chair. "Here, sit down and rest a minute," Daisy said gently. "Take a breath and let it out slowly."

"I'm not a kid, Daiz." Webb's anger intensified the throbbing in his skull.

"No, you're a grown detective who needs to lower his blood pressure. I've seen tomatoes paler than you."

"*Listen to her, Bud,*" Samuel whispered in Webb's ear. "*She can help you.*"

"Go away, Samuel!" Webb roared but quickly groaned. "Oh, God, I wish this headache would quit!"

Strong hands pressed against the side of his head. A moment later the thumping disappeared. He turned his head and gazed directly into Samuel's iridescent blue eyes.

"*Tell Daisy that Phoebe can help this situation,*" Samuel instructed.

"Phoebe? What?"

A startled look crossed Daisy's face. "What did you say?"

"Samuel says to tell you I need to see Phoebe. Who in the hell is that?"

She knelt beside him. "Phoebe is my aunt."

"What Aunt? How did she get into the act?"

"Phoebe's a psychic and swears we're surrounded by spirits."

Webb glared at her. "I don't believe in that bull."

"Phoebe's clairvoyant, and says these spirits are with her all the time."

"But Samuel's an hallucination…. He has to be. No one else can see him."

"I'll make an appointment with her," Daisy said, smiling. "She's a medium and takes clients."

"Hold on. I'm not ready for that weird crap."

"Webb, if you're seeing spirits, you're already into the weird stuff. My aunt can see auras and predict the future. You may have a gift here." Daisy turned to the window.

"Okay. Whatever," Webb said with a groan. "At this point, I don't care who this character is. I just want to get rid of him!"

"He must be here for a reason," Daisy said, removing her glasses, her eyes wide with wonder.

"There's more. I had this…I guess you would call it a…vision of some sort. I saw a bullet in Marc Lazare's brain."

Daisy leaned back in her chair. "Oh, Webb, that was all over the station."

"No. I had the vision before Rubel reported back from the coroner." He looked away from her. "How would I know about the bullet?"

Daisy's brown eyes gazed deep into Webb's. "I don't know what to say except maybe Phoebe can explain it."

Webb glanced at his watch. "I have to get this report going before Rubel has a shit fit. Thanks for listening, Daiz, and for God's sake don't tell anyone about this."

"You can trust me." She took a deep breath. "Believe it, I wouldn't tell a soul."

CHAPTER 4

THAT EVENING in Webb's apartment, the detective stepped out of his trousers, draped them over the back of a chair in his bedroom and went into the bathroom.

Samuel was right beside him.

At the commode, Webb turned his back to the spirit guide. "Can I take a leak without your prying eyes?"

Samuel snickered. "I've seen it all, Bud. Doesn't interest me in the least."

Webb finished his business and grabbed his toothbrush. With a mouth full of foam, he eyed Samuel in the mirror as he brushed his teeth. "If you know so much, Sam," he mumbled through the glob of toothpaste, "where is the gun?"

"I'm no killjoy."

Webb's eye's narrowed. He tossed his toothbrush on the counter, spat out the toothpaste, popped two painkillers in his mouth, and ducked his mouth under the faucet. "What in the hell does that mean?" He whisked past Samuel into his bedroom.

"Joy is in the discovery."

"You could at least give me a damn clue."

Samuel sprawled across his bed. "Sweet dreams, Bud."

Webb let out a tired sigh, slid in next to the guide and moved near the edge of the bed, away from the maddening spirit.

Soon he was fast asleep. His mind too hyper for his weary body, he tossed and turned in and out of odd dreams. Near morning he found himself walking in an expansive field with no trees or signs of wildlife. He peered into the distance but could see no end. "How do I get out of here?" he called out loud.

Walking onward he suddenly found himself at the opening of a cave. "Okay, this is what I'm looking for."

Inside, instead of being dark and dank he found it well lit and inviting. Warmth surged through his body and he stopped to rest on a rock. He found it cushiony soft.

"I'm hungry," he said, and instantly a meal was spread before him. A feast really. A platter of hearty steak, huge mounds of mashed potatoes swarming with butter, plump grapes the size of golf balls. Webb ate a grape like a plum, the juice dribbling down his chin.

Once sated, he began to explore the cave. With a feeling of elation, he seemed to float along over dagger rock formations and heavy boulders.

He came upon a door and his heart swelled with excitement. He pulled it open and stepped into a hollow room. Inside, straight ahead, a magnificent glow summoned him.

Webb moved toward the light. Slowly a wooden structure — a large wall unit of some sort — came into focus. He stepped closer. A gun cabinet. Rows of handguns were illuminated behind beveled glass.

"The murder weapon must be here," he marveled. "But which one is it?"

Suddenly one of the guns began to glow brightly. Webb reached behind the glass and carefully picked it up, admiring the smooth wooden handle.

"A Smith and Wesson." The brand name simply fell from his tongue. He ran his fingers along the barrel. "Stainless steel. They were first made in the early seventies," he said with authority.

Abruptly, he awakened.

Samuel was perched on the bed next to him.

Webb squeezed his eyes shut, engraving the image of the cabinet and gun in his memory.

*   *   *

Friday morning, a bolt of lightening crackled across the angry sky. A pesky summer thunderstorm pelted the windshield as Conrad pulled into his parent's driveway.

"My new suit will be ruined if it gets wet," wailed Jade. "You know how water spots silk. Pull into the garage."

"It's blocked." Conrad grabbed a golf umbrella from the back seat and stepped out of the car. A fishy smell assaulted his nostrils…it came from worms, actually, washed up from their homes in the soggy earth. The odor turned his stomach. Breathing through his mouth and bypassing the bloated night crawlers, he opened the door for his wife.

"Can't we go directly to the church?" Jade complained, hiking up her skirt against the splashing water.

Lightning slashed across the sky. Thunder crashed.

"Good God. Maybe Marc's thundering down from heaven," Conrad said and helped Jade up the front steps and into the house.

Katherine Lazare called from the winding staircase. "Oh, Conrad, I'm glad you're here. I'm concerned about Father." She looked worn, her eyes puffy and red.

"I see Teddy's here," Jade said, bending to wipe splash marks from the back of her stockings. "Where was he on the Fourth of July?"

"At school, according to Father," Conrad said. "He's taking summer courses."

The youngest Lazare brother, who had never outgrown his childhood name, sauntered in from the living room. "Jade, you look marvelous, as always." He kissed her gently on the cheek. Turning to his brother, he thrust out a hand. "This won't be easy," he said.

Conrad embraced his young brother, just twenty-two years old, trying to look older in a navy pinstriped suit that hung on his youthful frame. "How is school? We missed you at the Fourth of July show this year."

"I'm trying to graduate early so I can enter law school next spring." Teddy's brown hair and tanned face matched his brother's.

"Law school? Does father know?"

"Not yet." Teddy's face fell. "I can't believe Marc is—"

"Dead?" Conrad said.

Katherine approached her two sons. "Please join the others. We need to be at the church by ten."

In the living room, Conrad saw Laura, curly hair swinging across her face as she bent to kiss Austin.

The child pulled on her dress. "Mommy, where's Daddy?"

Conrad looked away.

Luc, dressed in a wrinkled tan shirt, a colorful, poorly knotted tie around his thick neck, leaned against the fireplace absorbing the scene.

"Luc," Pierre Lazare called from across the room.

"Laura is holding up well," Jade whispered to Conrad. "I'd be a wreck if I were her."

Conrad watched Luc follow Pierre into the study and close the door.

"Conrad, you're not listening again," Jade said, yanking on his lapel. "I need a drink. Funerals make me nervous."

"It's too early to drink. Wait until after the service."

Finally, Conrad strolled over to speak with Laura.

"I think I'm numb right now," she said. "I haven't been able to cry yet. Austin needs me."

Conrad hugged her stiffly, bent down and patted Austin on the head.

Katherine approached them. "Laura, I asked Teddy to escort you down the aisle, dear."

Across the room Conrad saw Luc, his face void of emotion, emerge from the study with Pierre a step behind. Conrad's heart skipped a beat.

*   *   *

At the police station, Webb hurried to his cubicle and sank into the chair behind his desk.

Rubel burst onto the scene. "Did you question Strickland? I want to mark him off the list."

Samuel popped behind Rubel, mimicking his irritating cackle.

Webb withheld a smile and offered Rubel a bored glare. "He's on *my* list," he mimicked.

"I'm on my way to pump the other employees for information," Rubel said in a raspy voice. "You'd better get cracking on your written reports. I've yet to see one."

Webb glared at him, his fists clenched. "Don't push it, Rubel. You aren't my boss."

"*I* did the ass busting on the murder scene. *I* watched the autopsy. That pretty much means, *I'm* leading the investigation."

Samuel's mouth yapped comically.

"Yeah, right into a brick wall. You're too textbook, Rubel. Try using your gut instincts for a change."

Rubel's face smoldered. "I'll have this case solved before you get your ass out the door," he huffed and fled from sight.

Samuel leaned against Webb's Rolodex.

Without thinking, Webb leafed through the worn file. "I'm calling the crime lab." He said smugly. "They should have traced the bullet by now."

He dialed the number. "Connect me with Sergeant Langdon. This is Webb Hannis, Detroit Detective Division."

Webb doodled circles on his notepad as he waited for the State Police Sergeant to come on the line. Samuel propped his feet on Webb's desk.

"Hannis," said the firearm expert, "I determined the gun used in the fireworks case is a Smith and Wesson revolver. Thirty-eight caliber police special, model ten with a four-inch barrel."

Webb jotted the information in his notebook.

"My gut feeling is usually right," Langdon said, "But you better add the Herrington-Richard and the Rossi to your list of possible weapons."

"Thanks for the information," Webb said and tossed the pencil onto the desk.

"I'll send the report by messenger," Langdon said and hung up.

Webb looked at Samuel. "A Smith and Wesson. Now where in the hell is it?"

"State a need and plant a seed," Samuel whispered softly. "Now trust the power of the universe."

* * *

As the family approached the church, rain continued to dribble down. Inside, weeping dotted the chapel. Several hundred mourners, dressed in somber colors, clutched handkerchiefs to their bosoms as Marc Lazare's casket was wheeled down the aisle, the entire Lazare clan trailing behind.

Laura, leaning heavily on Teddy's arm, walked directly behind the coffin followed by Pierre and Katherine, Conrad with Jade, and Luc at the rear with his hands stuffed in his pockets. The organ droned out a gloomy dirge until everyone was seated.

Katherine grasped Pierre's hand the moment he settled into the pew. His father's grief-drawn face pierced Conrad's heart.

He knew his parents were devastated by the loss of their first born. Family order was important to his father. It was tradition. Conrad's mind raged. Marc was so damned weak. I should have been born first.

Tears streamed down his mother's sunken cheeks and she reached for a dry tissue. Conrad barely heard the numerous eulogies. Everyone adored Marc.

The rain stopped on the way to the cemetery, but the temperature dropped sharply. Jade huddled against her husband during the short graveside service. He tapped his foot trying to speed things along. His mother frowned at him.

Laura, seated in a folding chair, stared straight ahead, seemingly emotionless.

After the burial the mourners returned to the church where the parishioners prepared a meal. Long tables were set with paper cloths, napkins, and baskets of rolls.

"Can't your dad afford a decent restaurant?" Jade whispered to Conrad.

"Are you kidding? And miss a free meal?" Conrad was embarrassed at the paltry layout.

The mood seemed to lift as family and friends ate fried chicken, baked beans and potato salad. After two bites Conrad threw aside his plastic fork.

At the end of the meal Pierre, with Katherine's assistance, slowly stood up. "May I have everyone's attention," his shaky voice called over the clatter. "We are so sad to say goodbye to our eldest son Marc. A father should never have to bury a child. But this is the Lazare family and we must carry on as we have for many generations." Pierre coughed violently.

Katherine grabbed his arm. "Really, Pierre, are you up to this?"

"Yes, yes." He brushed her hands away. "The family business must be passed on and according to tradition, that means I have named a new president."

Conrad held his breath.

"Luc will take over Lazare Fireworks. He is next in line for this position."

Thunderous applause echoed off the cement walls. "Luc," Pierre called. "Can you please step forward and say a few words?"

Conrad felt faint. The few bites of food in his stomach threatened to return. Jade jabbed him with her elbow.

"Luc!" Pierre shouted.

Everyone looked around for the new president of Lazare Fireworks.

He was gone.

*   *   *

The next morning Daisy Farrell curled up on her couch, clad in a white cotton bathrobe. Nine-thirty on a Saturday morning; she had already cleaned the bathroom and watered her plants. "I could veg here the rest of the day." She stretched her arms over her head and stared lazily at the ceiling fan.

The doorbell rang, encroaching on her freedom. Leaping from the couch, she padded barefoot to the door and peeked through the peephole.

Webb Hannis stood in the hallway, his features distorted by the curved glass. "Oh my God. What is he doing here?" She checked her robe.

The doorbell sounded again. Twice this time, followed by a loud rap on the door.

She opened it.

"I didn't mean to wake you," he said, his hair disheveled.

"You don't look so good. Come in." She threw the door open and stepped back, adjusting the tie on her robe.

"I could come back later, Daiz."

"No. Come on in." She motioned him to the couch. "Did you bring your invisible friend with you?"

"Oh, he's right here, damn it." Webb grabbed a decorator pillow, tossed it onto the floor, and sat down on the sofa.

"What's going on?"

"I can't even pee without him watching."

Daisy chuckled. "You need to talk to someone, Webb. It's obvious you're upset about this. If not Phoebe, maybe a doctor—"

"Oh sure! Can you see me going to some shrink and telling him about this? He'd have me committed."

"I'm just trying to help," Daisy said, shaking her head.

"There's more."

Her face softened. "I'm listening."

In a low voice, Webb told Daisy about his strange dream. "It was so vivid and real."

"You said Langdon told you about the Smith and Wesson later."

"I told Samuel I wanted to know where the gun is. He said, 'Sweet dreams'. Then I had this dream and I saw a gun in a cherry wood cabinet."

Daisy was enthused. "So it worked."

Webb hung his head. "I'm still confused. It's crazy, Daiz. Rubel realizes I know too much, and I'm not sure why I do."

"Did you ask Samuel about this?"

"I still don't get this Samuel business either." Webb leaned forward. "He's hangin' with me day and night. You say your aunt sees this stuff, too?"

"Phoebe's clairvoyant. She's had spirit guides since she was a child. I'm not sure if she sees them, but she's well aware they're there. Come on, Webb. Let me set up an appointment."

He took a deep breath. "Okay. But if it's too freaky, I'm out of there."

"I'll go with you. You'll love Phoebe. In the meantime, I'll fix us some breakfast. You'll feel better with a full stomach." She started toward the kitchen.

"Thanks, Daiz, but I'm not hungry." He headed for the door. "I'm going in to work. I have a murder to solve."

* * *

Inside police headquarters, Max Anglim flipped through the reports and press releases. Nothing new on the fireworks case. "Is Jake Rubel in this weekend?"

"No," the desk sergeant said. "Don't you reporters ever take a break? I saw Webb Hannis go back to the detective division. He's on the Lazare case with Rubel. I'll ring him."

Max was surprised when the towering Hannis invited him back to the detective office. "I talked with your news director on Friday," Hannis said. "He says we have to subpoena the footage you shot during the fireworks, if you haven't already recorded over it." Webb motioned him to a seat in the conference room.

Max met Webb's eyes. "What's it worth to you?"

"I'd like to comb through it. You never know what might pop up on news video."

"Anything new on the case?"

"We're still interviewing people." The detective was unshaven, course bristles shadowing his face. He seemed preoccupied, his eyes roaming around the room. "Nothing you could report."

"When there *is* something to report, I'd sure appreciate hearing it first." Max beamed, trying to establish eye contact. "I just may be able to dig out the original footage from the Fourth of July. You know Channel Three is the sponsoring station and my photographer Glen Gerard shot miles of tape before the fireworks. In fact you're in it, Lieutenant."

Webb appeared surprised. "Oh, yeah?"

"Here's the deal." Max's heart pumped. "I give you our original footage, and you come up with a scoop for us."

"Won't your news director have your ass?"

"He could damn well fire me," Max exclaimed. "But he has to find out first."

Webb shook his head and leaned back in his chair. "I can't give you anything that would hurt our investigation, but I can leak information a few hours before an official press release."

"Sounds like a deal," Max said, flashing his glistening white teeth.

Webb stood up. "When do I get the tapes?"

"I'll run over to the station now. Anything for our six o'clock show?"

Webb smiled. "Sorry, there's nothing right now. Ask the public if they have any information about the case."

"We did that the first night," Max said, and was out the door.

*   *   *

"Smith and Wesson revolver," Jake Rubel announced Monday morning in the briefing room as he slapped the folder down in front of Webb. "Langdon can't say for sure, but his hunches are right one hundred percent of the time. He's the best damn firearm expert in the country." Rubel beamed as if he himself had made the discovery, oblivious to Samuel looking over his shoulder at the report.

"An early seventies stainless steel," Webb mumbled.

Rubel crossed his arms in front of him. "How do you know that?"

"I talked to Langdon."

"It's not in the report." Rubel snatched back the folder, and combed through. "Not in here." He wagged his index finger at Webb.

"Maybe it wasn't the stainless steel. I thought I heard that. Anyway, I'll check gun registrations for the Smith and Wessons."

"I called on the fourth brother this morning," Rubel said. "Name's Teddy. He's in college taking summer courses at Purdue. Says he was at school over the Fourth of July. Had a big paper due."

"I'm gonna' talk to him," Webb said.

Rubel's eyes almost crossed. "I already did that!"

"Let me see the notes."

"No way. I'll tell you what you need to know."

"Did you do a background check on Harry Strickland? Have you checked with the other employees?"

Webb swatted the air in front of Rubel's face. Damned ant-brained idiot. "I've had enough of you," he yelled. "Get out of here before I lose it."

Rubel backed away.

Webb stood up, brushed past the angry elf, and returned to his cubicle.

Samuel sat with one hip propped on the edge of the desk clad in a white shirt with the tail dragging over jeans, his unruly hair glistening in the morning sun.

"So how do I know about the gun?"

"You dreamed about it."

Webb shook his head. "I still don't get who you are."

"I told you, I'm your spirit guide. You obviously don't believe me. Look it up for yourself on that computer you value so much."

Webb eyed his computer. "The Internet?" Quickly, he logged on and typed in psychic powers as a keyword. Up popped eleven site matches.

The first one was titled *Psychic and Paranormal Illusions with demonstrations of faked psychic powers.* "I'm not faking." He skipped that one. The next was *Scott LaRoche's Psychic Challenge. Test your powers over the Web and win a prize if you can demonstrate your psychic ability.* That was the problem. He couldn't prove anything. Another site talked about alien abductions and ghostly encounters.

He scrolled onward to a list of 1-900 numbers offering sessions with real psychics for a fee. He clicked into the site. "Maybe I oughta' talk to a psychic." But when he saw the cost was four dollars a minute he nixed the idea. "This shit's not for me."

Inside a site called *Crystalinks* he clicked on spirit guides and read aloud. "Spirit guides are pure energy entities who have chosen to aid others on the path to spiritual enlightenment." He shook his head at Samuel. "I don't even go to church."

"Church is outside, spirituality is within," Samuel said.

Webb continued to read. "Most spirit guides had incarnations on the physical Earth plane. They speak to you in many ways. Sometimes they are the little voice you hear in your head or loud thoughts. Often times they speak to you in dreams, meditation, or through the synchronistic things that occur in your life." Webb bit his lip.

Samuel beamed. "Read on."

"They can use art, music, dance, even television and movies to guide you. If they really want to make a point, they will do anything to get your attention."

Rubel breezed into Webb's cubicle. "Get your attention for what? Must be nice to play on the Internet while other people are working."

Webb clicked the exit button before Rubel could see what he was reading.

"I talked to Gallister, and he wants an update on the investigation," Rubel said. "I already gave him mine." He turned and left.

"Most people never see their spirit guides," Samuel said. "Remember, most follow the guidance without even knowing they exist. Do you get it yet, Bud?"

"Maybe," Webb mocked. He stood and headed toward Gallister's office. As he passed Daisy's cubicle, Samuel ran over, cuddled next to her, and pointed to a rock on her desk. The top was encrusted with violet crystals. Purple.

The brilliant color attracted Webb.

Samuel guided Daisy's hand to pick up the rock.

"Oh, Webb, this might interest you," Daisy said. "It's an amethyst. Aunt Phoebe gave it to me. It's supposed to help with spiritual awareness as well as protection." She handed it to him.

Webb rotated the sparkly gemstone. "What do I do with this?"

"*Pretty color*," Samuel said.

"I just thought you might like it," Daisy said. "Take it. It's yours."

"You said it was a gift to you."

"I have another one at home. It's supposed to enhance your psychic abilities, but it hasn't worked for me."

"That's all I need, more psychic abilities." Fingering the spiky crystals, Webb stared at Daisy.

She smiled. "Now would you like me to set up a visit with Aunt Phoebe so you can ask her about Samuel?"

"I was trained to follow logic," he said. "Not voodoo magic."

"Phoebe is not into voodoo," Daisy snapped.

"Okay, okay. I'll take the stone. I could use some protection. Mainly from Rubel." He grinned and started toward Gallister's office. Eyeing the amethyst, he stopped, headed back to his cubicle, and dumped it on his desk.

* * *

Later, Webb patted the tapes Anglim dropped off and prepared to scan through them. Daisy appeared. "I talked to Phoebe, Webb, and she can see us tonight. Does that work for you?"

"I guess so. At this point I need all the help I can get."

"Pick me up at seven-thirty," she said and returned to her desk.

Alone in the conference room, Webb dropped the first of the seven cassettes into the tape player.

Samuel milled around humming a cheerful tune.

"Rubel says this Anglim character's been around forever," Webb said "He sure took a chance bringing me these tapes. His news director was really tight-assed about sharing the unaired video."

"What a coincidence Anglim came to the police department on a Saturday you happened to be there," Samuel said.

"Oh, I guess you're going to tell me you set that one up."

"You need to pay attention to coincidences, Bud. They don't just happen. They are carefully orchestrated by God, spirit guides, and angels. It's called synchronicity."

"Synchro-what?"

"Synchronicity. Call it coincidences if it's easier. But it's time you learn what's behind them."

Webb turned away from him and studied the television screen. The first tape showed Luc Lazare explaining the launching equipment, plus several close-ups of the cylinders. Webb stilled-framed the tape. Some cylinders were twelve inches in diameter, large enough to blow off a man's head. Others were about three inches, yet big enough to be lethal.

Webb compared the video with the pictures Jake Rubel took at the crime scene. "Rubel says the body was found on the barge next to a row of twelve-inchers. The video provides a larger perspective."

Samuel smiled and nodded.

"You already know everything I'm saying, don't you, Sam? I wish you would damn tell me what I'm going to find on these tapes."

Moving on, he fast-forwarded through several interviews and a series of stand ups of Max describing the computerized control panel. "Sorting through this stuff could take all day. Come on, Sam. Save me some time. Is there anything significant on these tapes?"

"How did you feel when the reporter offered them to you?"

"Hell, I wanted them, of course. I've used news footage many times to search for clues."

"Trust your...what do you call them? Cop instincts?"

Webb stopped the tape. "I am trusting them, but it would be a hell of a lot faster if you would just tell me where to go."

"Trust worked in the past."

Webb yanked the tape from the machine and grabbed the second cassette marked July third. He jammed it into the machine and glowered at Samuel. The first part showed technicians busy with the computer board and some teasing shots of other media including a close-up of a female newspaper reporter's plump derriere. Webb scooted through most of that and slowed down to study an interview with a Coast Guard captain.

"Damn, is that me in the background?" Sure enough, he found a shot of himself mingling with the Lazare crew. He turned up the volume to listen.

"I've never actually seen how they shoot these things off. I always worked the crowds," he heard himself say.

"I vaguely remember being there, but it's more like a feeling of déjà vu. What did I see?"

Samuel simply smiled.

Next, the photographer panned a wide shot across the section of barge that held the launchers. The cylinders were lined straight in rows surrounded by sand. "No dead body out there yet," Webb said. "But this was taken on July third."

In the background of another shot, Webb saw himself climbing onto the Coast Guard boat. "That's how the newspaper got the picture of me. I was on the barge with the Coast Guard. Did I see something there?"

"Maybe."

Exasperated, Webb longed to give up, but something urged him on to view tape number three, shot on shore showing the gathering crowd along the riverbank. The Channel Three microphone cube bobbed in and out of the shot as Max interviewed a young woman in cut-off shorts and a bikini top. "I get such a rush from the fireworks," she gushed, displaying her skimpy top for the camera.

"I'll bet Anglim was getting a rush of his own." Webb snickered as he still-framed the curvy creature.

Moving on, he slow-motioned the panning shots of the crowd. A mother yanking an errant child's arm, teens lighting smuggled sparklers. One of the patrol officers was on a blanket with his family. His wife's hairdo looked like an erupting volcano, red with wisps springing out all over. "Americana at its best," he sighed.

Near the end of the tape, Webb scanned onward to another interview with a ditzy woman in a scanty stretch top that ended above her navel. "Max sure knows how to pick 'em."

Suddenly, his eyes shifted to the right. Puzzled, he zeroed in on something. Whirling around he saw Samuel nodding.

He turned back to the tape. In the background, the door to a navy blue BMW burst open and a woman with long, curly red hair stormed out of the car in an obvious snit, slamming the door behind her. She looked familiar. Webb stilled the shot. "That looks like Laura Lazare. I saw her picture at Pierre's house."

Webb felt the euphoric surge of adrenaline. "Okay, Sam," he exclaimed. "Is this it?"

"I guide. You stride," Samuel said. "Call it detective instinct."

"Now you're mocking me with that damn poetry," Webb said. "I've had flashes of insight since I was a rookie. I thought I was simply damn talented. Now you tell me it was you all along?"

"It works like magic."

"Come on, Sam, who works all this magic?"

"You do. With your thoughts. You simply ask a question, trust you'll get an answer, then follow the synchronicity."

Webb wagged his head, clicked on the tape again and studied the car. The driver appeared murky behind tinted glass. Scrutinizing each frame, the person's face was turned away. Though it looked like a man, it could have been a woman. "Is that Marc? Was he alive this close to the show?"

"Good question."

Suddenly Jake Rubel stomped into the room "What the hell are you doing looking at TV when there's so much to do? Do you have something I should see? Something from the Fourth of July?"

Webb hurriedly snapped off the tape player. "I was doing some research on the Fireworks industry." Rubel reeked, his shirt drenched in sweat, his straight, thin hair matted to his head. The stench permeated Webb's nostrils. "You smell like you just ran a marathon."

"I've been interviewing Lazare employees, which is more than you seem to be doing. "

Samuel crept up behind the frazzled Rubel pulling shanks of the detective's damp hair into spikes.

Webb laughed heartily.

Rubel's face contorted in anger. "You're an asshole, Hannis. Everyone in the division thinks so." Rubel backed away and caught his reflection in the window. Angrily smoothing the spikes from his hair he turned and left.

"That damn dwarf! I could ring his bony neck. I just hope Max Anglim's professional equipment can zero in on the guy in the car on that tape."

* * *

That evening, Pierre Lazare languished in his study with a glass of scotch. Slumped in his favorite green leather chair, Pierre's hand shook as he raised the glass to his lips, his mind mulling. Luc has been missing for a week, Katherine is on tranquilizers and sleeps much of the day, and the police are zeroing in on the family. He stared at the darkened gun cabinet.

Woozy from the spirits, he toiled up from the chair, knocking over the remaining scotch in the process. He staggered to the gun cabinet and switched on the light. His 1972 Smith and Wesson was not in its usual position. Pierre started to tremble.

Retrieving the key from the top of the gun cabinet, he opened the beveled glass doors, covered his hand with a handkerchief, and picked up the gun. He inspected it through blurred vision and sniffed the end of the barrel. Gasping, he clutched the revolver to his chest.

He placed the gun back on the rack, locked the cabinet and returned the key. Settling into his chair again, he rested his spinning head against the cushioned back.

After a few moments concentration, he knew what he had to do.

*   *   *

That same night, Conrad slammed his briefcase on the president's desk at the office and began stuffing documents inside. "Goddamn it, Father! How could you do this to me?" He sank into the chair and hammered his fists on the desk. Rage pounded in his head. He whisked the contents of the desk onto the floor.

Gathering his wits, he recovered a picture of Jade, the glass shattered. "Now isn't it just like Luc to up and disappear. It would serve him right if I got the presidency." He laughed. "Hell, as if he would care!"

Conrad knew Luc never wanted to follow Marc into the business. Who could blame him? Pierre thought Marc was a paragon. Luc went to the opposite extreme, dressing motley, skipping classes in high school, and, as a final protest, shirking college to join the army.

Conrad pulled out the blueprints for his new house. A whopping eight thousand square feet, all brick exterior, imported Italian marble in the kitchen, pool in the back. The house would cost more than a million dollars to build, and no telling how much the fag decorator would charge.

"Why did I let Jade talk me into this?" He rolled up the plans, knowing full well he wanted the showy house, too. "When it's finished, we'll have a big bash and invite all my college buddies. Let them see real success."

Opening a file drawer, he pulled out a folder marked life insurance and examined the fine print. The policy covered all four brothers. "In case of death, five million dollars to be evenly distributed among the surviving siblings. The amount to be paid in full within ninety days," he read. He patted the folder. "I'll have them start digging the basement soon. Enough money for the lifestyle is another matter. By then I might be president and you can bet, after I get the books in order, I won't be as thrifty as Father and Marc."

Conrad slumped in the chair at the thought of the homicide investigation. "Why didn't his entire head just blow off so police would have to accept it was an accident?" He returned the insurance policy to the file drawer, tucking it neatly in place. The clock on the desk glowed eleven-sixteen. "I wonder if Father is in bed." He switched off the lights, slipped out of the office, and drove to his parents' home.

The house was dark, all outside lighting turned off for the night. "Father, you'll never move beyond the Great Depression. Anything to save a stinkin' dime." Conrad tripped over a crack in the cement porch, spilling forward, his hands catching him with a thwack against the concrete. "Damn cheapskate," he spat as he picked himself up and brushed his hands on his pants.

Inside, the house was silent except for the irritating grandfather clock ticking in the foyer. He drew toward a light, down the hall to the back of the house. The eerie glow came from the study. His heart began to race as he tiptoed toward the room and peeked inside.

Pierre Lazare flinched to attention when Conrad entered the room, his eyes flickering open.

"I didn't mean to startle you, Father," Conrad said. "Maybe you should go up to bed." He mixed a scotch and soda at the wet bar.

"I'm fine," Pierre said, struggling upright in the chair. "What brings you here?"

Conrad sipped the scotch, his eyes roaming over the book-lined room. Despite weekly cleaning help, the room smelled musty, the heavy olive draperies oppressive. "Did you ever think of updating this house?"

Pierre cleared his throat. "Why? We built this house to last. The bulk of our money went into the business."

"I'm sure you have some assets besides the business," Conrad said, sitting down across from the slouched figure. "After all, you invested in the stock market for years."

"What are you getting at Conrad?"

"What I'm saying, Father, is you should start dispersing your wealth now while you're around to enjoy the fruits of your generosity."

Pierre twisted in his chair. "You and your brothers will get the business after I'm gone. Your mother inherits the rest of my assets." He raised his eyes casting a steady gaze on his son. "Do you need money, Conrad?"

"Jade and I are building a new home, Father, and yes, I could use some financial assistance."

"You have a substantial income. It's time you learn to live within your means like I always have. I tried to pass on those values to my sons."

Conrad's armpits prickled as he rose and strolled over to his father's elaborate gun cabinet. Lights illuminated the rows of rare weapons his father collected over the years. "These must be worth a Mercedes or two."

"Those guns are my only weakness," Pierre said. "When I was young, I dreamed of joining the police force, but my father insisted I take over the business."

Conrad eyed his father. "I didn't know that."

"The guns made up for that lost dream, particularly the police specials." Pierre's eyes brightened.

"Why don't you ever fire them?"

Pierre's hands trembled and he averted his son's eyes. "I'm tired, Conrad. I need to rest." He struggled out of the chair and shuffled toward the door.

*   *   *

Just after seven-thirty Daisy navigated Webb toward Phoebe's house in Sterling Heights.

"It will be interesting to see if Phoebe can see Samuel," Daisy said.

"*She's hip. I already paid her a visit,*" Samuel said.

"This whole thing is a pain in the butt," Webb grumbled. When they reached Phoebe's house he peered at the small bungalow painted cotton candy pink, lacy curtains draping the front windows. His eyebrows narrowed.

"I know what you're thinking. I'm warning you. She's different. She's psychic."

"Where does that put me?"

"Just as wacky." Daisy poked Webb's arm playfully. "Phoebe is excited about our visit."

At the door, nobody answered the ring. Daisy let herself in, leading Webb into a long living room decorated in more soft pastels.

Something hit him in the head. Looking up, a large crystal swung from the ceiling on a string. In fact, crystals of various sizes and shapes dangled here and there around the cluttered room. A shelf, several end tables, and the windowsill were lined with angel figurines from whimsical to realistic. In one corner a lounge chair stretched invitingly beside a babbling fountain. More angels and crystals were arranged under the waterfall.

"Remember...different," Daisy whispered.

"I guess Sam won't seem so goofy around here."

Webb heard a soft voice croon, "Oh, Daisy, my darling," and Phoebe Farrell swept into the room, a fuschia caftan billowing around her butterball figure, an eye-straining clash with her tinted red hair. "Sorry. I was journaling a vision. Do sit down."

Webb saw Phoebe's eyes sweep his height.

"You're a tall one. That means you're brimming with life."

"Interesting room," Webb said, his eyes meandering over the setting.

"Oh, the angels are gifts from various clients," Phoebe said. "Angels are always around us ready to help, but only if we ask,"

Phoebe said, a nostalgic look in her eyes. "Some angels and guides come for a short while to help with a specific problem. Others stay for your present lifetime." She gazed ethereally at the ceiling. "It's so comforting to know that."

"That's why we're here, Aunt Phoebe," Daisy said. "Ever since Webb was injured in an accident, a presence is with him and he's confused."

Samuel bowed like he was meeting a queen.

"Ah, yes, Samuel," Phoebe said. She motioned Daisy and Webb to the sofa.

The couch was lined with needlepoint angel pillows edged in eyelet lace. Webb pushed them aside, staring at Phoebe. "Do you see him?"

"Oh, yes. A colorful character," Phoebe said.

Suddenly Samuel was dressed like a clown, billowing green striped pants, a purple polka dot shirt, springy rainbow hair, even a red rubber nose. He began riding a three-wheeled scooter across the carpet.

Webb was abashed. "What the hell are you doing, Sam?"

Phoebe reached over and patted Webb on the knee. "I think he just wants you to lighten up a bit. You should pay attention to what Samuel does, as well as what he tells you."

Webb glared at Samuel, who had switched back to jeans and a shirt. He lay on his back on the floor, his arms pillowing his head.

"So you do see him?"

Phoebe shifted her girth on the couch next to them. "Oh, yes."

Webb groaned, but Phoebe laughed heartily. "The big fellow needs to get on with his mission on earth," she crooned.

Puzzled, Daisy moaned, "This isn't fair. I can't see or hear what's going on."

"Your own guide is in touch with you all the time, Daisy," Phoebe said.

"You told me that many times, but how can I know?"

"Sometimes a spirit guide will brush against your leg or touch your neck."

"Every so often I feel a fluttering on my cheek," Daisy said.

"That's it, child. No matter how they communicate, everyone can tap into their guidance. You use it every day without even knowing it. Most of us have more than one guide. Gracious, I have a dozen."

"A dozen Sams! That's all I need," Webb sighed. He stretched his long legs and stood up. "Thanks for your time, but I have work waiting for me at home."

Phoebe's eyes widened. "Leaving so soon? I'm just getting warmed up."

Samuel switched to his clown outfit in a flash and landed a perfect cartwheel across the living room.

Phoebe roared hysterically. "Don't be so serious, Webb. This is fun stuff."

Daisy wrinkled her nose. "Why are you laughing?"

"*Because life is fun,*" Samuel said, juggling four colorful balls.

"Oh, Sam is being a clown." Webb headed toward the door.

Samuel gave him an exaggerated smile.

"I know you'll be back, Webb," Phoebe called to him. "We have much more to discuss."

CHAPTER 5

TUESDAY MORNING, July eleventh, the list of Lazare employees in hand, Webb rapped on the peeling screened door at Harry Strickland's house. Grayed paint flecks sprinkled onto the sagging porch. "Okay, Sam, so what are we looking for here?"

Samuel smiled. "Discover for yourself." The spirit hopped onto the porch railing and began to walk the tightrope. "It's more fun that way."

The door whipped open, and Webb viewed a slender version of Grisly Adams through the grimy screen. Sharp brown eyes, narrowed with suspicion, and a thin, piggish nose were the only visible facial features beyond the bushy beard.

The man pushed the screened door open, shooing Webb backwards, and stepped out onto the porch. "What do you want?"

"Harry Strickland?" Webb offered a hand but immediately regretted it when he saw the curled hook protruding from Strickland's sweatshirt.

Strickland ignored the gesture, and pulled the door closed behind him. "The name's Purp. You might as well get used to it. Everybody calls me Purp."

Samuel hopped down from the railing.

"I'm Webb Hannis with the Detroit Police Detective Division."

"I know who you are." Strickland jammed his good hand into the pocket of his grungy jeans, his shoulders hunched forward. "We met before."

An odd chill rippled through Webb's body. When was that? Suddenly he remembered the picture in the newspaper. Purp Strickland was one of the fellows in the photo with Webb in the background.

Samuel nodded vigorously.

Webb tried to swat the spirit away like a pesky fly.

Strickland eyed him suspiciously.

"So, you're a fireworks color," Webb said.

Strickland lifted his head, the brown eyes rounding for a brief moment. Pulling his hand from his pocket, he leaned against the porch railing "Don't see much purple in a fireworks show, do ya?"

"I guess you're right. Why not?"

"Purple takes a precise mixture of red and blue to get the correct balance of emission in the visible range for purple."

"Very interesting. I take it you're an expert at making purple."

The semblance of a smile buried beneath the burly beard caught Webb's trained eye.

"That's right. I perfected purple," Strickland said with obvious pride. "I'm still the only one in the country who can mix it just right. Had a special purple feature in the Fourth of July show."

Webb, still woozy from his head injury, had a vague memory of purple fireworks erupting in the sky. "I think I saw it." He scowled. Why can't I remember? He eyed Samuel hoping for prompting, yet the guide was intent on Strickland. Webb stared at the purple man. "I see why the Lazares value your expertise. Tell me about the oldest brother."

"You mean Red?"

Webb nodded.

"He was a kid, sixteen or so, when we gave him his color name. He was a whiz with the red fireworks. Ain't nobody ever got a color that young."

"What color is Luc?"

Purp's eyes narrowed again, and he stuck his hand back in his pocket. "He wanted purple. It was already taken. He never got another color."

"What about Conrad?"

"He preferred the business end inside the cozy headquarters. He never liked to get his hands dirty."

"Did Conrad get along with Red?"

"As well as any brother tryin' to take over the old man's company."

"Did they compete in the business?"

Purp gazed over the crab grass in his lumpy front yard. "I don't know."

Out of the corner of his eye Webb caught sight of Samuel back up on the narrow porch railing. He was peering through a tiny rip in the front window shade.

Purp, following Webb's gaze, whipped around, his eyes flittering.

Webb cleared his throat audibly. "Was Conrad jealous when Red took over after Pierre's stroke?"

Strickland straightened. "I can see where this is goin', and I don't know nothin'." He pushed past Webb and opened the door.

Webb grabbed the screened door. "How can a body end up over a mortar tube without the crew seeing it during the launch?"

Purp glared at him through beady eyes. "Can you see in the dark?" With that, the man who was an expert at purple slipped into the house and slammed the door.

Webb heard the deadbolt turn.

* * *

Purp Strickland pulled the window shade aside and watched the detective raise dust pulling out of the dirt driveway. After fixing instant coffee in his grubby kitchen, he returned to the living room and sat down on the sagging couch. Why would that cop man think I'd give away any secrets? "I gotta keep old man Lazare on my side. No way am I lettin' anyone sabotage my masterpiece."

He laughed out loud.

* * *

On his way back to the station, Webb considered the man he had just questioned. "What a creep. I wanted to get into the house. It's probably as cruddy as the front yard." He stopped for a red light and glanced in the rearview mirror at a slouching, silent Samuel, his head tilted upward.

"I have a feeling Purp hates the Lazare brothers," Webb said. "He probably wants to take over the business." Webb looked over his shoulder at his spirit guide who didn't offer a word. "Dammit! I thought you were supposed to help me solve this murder. All you ever do is lounge around."

"If I tell you everything, what do you have to work for? You state a need, and that plants the seed."

"Yeah yeah, yeah ...you said that before. What exactly do *you* do?"

"I provide the feed. It's really very simple."

"Simple? This poetry shit is making me nuts."

"Actually, you followed my guidance with ease all along. It's so natural, you don't even recognize what's happening."

"Huh?"

"Remember at the Lazare's when I led Katherine to that picture and had her give it to you?"

"So."

"She had no idea I guided her to do that because she can't see me, Bud."

"So what does the picture mean?"

"Before you could see me, Katherine would still have handed you that picture and you would never know I was there. Later, you would simply remember what you saw in the photo, when you recognized Laura at the fireworks on Anglim's tape."

Webb scowled. "I wonder if I ever did anything on my own." He waved Samuel away, turned on the radio, and revved up the volume.

*   *   *

That evening, Conrad Lazare stood mesmerized by the flickering torch lights that reflected from the water in the luminescent swimming pool. I could be out sailing with my own friends right now, he thought, instead of helping Jade scale the social wall. This party is a damn bore. Surrounded by cliques of beautiful people dressed in summer finery, cackling mindlessly, Conrad, nursing his whiskey and soda, felt alone and irritated.

"Darling," Jade called from a pink-cushioned lawn chair. "Gillian has a great proposition for us." Jade looked spectacular in a white crinkle-pleated tank dress, her blonde hair, a golden halo curled into tiny ringlets, tied away from her face with a turquoise kerchief. She sipped a strawberry Daiquiri garnished with a skewer of fresh fruit.

Sitting next to Jade the goddess, Gillian Rosemont looked fleshy and bloated in her red designer frock, ruby fingernails and lips to match. Conrad thought she was a mess with her choppy black hair. He detested small talk, unless people could be of value to him personally.

Dumping his highball into the pool, he waved the empty glass. "I need to freshen my drink," he called, and headed for the Tahiti bar edged in bamboo, complete with potted palm trees and a basket overflowing with coconuts and spiky pineapples.

"Whiskey and soda," he told the tanned bartender.

"Conrad, I was looking for you." It was Gillian's husband Richard wearing an obnoxious floral shirt. "Jade says you two can join us in Hawaii."

Conrad almost spilled his drink. "What?"

Richard's sunburned bald spot was peeling, flakes of skin clinging to what was left of his thinning brown hair. It sickened Conrad.

"We rented a luxury condo in Kona, a remote part of the big island. It's big enough for four. If we split it, that's just twenty-four hundred apiece for the week."

Conrad stared into Richard's bulging, blue eyes. "In case you haven't heard, Richard, my brother was murdered. I need to stay near my family in case there's a new development."

Richard stepped away fidgeting with his belt buckle. "Gillian told me about your family problems. I would think you need a break from that depressing scene."

Conrad placed his drink on the bar. "We won't be going to Hawaii with you, Richard." Find another sucker to foot half your bill, Conrad thought as he moved away, scanning the pool patio for his wife. He spotted her laughing with a coterie of fashion mavens, her long legs outlined beneath the sheer dress.

He tugged at her slim arm. "My stomach is upset. We're leaving," he whispered loudly.

She looked alarmed. "Oh, honey. What did you eat?"

"Say goodbye, and I'll meet you at the car." Conrad slipped out the patio gate.

On the way home, Jade fawned over her husband. "I'm sorry you're not feeling well, darling. Do you have a fever?" She wiped her hand over his forehead.

He pushed it away. "I can't see to drive."

"Gillian looked nice, didn't she? She lost six pounds on the spa diet."

"She needs to lose about fifty more."

"She does have a big butt…and her arms in that sleeveless dress!" Jade laughed loudly. "Did Richard mention renting the condo with them in Hawaii?"

Conrad pounded the steering wheel. "Damn it Jade. We don't have the money."

She cuddled next to him, nuzzling his arm. "What's the big deal? I thought we were getting a big settlement from Marc's life insurance policy."

Conrad turned into their driveway, and clicked the garage door opener. "That doesn't pay off until September and that money is for the house."

As she stepped out of the car, Jade gathered her flowing dress. "We need a vacation, Conrad. We never go anywhere exciting. You're the head of a big company now."

"Not yet. Father is holding out for Luc."

"Where in the hell is he? Why don't you track him down? If he doesn't want Lazare Fireworks you should make him tell your father."

"And just how do you expect me to find him? If he stays lost long enough Father will have to relent."

"Surely we have as much money as the Rosemonts."

"Gillian and Richard are both working and making a killing in posh real estate."

Switching on the light in the kitchen, Jade pulled the kerchief from her hair, the unleashed curls swirling around her face. "Conrad, you know I'm not career-minded. Besides, if I work, who would decorate the new house?"

"I'm not asking you to work. I'm simply telling you we can't afford a week in Hawaii right now." Conrad melted at Jade's sensuous pout and took her in his arms. "Eventually we can buy that condo, but we have to watch our finances right now." He squeezed a handful of curls.

She pulled away from him. "We can't join the country club. We don't have enough money to take a vacation. Gillian probably pities us." She wrinkled her nose. "You promised when you asked me to marry you, that we would have enough money for anything we want."

Conrad turned and started up the stairs. "I love the good life as much as you, and we will live it soon."

Jade followed him and peeled off the dress, leaving it in a heap on the bedroom floor. She carefully rotated her body to show off a white silk lingerie set, the bra a lacy uplift.

Conrad, frustrated by the boring evening and his wife's harsh words, averted his eyes and undressed quickly.

"I had Tristan go ahead and order the English gossamer fabric for the master suite. He wants a light, airy look in there," Jade said as she sprawled provocatively across the bed.

Conrad gritted his teeth. "How much will that cost?"

"Don't go cheap on me now where the house is concerned," she said. "Tristan says only the English fabric will do in such an elegant suite."

"How much?"

"Conrad, honey, we have credit cards." She pulled him down on the bed and buried her nose in his hair before her hand slid down to his groin.

*   *   *

The next morning, Jade, silk panties peeking from beneath her shorty nightgown, fluffed her disheveled hair as she entered the kitchen.

Dressed for work, Conrad sat at the table writing checks. "You're up early."

Jade poured a glass of fresh tomato juice and carried it to the table. "Gillian wants me to go shopping with her today." She rubbed her temples. "I have a headache."

Conrad ripped off a check and handed it to his wife.

Jade stared at the amount in disbelief. "Ten thousand dollars?" Her eyes glistened. "Is this for today's shopping?"

"Don't be ridiculous," Conrad said closing his checkbook.

"It's for the decorating. Now you have something to work with."

Jade moaned. "This won't even cover the draperies. That imported material costs a hundred thirty dollars a yard."

"That's all I can spare right now. You and Trisket can at least get started. If you just relax, when the settlement comes in, we'll be loaded."

"His name is Tristan." Jade's hand tightened around the juice glass. She had a sudden urge to fling it at him. She saw her mother throw things at her father many times. Instead she stood up and slammed the glass against the table, juice spewing everywhere. "A decent sofa costs this much. I'll never live in a chintzy house again, Conrad. You have no idea what it's like." Her eyes filled with tears.

Conrad blotted at the mess with a napkin. "I know how to budget. I learned that from my father." With a smile, he coaxed her onto his lap, touching the tip of her tiny nose. "You know, you're awfully cute when you're mad. You're out of that trailer, darling. You'll get everything you want if you can just wait this out."

"Talk some sense into your father. He's crazy if he waits around for that damn Luc to come back. Make him give you the presidency."

"It's not that simple. Father is set in his ways."

She jumped up. "You're a wimp. You can't even stand up to your own father."

"He doesn't react to pressure, Jade. Let me show him how good I am at the job."

"That could take months." Jade wanted to pound on his chest, rip at his hair. "I'm sick of waiting for everything." Her body stiffened.

"I need to get to work," he said. "Ask your decorator friend what really has to be done first. You won't need furniture for awhile."

Jade scurried in front of him as he reached for the door. "Custom furniture takes months to build and ship. We need to order now." She pummeled his chest. "I'm going ahead with this." Out of control, anger was taking over, possessing her. She knew the feeling well.

Conrad nudged her aside, rushed out to the garage, and was gone.

Sucking in deep breaths, Jade fought to quell her wrath. She detested this feeling. She swore she would not end up like her mother. "But damn it, Conrad, you said we'd have the most beautiful house in Grosse Pointe."

Padding across the ceramic tile in bare feet, she stubbed her toe on a chair leg. She winced and waited for the throb to subside. "I hate this place," she hissed. With her head aching and the toe smarting, she fell into a chair and began to cry. "Conrad's probably hoarding all our money for that antique pool table he's been eyeing." She hurled the juice glass across the breakfast nook. It shattered against the ivory flocked wallpaper, a blood-like river running down over the baseboard. She dropped her throbbing head onto the table.

The phone shrilled.

"Shut up!" Jade screamed. On the fourth ring the answering machine picked up the call.

"Jade, this is Gillian. I hope you're in the shower. I'll pick you up at nine-thirty so we can be at the mall when it opens. See ya."

Slowly lifting her head, her mood changed. She smiled, an idea crossing her mind. "If I hurry, I can easily be back here by nine-thirty for Gillian."

She scampered upstairs into the bathroom, and stared at her peaked complexion. "Nothing a painkiller, shower and makeup can't fix." She sprang into motion.

* * *

That morning Pierre Lazare took the Smith and Wesson thirty-eight-caliber revolver from his gun cabinet. The police special was highly collectible since it was one of the first stainless steel made by the company in the early seventies. He had searched for this beauty, with its showy handle and four inch barrel. Slowly and lovingly he polished it with a clean handkerchief.

Purp Strickland walked into the room and stopped when he saw Pierre with the weapon. "Mr. Lazare, I hope I'm not buggin' ya. I just wanted to stop by and see if I could help. With Marc's death and all—"

Waving the gun in the air, Pierre said. "I'm headed to the shooting range. It's been awhile since I did any target practice and I'm probably pretty rusty." He tucked the revolver into a leather satchel. "Do you shoot, Harry?"

"I had a few lessons." The bushy-faced man moved to the gun cabinet, admiring the collection.

"Maybe you'd like to join me at Rafferty's," Pierre offered, opening the cabinet. "Pick your weapon."

"I thought these were for show. Do you really want to fire them?"

Pierre chuckled. "Purp, I'm getting too old to simply show them. The boys aren't interested in my guns, so I might as well enjoy them myself."

Purp selected a Colt Model revolver.

"That's a 1917 Army," Pierre said. "It's a forty-five caliber, so it packs a punch."

The scruffy man admired the pistol, turning it over and over in his hand. Pierre added it to the leather bag.

He jumped when he noticed a figure in the doorway.

"Hello Father." Jade paraded into the study, an amazing sight dressed in a pair of chamois slacks and a black sleeveless shell, her blonde hair a finishing touch to the striking package. "I thought I'd drop by and check on you and Katherine."

Pierre coughed, pushing the gun satchel behind him. "How long have you been here? Purp and I are discussing business."

Purp snatched the leather satchel, nodded to Jade, and left the room.

"I'd like to discuss business too," she said to Pierre.

Pierre's hands started to tremble. "I'm on my way out, Jade. Is there something you need?"

"This won't take long." She set her purse on a side table and took a seat near Pierre's favorite chair. "It's about Conrad."

"Yes? What about him?"

"He can't sleep. He goes into work early every day and stays until all hours. I'm worried about him."

"That's the way it is when you run a business."

"Oh, that's not what I mean. He's the perfect choice to head that business. I'm worried that he'll work himself to death fixing all the problems just to have Luc come back and take over. That's not fair, Father."

Pierre closed the gun cabinet door. "Conrad knows the score Jade. Luc is next in line to run the company. Conrad is merely managing on an interim basis."

Jade clucked her tongue. "So he's working his butt off for nothing?"

"I don't have time to discuss this with you now. This is Conrad's business, not yours."

Anger slashed across Jade's face. "You know Conrad is perfect for that job. Luc doesn't even want it. Anyway, that slob wouldn't run the business any better than Marc." Tears streamed down her face. "Either you recognize my husband's talents, or you'll be sorry."

Pierre stifled a smile. "My dear, you don't tell me what to do. I own the place. That means I make the major decisions at Lazare Fireworks."

Jade shot from the chair, slamming her hand against the beveled glass on the gun cabinet. The entire room seemed to rattle. "I won't stand by and let you make a fool of my husband!"

Grabbing her arm, Pierre wrenched her away from the cabinet.

She jerked from his grip, backing away from the tottering man.

He fought to keep his balance. "Please leave my house now," he said, his body rigid. "I will not tolerate this abuse."

Heaving for breath, he glared at Jade. "We both need to forget this ever happened."

Eyes flashing, chin trembling, she grabbed her purse and raced out the door.

* * *

Later, Jade sat back against the leather seat in Gillian's Mercedes.

"I'm loving this," Gillian gushed. "It's fun to shop with someone who can keep up with me. So many of my friends have to watch their budgets. That's no fun."

The shopping frenzy energized Jade. For once she was in charge, not Conrad, or Pierre for that matter. Why doesn't Conrad have the guts to stand up to his father? I have to do everything. I made an impression on that old man. I saw how he was shaking. Now I'll just give it time. Conrad will thank me when Pierre offers him the presidency.

Gillian seems to really like me, she thought, the summer breeze gusting through her hair in the open car. Her total for the day's shopping was more than six thousand dollars.

The best part; she kept up with Gillian.

* * *

Inside the Rafferty Shooting Gallery, Pierre and Purp were settled into adjacent pistol ranges. Sweat pooled around the old man's neck, and with his hand quavering at the low end of the Richter scale, Pierre felt the gun's power thunder in his chest. He never hit the target. He hadn't shot a gun since his stroke.

He made a point of calling Purp's attention to the Smith and Wesson. Pierre purposely brought along several other pistols, and just for show, raised each one toward the target, missing every time. The arduous therapy sessions after the stroke failed to improve the strength on his right side. His once dominant side. His strong side.

Each squeeze of the trigger was exhausting. He longed to pack up the guns, go home, and collapse in his chair with a drink. No. He had to keep shooting. Think of Jade as the target. That ignorant woman-child. What gall she has coming to my home and trying to tell me what to do.

He aimed the gun and pulled the trigger with angered strength. The bullet clipped the outer circle on the target. You can tell your husband, who you lead around by the nose, Jade, that you ruined his chances for even a raise.

Pierre suddenly felt drained. He wiped off the gun and placed it back in the satchel. Did she see the guns? She knows I don't use my collection. God, I need to be more careful.

It was just his luck that Purp showed up and agreed to join him this day. Did he notice the Smith and Wesson?

He looked at Purp's target. The center circle was obliterated.

*   *   *

Jade carefully hung the new purchases in her walk-in closet, pausing to admire the fabric on a melon colored jacket. She loved the feel of new clothes, smooth and sleek against her skin.

She pulled a pair of Nubuck leather sling pumps out of the box. Gillian spotted them at a cool two hundred dollars. Holding the shoes against the jacket she marveled at the perfect match. Gillian insisted she buy the faux crystal pendant in the same color and a crème silk handbag with a shoulder strap for daywear. She felt elegant and sophisticated just clicking the expensive clasp.

A pang of guilt stabbed her.

"No! I deserve these clothes. We have the money." She so desperately wanted to let go of her muddled childhood, the raging fights between her parents over money. Her mother always won. Not that she bought anything decent. She was hooked on garage sales. With newspaper ads in hand, they followed the trail, buying other people's junk. How Jade hated wearing the faded, used clothing her mother hauled home.

Truly, she felt great spending real money today. Finally she had arrived. Jade placed the new pumps in her shoe rack and tucked the purse into a lower drawer. Gathering the price tags, she stuffed them into one of the shopping bags. She scolded herself. Why do I always feel I have to hide the evidence?

At that moment Conrad breezed into the bedroom, his shirt already unbuttoned, his tie over his shoulder.

Jade sat on the bed hoping to hide the wreckage. "You're home early, honey."

"Actually I'm late," he said tossing his tie on the dresser. "I was with the builder. Now he wants the money for the lot up front before he'll start digging the basement. He says people are lined up to buy those exclusive lots, so he'll only take cash."

"I thought we agreed to pay on installments."

"Nothing in writing. We'll have to come up with the dough if we still want that wooded lot."

"How much?"

"One hundred-eighty thousand. If we keep the bills down this month we might eke out that much. The builder can begin digging the basement in early August."

Jade stiffened. The bags littering the bed throbbed in her mind. I don't care. I deserve to spend our money, too. "Ask your father for a raise. Better yet, insist he make you president. You need to get tough with that old man."

"I already talked with Father. He said to live within our means."

Jade's mouth went dry. "That bastard! Why should you do all the damn work while Luc cashes in?"

"Father is still holding out for family tradition. No matter what I do, Luc will get the job. That is, if he ever comes back."

"What if he doesn't? Will Pierre finally decide you're good enough after you save the company?"

Conrad went into the bathroom.

"Did you have fun shopping with Gillian today?"

"Don't change the subject." Jade grabbed the bags and stuffed them under the bed. "Get out here and discuss this with me. Why can't you be tougher with your father?"

Conrad walked back into the room patting his face with a towel. "Father is too distraught to press him right now. He knows where I stand. I'll talk with him later."

"When?"

"Calm down, honey. I'm bushed. I had to deal with angry people at work, I don't need it at home. I hope you didn't spend any extra money this month. If you did we'll lose the lot."

* * *

Purp Strickland reclined on his couch, ruffling his scraggly beard. "Why in the hell would Old Man Lazare go to the shooting range with barely the strength to hold a gun?" He stared at the ceiling, paint peeling in the corner. "Damn. Who cares? I got some free target practice, and scored some points with the old geezer."

"Better stay on Lazare's good side. I need his solid support for my masterpiece." Purp enjoyed his intimate knowledge of Lazare Fireworks. He relied on it. He thought back to April when he used it wisely.

Long after midnight on that spring night he used a passkey to enter the fireworks compound. He knew the place was deserted after dark and poked around, checking the windows to the main building for lights, listening here and there for movement.

Satisfied he was alone, he opened the gate on the chain link fence and drove his pick-up truck inside. He didn't dare move it any closer to the bunkers. A simple spark could blow the place sky high.

He lowered the tailgate. Flipping his head back and forth, he checked once again for signs of life. A security light flickered, making him flinch. Nobody's out here at two in the morning unless they're burglarizing the place, he thought.

He stole quietly to bunker number fourteen and used another key to enter his private domain. Immediately, he set to work pulling folded boxes from beneath his worktable. It took him months to gather enough boxes without being noticed, tear them down and store them for this night.

He pulled a roll of packing tape from a drawer and painstakingly assembled the first box, taping the bottom together for extra strength. Consumed with his plan, he had built the boxes hundreds of times in his mind, in his dreams. Four strips of doublewide tape on the seam, four strips crosswise for support. The boxes were important.

Soon the floor space in his small bunker was littered with boxes. He meticulously packed each one with three-inch paper bombs, each a different piece to the puzzle.

His heart pummeled as he carried the first box to his truck. He placed it in the back of the pick-up. It took more than an hour to haul the next ten boxes and pack them on the truck. His chest heaved with exertion.

Once the truck was loaded he was only half-finished. He would have to drive this load home and return. He held his breath as he started the car. "One spark—"

It was grueling inching the truck out of the lot, shutting the gate, and driving the few miles home. He stored the boxes in a shed in his back yard and returned to the compound for the remaining ones.

At six in the morning he finally hauled the last load and stashed it in the shed. Afterwards, he pulled out his trusty video camera. Tomorrow night he would record the test round.

Every detail was important for creating his perfect masterpiece.

He fell into bed.

CHAPTER 6

WHEN THURSDAY morning dawned, the oppressive heat returned. At nine in the morning, the detective office was already seventy-seven degrees. Webb squirmed at his desk, tugging at his tight collar, wishing he could turn down the thermostat. He longed to dive into a refreshing swimming pool.

The phone rang, rattling his head. He lunged for it. "Hannis here."

"Lieutenant, I'm with the Wayne County Sheriff's Department. I checked the gun registrations and found two Smith and Wessons from your description registered to owners in Wayne County. I have the addresses and phone numbers."

Webb grabbed a pen and wrote on an envelope. "That's great. Go ahead."

"The first is a Carl Kaiser and the other is Pierre Lazare."

Webb's heart pounded in his ears. My God. This is the break we need. "Is the Lazare address on Pinecrest in Grosse Pointe?"

"Yes, that's the one. I hope that helps."

"Hell yes. Thanks."

Webb looked up at Samuel. "The sheriff's department just...oh, you know what they said." Webb's adrenaline soared. He flew into Gallister's office.

Fred jerked to attention. "What's going on?"

"I think the Lazare family is hiding something...at least they're most likely harboring the gun used to murder Marc," Webb said in a rush. "I just found out the patriarch of the clan owns a Smith and Wesson, the exact kind that killed his son."

"Hot damn!" Gallister pounded his desk. "Get down to the courthouse and grab a search warrant. I'll call ahead and move things along."

"I'm on my way." Webb was out the door.

At the courthouse, the judge granted the warrant without problem. It seemed everyone wanted the Lazare murder solved without further delay.

On his way to the Lazare's home, Webb turned to Samuel. "I'm glad Rubel was out of the office during this coup. All we need is that twitchy little bastard tagging along when we confront Pierre Lazare. Wouldn't that moron love to burst in and make a scene?"

As he pulled into the circular driveway at the Lazare home, the grounds were even more unkempt, the shrubbery overgrown, spent flower heads dropping from the urns.

He rang the bell.

After an interminable wait, a sullen Pierre Lazare opened the door. "Detective...I'm sorry, what was your name?"

"Lieutenant Hannis. I need to speak with you."

"I told you our attorney is handling the case." He attempted to shut the door.

Webb jammed his foot over the threshold, stepped inside the foyer, and reached in his jacket pocket. "I have a search warrant for a Smith and Wesson revolver." He handed Pierre a copy.

Struggling for breath, the elderly man took the paper. "What is this all about? I haven't been feeling well since all this trouble started," he said, his voice trembling. He swiped at his perspiring forehead. "Did you trace the bullet that killed Marc to that gun?" The old man shuddered and leaned against a hall table for support.

"Mr. Lazare, it would be easier on both of us if you would show me where you keep your gun."

With great aplomb the man stood tall. "Oh, yes. It's part of my collection." Pierre shuffled down a hall toward the back of the house, and led Webb into an impressive study. Bookshelves lined the walls. Heavy oak wainscoting climbed the wall behind an ornately carved desk.

Webb looked around for Samuel. The guide was sprawled on top of a now familiar cherry wood gun cabinet, the one in his dream. It displayed an arsenal of weapons. Webb immediately spied the Smith and Wesson.

Samuel jumped down from his perch.

Pierre retrieved a key from the top of the cabinet and unlocked the glass door.

"I searched a long time to find a Smith and Wesson from this era," he said, his hands shaking.

"Don't touch it," Webb warned and pulled out a pair of latex surgical gloves.

"Oh, my fingerprints are all over it. I had that gun at the shooting range this week. My friend Harry Strickland and I had a little target practice." Pierre paused to catch his breath. "I'm almost sure I used that gun. You can ask Purp. His memory is sharper than mine these days."

With a gloved hand, Webb carefully lifted the gun by the trigger guard and dropped it into a plastic bag. "You say Purp Strickland saw you fire this gun recently? Which shooting range?"

"Rafferty's. I have a membership. They'll tell you when we were there."

"Mr. Lazare, does anyone else have access to this gun cabinet?"

Pierre slowly lowered himself onto a leather chair. "Sorry. My legs are still weak. My sons aren't interested in guns."

"Could anyone have opened the cabinet and taken a gun?"

"The key is right on top. I don't know how many knew that. Surely you don't think someone in the family killed Marc?" The man's eyes misted. "That couldn't be. My sons were very close."

"Do any of your employees have access to this cabinet?"

Pierre fingered his sagging chin. "I suppose so. Various people have been in and out of the house since Marc's funeral."

"I'm talking about before the funeral. Before Marc was killed."

"I can't say who for sure."

Webb studied the old man's mannerisms. "Where were you during the day of the fireworks show, Mr. Lazare?"

Pierre shifted in his chair, averting eye contact with the detective. He cleared his throat. "I was here at home. Katherine and I didn't go to the park until about seven o'clock. It's a relief to be a spectator after so many years of worrying about the launch. Now we can just watch the crowd's reaction."

"Did you see Marc that evening?"

Pierre stared over Webb's head. "I don't think so. I can't remember. My memory fails me from time to time. I had a stroke you know. I take a lot of medication," he droned on.

"Mr. Lazare, do you have any heart problems?"

Alert once again, Lazare looked Webb in the eye. "My ticker's as strong as ever." He puffed out his chest with pride.

"I'd like to offer you a polygraph test."

"Do you mean a lie detector?" Pierre's eyes widened. "Whatever for? You don't think I killed my own flesh and blood?"

"The polygraph will help us eliminate you as a suspect. It's totally up to you, but I would suggest you take it to prove your innocence."

"Absolutely not!" Pierre stood up, swaying for balance.

"Unless you're going to arrest me, I want you to leave. My wife is ill and I don't want her to know why you're here. You had no right to barge in like this before I had time to contact my lawyer."

Webb started toward the door. Samuel was already there. "I'll be in touch, Mr. Lazare." He let himself out.

In the car, he exhaled deeply. "So, the dream was right on target. The murder weapon was in that cherry wood cabinet, and damn if it wasn't in Pierre Lazare's house."

"Good instincts, Bud," Samuel said. "What's your next question?"

"Motive."

Buoyed by the latest discovery, Webb returned to the courthouse. "I need another search warrant. One for Lazare Fireworks. I want to see every insurance policy that company has on the family members."

* * *

That evening, a cold front shifted in from Canada smacking into the hot and heavy air. The result, an old-fashioned summer thunderstorm. Webb raised the blinds in his living room to study the menacing sky, already dark at eight o'clock in the evening.

Neon daggers of lightening stabbed through the clouds; nature's fireworks. Webb loved a good storm. Thunder drummed overhead as he searched the parking lot, expecting a visitor. Only the familiar vehicles of fellow tenants were lined up like matchbox cars in a child's playroom.

Dressed in a Cincinnati Police T-shirt and blue jeans, Webb was glad to be home. The Lazare case occupied his days, and despite his efforts to let it go at night, Marc Lazare invaded his thoughts.

"Tonight should be interesting." He glanced out the window again. "Where the hell is that character?"

"Patience, patience," Samuel droned. "Trust or bust."

"I hate waiting for anything," Webb said, swatting the air. He looked around his small apartment, cluttered with mail and paperwork. His bedroom was a disaster area with laundry spilling from the hamper. He would tackle that on Saturday. Maybe take it to the laundromat so he could do four loads at once rather than vie for the one machine in his building. He despised the laundromat. Everyone competing for the few dryers, strangers studying each other's underwear.

"Did you know that you and I are authors?" Samuel asked. He held up a large book bound in black leather. *Webster Martin Hannis* was embossed in gold on the cover.

"What the hell is that?" Webb reached for the thick volume, his fingers grasping only thin air.

"If you read it, you'll know your entire life," Samuel warned, holding the book aloft. "What a bore that would be. You're here to discover, Bud. You made that choice before you were born."

"You're telling me I *chose* to come here and have all this crap happen? I *chose* to get zonked on the head? Give me a break, Pal," Webb snorted. "I'm not that dumb."

Samuel ran his hand over the shiny cover. "We wrote this together, with God's guidance."

"Not that God crap again."

"I use that word because you recognize it. God is really the wondrous universal energy within every person and every thing."

"God, Samuel—"

"See, you do recognize God. Others call this energy Allah, or Buddha, or Divine energy. It's all the same. Everyone can tap into it just by believing they can."

"Okay, okay. So what's up with the book?"

"You came to earth with an agenda. You learn important lessons from each lifetime. Always remember, you're never alone."

"That's for sure," Webb said with a wry grin.

"Lighten up, Bud," Samuel teased. "Remember, I'm here

too until you leave this body for good." The book disappeared.

Webb scowled. "I solved hundreds of crimes without you around. I'm a damn good detective." He eyed Samuel. "Okay, I know you said those hunches came from you."

Webb threw up his hands in frustration. He went to the coffee table, swiping the dust off the oak top, grabbed the Lazare case file, and opened it. He was anxious to add more to it. "Where is that guy? He should be here by now."

"You'll save yourself an ulcer if you just calm down, Bud," Samuel said.

Turning on the television, Webb popped in a tape to check the VCR. "Working fine." He flipped through the sit-coms on network television, groaning at the canned laughter.

Suddenly he heard a knock on the door. "Almost an hour late. Probably couldn't see the address in this weather."

Webb sprang to the door and tore it open.

Max Anglim glistened from the rain. He clutched something under a knit shirt. "I hope nobody saw me come in here," he teased. "Wouldn't want anyone to think I'm some kind of narc."

Webb ushered the reporter into the living room and brightened when Max pulled a videotape from beneath his shirt.

"I ran this through the super editor. See what you think."

"Want a beer?"

Anglim brushed the rain off his shoulders. "Sure."

When Webb returned from the kitchen with a Budweiser, Anglim was seated on the couch eyeing Webb's notes. The detective whisked the folder away and tossed it onto a chair across the room. Then he pushed the tape into the machine and pressed play. There on the screen was a still frame of the BMW at the fireworks, much closer than the original footage.

"Let this roll," Max instructed. "I still-framed the video in multiple places so you can study different angles."

"Good, good." Though the image was closer, the tinted windows on the vehicle still obscured the driver. He forwarded to the next frame. "The person appears to have dark hair, but I can't really tell through the tint. It would help if whoever it is would look this way."

"It could be Marc Lazare," Anglim said.

"What time did you shoot this video?"

"Oh, an hour or so before the show."

"If this is Marc, he was alive at that point." Webb examined the rest of the tape.

"I did a little color correcting on the tinted windows, but that's as good as I could get," Anglim said. "The boss would shoot me if he knew I'm helping the cops without his permission."

"I had a good working relationship with the TV reporters in Cincinnati. Your video is invaluable. Can I keep this tape?"

"It's yours. Now do you have anything for me?" Max leaned back on the cushions.

"Actually nothing you can air," Webb said. "What do you know about Purp Strickland?"

"He's a weird dude. Kinda keeps to himself. I wouldn't trust him. He's in cahoots with Pierre Lazare."

"Does he have anything against the brothers?"

"There's some friction. I don't know that much, but he's a damn good pyrotechnist."

"What kind of friction?"

"Purp's a real expert and knows it. But Pierre won't let anyone outside the family be a partner in the business. Must be tough on old Harry."

Webb switched off the television and ejected the tape. "Very interesting. I wonder why Marc's wife stormed out of that car?"

"I don't know her," Max said. "Can you tell me anything off the record?"

"We're mainly looking at the family right now, but don't air that yet. We have other leads as well."

"Like what?"

"I can't say at this point."

"Come on, man. I thought we were sharing here."

"When we have something to share, you'll be the first to know."

Anglim stood, shaking his head. He left without comment.

"Okay, Sam. Who in the hell is the driver in that car?"

Samuel smiled. "Won't it be a real kick to find out?"

"So much for guidance tonight." Webb went back to his notes.

Just before midnight, he stepped out of the shower and reached for a bath-towel. He rubbed his body vigorously. Back in his bedroom, he stood naked under the ceiling fan. Samuel lounged in a chair.

"God, Sam. Just give me one moment of privacy."

Samuel rolled his eyes. "Your body doesn't interest me, Bud. I'm more interested in what's on the inside."

Webb wrapped the towel around his waist.

"God, I'm bushed. How could my life get this complicated?

"Watch the negativity," Samuel said. "Eventually you'll understand everything."

"Why do I have to wait if I'm eventually going to understand everything? That's nuts. Why not explain it now?"

"You're learning patience, remember?"

"I'm tired of being patient." Webb turned the ceiling fan on high. "Damn this humidity. The AC in this apartment stinks."

Sam got up and ambled across the room. "Sleep tight, dream right."

Webb dove into underwear, pulled back the bed covers, and lay down on the cool sheets.

"Monitor your dreams. They contain a wealth of knowledge," Samuel said. "Dreamstate is a great way to gather information from the spirit realm."

"When do I get a break from all this?"

"When you die."

Webb sighed and doused the light, aware Samuel would be

with him all night. He had to admit that in a way it was comforting. He nested into a comfortable position. Within minutes the fan's soft whirring mesmerized him, and he drifted off.

Later that night Webb found himself in the parking lot at the fireworks. People milled around in slow motion. He felt weightless, as though gravity had disappeared. He leaped into the air and slowly floated back to earth. The sensation delighted him.

In the distance a car approached...a navy blue BMW. It stopped a few feet from him. The door opened and Laura Lazare got out in the same slow motion, her face contorted like it was on Max Anglim's tape. She slammed the car door and began her labored trek toward the park.

Webb yelled, "Wait! Come back, Mrs. Lazare."

She turned slowly and eyed him.

Webb called to her. "Who's that in the car?"

She turned and started toward him, a look of fury in her eyes.

Webb plowed toward the car like he was wading through high water. It took every effort to move his legs. He peered through the tinted glass but couldn't tell who was inside.

Laura reached the car and began clawing at him.

He shoved her away and opened the door. Inside, another shield of tinted glass appeared. He pushed it away only to see still another.

Laura screamed and beat on his back. Her touch was feather light. "You can't do this! Stop!" she cried, her voice hollow.

Webb pressed his forehead against the menacing shield straining to see through the dark tint.

The driver covered his face with both hands, but Webb could see a medallion in the shape of a sunburst hanging around his neck.

He woke with a start, gasping for breath, perspiration running down his chest. "My God. What a dream." He sat up and threw his legs over the side of the bed.

Samuel stood near the moonlit window.

"Why were all those shields in my way? I couldn't see the driver! Come on, Sam, you know damn well who was in that car."

"Calm down and rehash the dream, Bud. What did you see?"

Webb leapt out of bed, padded into the kitchen and rummaged through the cupboard until he found a pack of cigarettes. "I haven't had one of these in months, but I need one now."

"Those things can be fatal," Samuel said. "I helped you quit. Don't mess it up."

Webb lit the Camel, went into the living room, and stared out the window. The storm had cleared out. Tree branches now cast eerie shadows on the starlit lawn. He drew in the smoke, inhaling deep into his lungs, and slumped down into a chair. "God, these cigs are stale."

He stayed there until dawn, the ashtray beside him littered with butts.

* * *

The next morning, Max Anglim and his photographer were on their way to cover a teacher's strike in Southfield. After the thunderstorm, temperatures dropped into the seventies. Max reveled in the breeze wafting through the open windows. "My eyes get so dry in the air conditioning."

Glen drove with one hand on the wheel, popping pretzels into his mouth with the other. "Anything new on the Lazare murder?"

"The company had a whopper insurance policy on Marc. Sounds like a good reason to murder him."

"Where did you get that information?"

"I pick up on things."

"Did Hannis give you a scoop yet?"

"I was at his apartment last night. We're tight. I have him right where I want him."

Glen spun the news van off the Lodge Freeway onto Lahser Road, tossing the pretzel bag onto the floor. "What does that mean?"

"He needs me, man. I enlarged that video of Marc Lazare in the car, and he about pissed his pants," Max boasted. "Hell, I could fake some evidence with our camera and he'd eat it up."

Glen looked at Anglim and cocked his head. "Don't even think—"

"I'm gibing you. But consider the possibilities."

Glen grabbed the two-way radio and checked the on/off switch. "I hope they're not hearing this back at the station. You worry me." Glen stopped at a light.

Max stared him straight in the eye. "I'm not kidding about that Emmy. It's mine," he said. "I've been thinking about taking a job in public relations. Maybe at some hospital where there's more blood and gore. That should be exciting."

As the news van pulled up in front of the school superintendent's office a mob of sign-toting teachers leaped from lawn chairs and began their chant. "Better benefits for better education!"

"It's always like this," Glen chafed. "These guys sit on their duffs until we get here."

By the time Glen gathered the equipment, the picket line was in order, circling in front of the Board of Education sign.

Max rolled his eyes. "I'm tired of this stupid stuff. This is my last year as a media whore. But I won't let it end without the Emmy."

Glen eyed him warily.

*   *   *

Wind chimes tinkled in the cool breeze as Webb Hannis pumped the doorbell on Marc Lazare's front porch. He waited, tapping his foot. Breathing deeply, grateful for a break in the weather, the scent of roses wafted across his nostrils. The front yard abounded in fragrant bushes.

"So you stopped to smell the flowers," Samuel said.

Webb hit the bell again and banged on the door.

Finally it opened and a petite Mexican woman in a black maid's uniform smiled at him. Webb flashed his badge. "I'm detective Webb Hannis with the Detroit Police Department. Is Mrs. Lazare home?"

Laura Lazare, tall and regal in a riding outfit, appeared at the door, ringlets of red hair falling over her shoulders. Her lips, a delicate pink in spite of no makeup, pursed when she saw him. "May I help you?"

"I have some questions."

"I'm on my way out, Detective. My son has a riding lesson in fifteen minutes."

"Cancel it," he said.

Her eyes narrowed. She stepped back and motioned him in. "Rosa, please call and leave a message at the stables."

Webb waded through thick carpeting into the living room. Furnished in exquisite taste, an array of antiques spread before him, some so delicate, he chose a velvet tufted sofa with cabriole legs and hoped it wouldn't collapse under his weight. He scanned the room. Wow! This place is certainly different from the old man's house. It took a pretty penny to put a room like this together.

Laura slipped into a chair opposite him, crossing her long legs. "I wish you called before showing up at my door."

"I'm sorry to inconvenience you, but we are trying to solve your husband's murder."

She sat up straight in the chair. "I'm trying to keep life as normal as possible for my son," she said tersely. "He doesn't understand death."

Webb opened his notebook, plucking a pen from his shirt pocket.

For once, Samuel, sprawled casually across a needlepoint chair, was behaving.

Webb directed his gaze at Laura. "Where were you the night of the fireworks, Mrs. Lazare?"

She grabbed a tissue and blew her nose. "I was...right here."

"All evening?"

"Yes...ah...Austin was sick that morning and I didn't want him to go out." She fumbled with her wristwatch.

"Don't lie to me."

"Why are you asking?"

"I saw you on a videotape. You got out of a car and went into the park that night."

She rose and ambled over to the window. "How do you know it was me? We never met."

"I saw a picture of you at your in-law's house."

She turned to face him, her chin trembling. "I can't bear this invasion of privacy. What difference does it make if I was there or not?"

"Plenty. A man was driving the car. Was it your husband? Was he alive at that time?"

She clutched the back of an antique chair, her face twisted in anger. "What are you getting at, Detective?"

"Was your husband the man in that car?"

She turned away from him. "Yes! Who else would it be? We had a fight and I...I left in a huff. Now, are you satisfied?"

"Was that the last time you saw him?"

She lowered her head, her self-control waning. "Yes...my God, yes."

"How did you get home that night?"

She stared at him, her eyes wide, her mouth open. "I...I don't remember." She came back to the chair and sank down. "Oh yes. I...I...took a cab."

"Which company?"

"How should I know?" she shouted. "I hardly remember the night at all with all that's happened since."

A small boy, about three years old, rushed into the room. Samuel dropped to the floor and somersaulted over to the child.

The boy clapped his hands in delight. "Mommy, I wanna' ride my pony."

Laura scooped the boy into her arms. "A little later, Austin. Run along and Rosa will give you a cookie."

The child approached Webb. "Hi. You gonna ride, too?"

"No," Webb said. "I'm here to—"

"Austin! Go to Rosa," Laura cried. "Mind Mommy, now."

The child's face fell. He turned and scooted out of the room.

Samuel, sitting in lotus position, remained on the floor, listening intently.

"Surely you weren't going to tell my son why you're here," she said.

Webb stood abruptly and put his notebook away. "Do you want to take a lie detector test?"

Laura's face reddened. "Absolutely not. I know those things are unreliable, especially when you're upset. Are you trying to say you suspect I killed my husband?"

"No, but if you didn't kill him why not take the polygraph?"

"I'm not saying another thing without my attorney. Please leave, Mr. Hannis."

Slowly Webb stood. "Keep yourself available in case I have more questions."

"Next time, call in advance so I can contact my attorney," she said.

He headed for the door and let himself out.

In the car he gunned the engine and pulled out of the driveway.

"What is it with this family? Why was she so skittish? One thing for sure. I'm not through with her."

"Good job, Bud," Samuel said as he rolled down the window and hung his head out.

"You look like a damn dog hanging out the window like that," Webb snapped. "I suppose you prompted me in there," he said with a smirk.

"You don't need much prompting in your work, Bud. You do a lot of it automatically now." Samuel smiled. "I trained you well."

Back inside the department Webb met with Jake Rubel in the conference room. Jake spread papers out in front of him on the Formica table. "I interviewed just about every employee that was working the night of the fireworks. Would you believe they don't even have the names of most volunteer pyrotechnists? Those guys are wacko. They like to blow things up, and they do it without pay. Next I'm going to talk to the retirees."

Webb only half-listened.

"I don't want to leave a stone unturned," Rubel expounded. "What have *you* done?"

"I got a warrant and picked up the Smith and Wesson at the Lazare's house," Webb said casually, swinging the paper sack that contained the gun. "It's registered to Pierre."

Rubel leaped from his seat. "Why did you do that without me?"

"I guess you were out on one of your interviews."

"I'm going to talk to Gallister about this. We're supposed to be partners."

"Then how about sharing these with me?" Webb flipped through Rubel's folders.

Rubel grabbed them away. "I'm working on a report for Gallister."

Amused, Webb stood up and calmly left the room.

Out in the break room, he poured coffee into a foam cup and sat down at a table in the corner.

Daisy appeared, her hair caught up in a loose ponytail. She punched a candy bar from the vending machine, peeled off part of the wrapper, and sat beside him. "What's going on?"

"Daiz, we traced the murder weapon to Pierre Lazare."

"No kidding? What a great break."

"You won't believe this." He leaned toward her and lowered his tone. "Remember that dream I had about the gun in a cherry wood cabinet? Well, I saw the exact one. It's in Pierre Lazare's study."

Daisy slapped the table. "Wow!"

Webb thought about the big black book. That's too far out. A prewritten script for my life?

"*Not a perfect script,*" Samuel said. "*More of a framework to help you stay on your chosen path.*"

Webb sighed heavily. "A week ago I thought I was doing okay. Now I'm confused."

Daisy patted his arm. "Webb, you look exhausted. Take the day off and sleep."

"I have too much to do," Webb said, rising. "I need to interview each family member again. Finding the murder weapon was a gift. Ballistics is testing it." He turned away from her.

Daisy took one bite of the candy bar, wrapped up the rest, and returned to her cubicle.

* * *

That evening on the five o'clock news, Max Anglim was the lead story. Standing on the street in front of the Lazare Fireworks complex, he told about a huge insurance payoff to the surviving brothers. The live microwave truck beamed his story into living rooms across Detroit.

When the report ended, Max whooped into the air. "Best goddamn work I ever did. This story keeps getting better and better."

Glen Gerard carefully folded the giant silver reflector.

"Man, I hate that thing," Max complained. "It's like a big mirror burning the sun into my eyes."

"With your dark skin, you'd look like a black blob without it. The reflector gives you some facial features in the sun." He zipped the cover over the folded disc. "You better hope the news director doesn't find out you gave those tapes to Hannis."

Max chugged a cold soda, belching loudly. "Nothing to fear, man. You're the only one who knows." He glared at Glen. "So if he does find out I'll know who blabbed."

The two-way radio blared from the live truck. "Great work, Anglim." It was the news director back at the station. "The competition had nothing on the murder. They led with the teacher's strike."

Anglim beamed at his photographer and went to sit in the air-conditioned truck while Glen tore down the equipment. His chest bulging with pride, he gazed at the Lazare complex spread over a vast fifty acres. The operation was split between one hundred fifty small, separate buildings. He knew each step in the manufacturing process was segregated. That way, an accidental explosion in one building wouldn't destroy the entire complex. The buildings were constructed so that if an explosion occurred, it would blow upwards instead of bursting through the walls.

The white wood-framed structures reminded Max of little chicken coops. He and his cameras were forbidden to enter the individual bunkers. The federal government prohibited unauthorized people from going inside because of the danger. Max longed to view the intricate chemical mixing.

Suddenly, his eye caught the door to one of the bunkers. Slightly ajar, a bushy face peered out.

He recognized the shrubby beard. Purp. Bounding out of the truck, Max approached the chain link fence. "Purp," he called out. "Hey Strickland, can I talk to you?" Come on, man, let me inside just this once, he pleaded silently.

The door to the bunker slowly shut.

*   *   *

Saturday morning in Webb's cubicle at the station, the purple crystal was missing. He slammed his fist on the desk. "Damn it! Where the hell did that thing go? It doesn't even belong to me." He rattled papers and folders on his desk, searching for the glittery stone. He kicked at some fallen papers.

Samuel began slow dancing across the room. His head tilted as if in a tranquil trance.

Gallister appeared in the hall. "I see you're here on a Saturday too, Hannis. Good. It's a perfect time for us to talk. Let's go into my office."

Another folder dropped, spilling papers about the floor. "What a lousy day," Webb groaned.

Samuel wagged his finger. *"Negativity."*

Webb followed his boss into the glass-walled office and sat across from him. "What's on your mind?"

Gallister lifted his glasses off the desk and placed them on his nose. Folding his hands in front of him he looked grim.

Webb shifted uncomfortably in the chair.

"Webb, I'm wondering…have you totally recovered from your accident?"

"I still get headaches, but I'm fine. They certainly don't get in the way of my job."

"Jake Rubel seems to think you're not quite up to par." Gallister raised his eyebrows, deep furrows rippling across his forehead. "He's interviewed dozens of people and taken copious notes. He thinks you're slacking."

Webb rolled his eyes. "C'mon, Fred. Haven't you figured out Rubel by now? Sure he's out gathering information, but he has no idea how to process it. He has absolutely no instincts. He won't even share the notes with me, his own so-called partner."

"I didn't know that," Gallister said. "I'll get on his ass. He said you told the Channel Three reporter about the Lazare's life insurance policy."

Webb swallowed hard. "Anglim probably has an inside source. I certainly didn't tell him." He wanted to strangle

Anglim, knowing the bum got the information that night at the apartment from the folder on the coffee table.

Samuel leaned against the bookcase, his arms crossed over his chest.

Webb glanced at him hoping for assistance.

Gallister cleared his throat. "The prosecutor is hounding me for a breakthrough in this case. Lucky for you the gun was easily traced to Pierre Lazare. Do you have it in for firearm identification?"

"Of course."

Gallister pulled the purple stone from a desk drawer. "Rubel found this on your desk. Says it's one of those magic crystals. I must say I'm concerned about you, Webb."

"Uh, Daisy put that thing on my desk as a joke," Webb fumbled.

"Rubel told me you're spending time on the computer rather than hitting the pavement," Gallister said. "I felt I had to look into your time on the Internet."

Gallister pulled a printout from the folder. "It says here you were investigating psychic call-in lines. Rubel thinks you're trying to get psychics to figure out this case. Is that true?"

"No! I mean, yes, I was checking out that website, but it's not what you think."

Gallister adjusted his glasses. "Then what is this all about?"

"I can't tell you, Fred. At least not now. I may be onto something big."

Gallister shut the folder and glared at Hannis over his glasses. "We go back a long way, Webb. I'll give you the benefit of the doubt for now. Don't disappoint me."

Webb stood. "I hope to have something important soon, Fred. In the meantime, keep that asshole Rubel off my back."

Gallister chuckled and tossed the crystal to Webb. "This looks better on Daisy's desk."

Back in his cubicle, Webb stared at Samuel. "What good are

you if you keep causing me grief? I've had more problems since you arrived."

"Life's lessons. Would you want to miss them?"

Samuel's gray shirt slowly morphed into a shiny red satin with black trim. The spirit guide shouted, "Do the tango!" and began a frenzied dance.

Webb's heart beat picked up to the rhythm as he stared at Samuel. "Enough is enough," he declared. "If that damned family won't talk, I'll use some persuasion. This is no time for privacy."

Samuel stopped in the middle of the cubicle, arms in Flamenco position. "Now you're doin' the tango, Bud."

Ignoring Samuel, Webb slipped his tape recorder into his pocket and hurried to his car. A moment later, with renewed vigor, he was on his way to Laura Lazare's home.

He rang the doorbell and listened. "This gal knows something, and I intend to squeeze it out of her today. You keep your trap shut in here, Sam."

When Laura saw Webb at the door, her eyes widened. Dressed in a gauzy, shapeless dress that flowed to her ankles, the pale yellow color complimented her strawberry ringlets. Even without a trace of makeup, Laura Lazare was a natural beauty. "Mr. Hannis. I thought my father-in-law made it perfectly clear, you should direct all inquiries to our attorney."

"This has nothing to do with your attorney, Mrs. Lazare. I'm here because you lied to me during my last visit."

Laura's face flushed. She tried to push the door shut. "Please contact my lawyer."

Webb grabbed the door and shoved his foot in the way. "I'm here to keep you out of prison." He pushed his way into the foyer.

"What is this all about?" she demanded, lacing her fingers across her bosom. "I don't have to say anything without my attorney present."

Webb strolled into the plush living room, sank onto the couch, and turned on the tape recorder. "You're hiding information about your husband's murder. That means you're an accessory after the fact. Do you know what that means, Mrs. Lazare?"

Laura stood in the middle of the floor. "I'm not saying anything," she said, hands on her hips.

"I don't think you murdered your husband, but you are obviously hiding something that could help us."

Samuel moved over to Laura.

Webb stood up to his full height, towering over her, and avoiding eye contact with Samuel, he looked deep into her eyes. "That means if you don't tell me what you know, as an accessory, you'll serve the same prison term as the person who pulled the trigger."

Laura dropped into a chair, running long fingers up and down her arms. She looked past him, refusing to meet his gaze. "I don't know anything about Marc's murder. I swear I don't."

"Let me put it this way. I could get up on the stand and expose your lies before a jury. Is that what you want?"

"I told you. I don't know anything," she said firmly. "I'm innocent."

Webb sat down. "I spoke with the prosecutor about a deal. He promised, if you cooperate with us now, he won't press charges against you."

Webb leaned against the cushions, comfortably propping one leg on the opposite knee. His natural abilities in full throttle, he felt in control for the first time in days. "If you're as bright as you appear, you won't risk maximum security prison to protect somebody else."

"I'm not protecting anyone," she said, her voice a bit shaky. "I'm telling you the truth now. I'm as puzzled as you are. Marc and I loved each other."

"It didn't look like it on that tape," Webb said. "Why not tell me the whole story and save yourself a lot of grief. It would be so sad for your young son to lose his mother."

"Stop!" Laura's voice dropped an octave. "I know what

you're trying to do, Detective. You won't frighten me into talking to you."

"Why? Do you have something to hide? You say you don't, so why not tell me everything that happened on the Fourth of July?"

Laura hunched her shoulders.

She's definitely scared, he thought. But she's stubborn. Highly intelligent. Most suspects break down at the mention of prison.

Webb remained calm. "What happened to your husband after you stormed out of the car?"

"How should I know? I didn't see him after that."

"Did he own a silver medallion?"

Laura looked genuinely puzzled. "What?"

"A medallion on a silver chain in the shape of a sunburst. Did your husband own one?"

"I'm calling my lawyer."

"I'll call him for you. What's the number?"

She reached for the phone.

He pulled it out of her hand and lifted the receiver. "The number."

Her voice rose. "I told you all I know," she shouted. "Marc and I had a fight and I left him in the parking lot at the fireworks. That's everything."

Webb pocketed the recorder, stood and started toward the door. "I'll give you another day to think about this, Mrs. Lazare. After that, the deal with the prosecutor is off."

CHAPTER 7

MONDAY MORNING, Jade Lazare rummaged through the latest Neiman-Marcus catalogue. "These shoes would be perfect with that dress I got at the mall with Gillian." She winced. "Conrad will have a stroke if I put any more on the credit cards."

The phone rang. "Maybe that's Gillian. I can't possibly go shopping again." She grabbed the receiver.

"Jade, it's Pierre."

"Yes, Dad. I do know your voice," she snapped.

"Is Conrad home? I called the plant and he was gone."

"He's at the hair salon."

"Well, I have something to discuss with him."

"Is it about the business? I hope you've come to your senses. It's selfish for you to toy with our future. Your son won't stand up to you, but I will."

"This concerns his mother," Pierre said. "She's deteriorating fast since Marc's death. She doesn't eat, and sleeps most of the day because she's so depressed."

"I'm sorry to hear that."

"I forced her to see our doctor yesterday, and he recommends the Mesa-Verde Clinic in Arizona. They specialize in these cases."

"That's so far away," Jade said, dollar signs floating through her head.

"I know. It's very expensive, but I don't know what else to do. Please have Conrad call me."

"Sure, sure." She hung up and sank back onto the couch. "Big bucks to treat that old lady in style. When will it be my turn?"

She propped against pillows on the couch, with her feet on the coffee table. A morning talk show droned on the television as she dabbed into the nail polish bottle and slicked the brush over her oval fingernail.

The phone rang. "God! I can never get through a manicure without ruining it. It better not be Pierre again. I'm not giving in until he meets my demands." Her fingers splayed like wheel spokes, she delicately lifted the cell phone off the couch cushion and balanced the phone against her shoulder. "The Lazare residence."

"Mrs. Lazare?" The voice was deep and pleasant.

"Yes. I'm Jade Lazare. Who's calling?"

"This is Max Anglim with Action News, Channel Three. You probably see me on the six o'clock show."

"Oh, I'm actually talking to a real celebrity?" Jade placed the bottle of polish on the table and blew on her nails.

"Sorry to bother you, but I'm working on a follow-up story about your brother-in-law's murder. Were you close to Marc and his wife?"

"Yes. I know them — knew him — well." God, a news reporter chose me for information.

"Did they get along? I mean, do you know if there was trouble around the Fourth of July?"

"Aren't you blunt with the questions? They got along as well as any other married couple. Laura thought Marc worked too hard."

"Did they fight about that?" the reporter persisted.

"Now that I think of it, Laura didn't even want to go to the fireworks that night because she was mad at Marc."

Anglim's voice sounded excited. "Did she attend anyway?"

"I really don't know. I always join my husband on the barge. I never saw Laura or Marc that night."

"Jade, you've been very helpful to me. Would you mind if we swung over and interviewed you on camera?"

Jade's heart skipped a beat. "Me on television? I don't know about that."

"Oh, I can tell by your voice you would be great. We can be there in half an hour if you give me the address."

"I'm not sure Conrad wants me to talk to the media."

"It's up to you, Jade. The police want us to keep the case before the public in the event people have information."

"Oh, then I should probably cooperate."

"I won't ask you anything more than what we've already discussed. In television we need to videotape your response. If I were from the newspaper, I could simply write it down with quotation marks. What is your address?"

Jade gave him detailed directions to the house, all the while contemplating what to wear on television. When she hung up, the polish on her index finger was smeared.

* * *

Max Anglim throbbed with excitement. "Glen, get off your butt. We gotta get across town, now! I just set up an interview with Jade Lazare, Conrad's wife. She could change her mind in a heartbeat. Maybe even call her husband. He'd definitely nix the interview, especially after that story about the insurance policy. We gotta be there now."

Grabbing his suit jacket and a notebook, he sailed out to the garage. Glen opened the hatch back and inventoried his equipment.

"As long as we have the camera and a microphone, we're set. Let's get going." Max leaned over and cranked the key in the ignition.

Once on the road, Glen eyed his reporter buddy. "Why is this interview so pressing?" He ran a yellow light and turned onto the highway.

"Conrad Lazare's wife has agreed to go on tape about Marc and Laura Lazare's relationship."

Glen rolled up his window and turned on the air conditioner. "Why do we care about that?"

"Remember that footage we shot on the Fourth of July?

"Vaguely."

"I'm talking about the part where Webb Hannis spotted Laura Lazare in the background, storming out of a car with Marc in the driver's seat."

"That stuff you still-framed for Hannis?"

"Yes. Now's my chance to use that great video. Well, we don't know for sure if it's Marc, but it sure looks like him."

"Wait a minute. If you can't positively identify him, we shouldn't say it's Marc Lazare. That's tabloid journalism."

"I'm the reporter. Leave it up to me," Max said as they turned into the driveway at Conrad Lazare's house. Anglim's heart fluttered. He hoped Jade would still be responsive. He jumped from the car, hurried up the front walk, and rang the doorbell.

He could hear high heels clicking against the hard floor before the door opened.

Jade Lazare was stunning.

Max gulped.

Dressed in a tank dress splashed with bright red and orange flowers, the narrow cut outlined her curvaceous figure all the way down to her ankles.

"Jade? We're going to do the interview outside since the weather is so nice," he said before she could protest. If they hauled in lights and set up inside, she might be intimidated and back out of the interview.

Jade stepped onto the porch, gold teardrop earrings reflecting the sunlight. Glen walked up, the camera already on his shoulder, and handed the microphone to Max.

"Just relax and look at me rather than the camera." He brushed a blond strand away from her eyes. "Want you to look your best on television," he teased.

Max launched into the interview with gusto.

Jade was a bit more reticent than on the phone. Interview subjects always were. It was frightening to face a camera with no experience.

"You're doing great," he coaxed. "In fact you're a natural for TV. Did you ever consider a career in news?"

Jade dropped her chin, obviously flattered. "Really? When will this be on the air?"

"Probably tonight, if we can get the facts together. Just a little background story about the family. Nothing really big."

Anglim was amazed when Jade agreed to let Glen videotape her inspecting a flower garden in the backyard. "This is just extra footage we use for editing."

Glen zoomed in for a close-up of the flowerbed. "I want you to reach in and pick the largest blooms, Mrs. Lazare. Wait until I count to five."

Jade really was comfortable on television. So many people were confused when the photographer sequenced video, especially the close-ups. "Great. Continue with what you're doing." He shot a close up of her face, then a medium shot that included the flowers and Jade from the waist up. Finally, he lowered the camera. "I think I have everything I need."

Max shook her hand warmly. As they pulled away, Jade waved from the porch, unaware the sun filtering through her dress exposed the absence of underwear.

*   *   *

When Conrad returned home for dinner, Jade was in the kitchen preparing a salad. Nibbling on celery, she chose a ripe tomato and sliced it into chunks. "Franciois did a super job on your hair, honey. I told you he was good."

"Good and expensive," Conrad said with a wry smile.

Jade tossed the tomato pieces into the salad, covered the bowl, and slid it into the refrigerator. "Your father called."

Conrad stopped and turned toward her. "He must be pissed about that report on Channel Three last night. The employees were all talking about it today."

"What report?" Jade felt suddenly uneasy.

"Supposedly the reporter found out about our big insurance policy. Makes us look guilty. The media is so damn destructive."

Jade cleared her throat. "Your dad called because he wants to put your mother in some big expensive place out in Arizona."

"What kind of place?"

"It sounds like a fancy spa," Jade said, folding her arms. "Why don't they just put her on an anti-depressant drug? Half the people I know are on one of those."

"I'm sure Dad's following doctor's orders," Conrad said, his forehead wrinkling. "You know he wouldn't spend money unless it was necessary. My mother looked awful the last time I saw her."

Jade stomped back to the counter, swept the remains of the salad into her hand and dumped them into the sink. "There's always money for everyone but me. What about the new house? Do we just scrap those plans?"

"When the insurance money comes through we'll have our money. You're acting like a real bitch, Jade. We're talking about my mother here." He started out of the room.

"I told Tristan to go ahead and order that material from England."

"How do you plan to pay for it? When the well is dry Jade, the water is gone."

"I'll...I'll use the ten thousand you gave me and put something else on hold."

"Now you're talking sense," he said, smiling, and left the room.

Damn! Why did I say that? I already ordered custom furniture that costs more than that ten thousand, she thought, swatting the towel against a cupboard.

She glanced at the clock. Five until six. Tossing the rag on the counter, she rushed to the family room and switched on the television.

*   *   *

Laura Lazare's days at home seemed interminable with the endless demands of a three-year-old. She adored Austin, who looked so much like his father. But his constant chatter almost drove her crazy. She longed for quiet so she could gather her own thoughts without interruption.

With Austin on the floor banging pots and pans from the cupboard, and the television on the counter top tuned to one of his kiddy shows, peace would have to wait tonight.

Austin dragged a kitchen chair across the hardwood floor. "Me play in the sink, Mommy."

"You're scratching the floor, honey. Let me handle that chair." All I need is a wet mess, but it's better than dealing with another tantrum.

"Wash these plastic cups for Mommy." She dumped the cups into the dishwater, then went to retrieve celery and carrots from the refrigerator.

"Austin, how about me cooking the carrots tonight?"

"No, no. I want dippy."

She sighed and retrieved a bowl of vegetable dip from the refrigerator. Pulling out the under-counter cutting board, she began scraping carrots near the television where the cartoon show was winding down. A vegetarian herself, she was adamant about feeding her child healthy foods.

As she reached for the celery, she thought, how many nights did I hold dinner for Marc, only to have him return home after midnight? At one point she suspected an affair, but realized that just wasn't Marc's style. Oh, I know he loved us, but his job came first. The classic workaholic. What a bore.

"Austin, this show is driving me crazy."

He continued to splash in the sink as she switched on the six o'clock news to catch the weather. "If it stays cool we can go to the stable at mid-day this week. I'm so glad you like horses."

"Me like ponies."

When the anchor mentioned Marc Lazare's name, Laura almost sliced her finger.

"Mommy, see bubbles?"

"Please, Austin. Mommy needs to hear this." She turned up the volume as reporter Max Anglim began his report.

"Detroit Police still don't know what time Marc Lazare was murdered and his body placed over the mortar tubes," Anglim said. "But we have exclusive footage that may prove the president of Lazare Fireworks was alive just hours before the Fourth of July show."

Laura watched in horror as the reporter showed video in slow motion of her bursting out of the BMW. They closed in on her angry face. "Oh, my God!"

Pulling his sudsy hands from the water Austin climbed down from the chair, glopping water and soap onto the floor. "Me watch TV?"

Anglim continued. "Police have tentatively identified the driver of this car as Marc Lazare."

Up popped an interview with Jade. "Laura didn't like it when Marc worked late, and they often fought about it. She told me she wasn't going to the fireworks because she was mad at him."

Laura's mouth fell open. "Where in the hell do you get the nerve to talk about me to the media?" She grabbed for the counter, her mind suddenly whirling in disbelief. "That must be the video the detective was talking about." Laura felt exposed. Naked.

"Mommy, Mommy, look at me." Austin slid across the floor in the water and hit his head on the kitchen table with a resounding thud. He burst into tears.

Stunned by the television report, Laura wanted to scream. Instead she picked up her soggy child and hugged him against her thumping chest. The thought of Jade's exposé sickened her.

The moment the news ended the phone rang. It was Pierre. "What was that all about? Where did the television station get such footage?"

Laura searched for an answer, but her mind and mouth worked against each other. "I'm as dumbstruck as you."

"I won't have this family telling tales on a news program. We must pull together." Pierre softened a bit. "We're talking honor here."

"I agree with you, Father. But you need to talk with Jade. She's the one who did this."

"Was that Marc in the car with you?"

"Ye…Yes. It's true we were arguing."

"When was that footage taken?"

"I'm not really sure. I was upset and took a cab home. I never did see the fireworks that night."

The line was silent except for Pierre's labored breathing. "Katherine is not well. I would prefer she doesn't hear about this." He hung up abruptly.

Austin whined on her lap. "I'm hungry."

Setting him down in his junior chair, she gave him the celery sticks and dip.

Laura snatched up the phone to call Jade. She hesitated. Slowly she set the receiver down in the cradle. "Let Pierre have a stab at her first."

*   *   *

Over at the television station, Max Anglim was fielding his own call. Fresh from the news set, sweat shining over matte makeup, he answered the ring.

"What in the hell are you doing, Anglim?"

Max recognized Webb Hannis.

"We don't know if that was Marc Lazare. You could've damn well ruined our investigation."

Max loosened his bright tie and sat on his desk. "It's our video, and I said *tentatively* identified—"

"I don't give a shit what you said," Webb bellowed. "You were wrong! After this you better damn check with me before you do something that stupid!"

"I don't have to check with anyone," Anglim said, a sly smile on his face. "I have my sources too. Jade Lazare knows a lot of juicy details about your murder victim, or haven't you talked with her yet? I could let you see my interview. Want me to drop it by your apartment?"

"So you can stick your nose into my files again? I know where you got that information about the insurance policy. I'm warning you, Anglim. Don't botch this case for your glory." Webb slammed the phone in his ear.

"Who was that?" Glen Gerard asked.

"Webb Hannis thinks he can control the media. Not so. I know more than he does about this murder."

"Oh yeah? Like what?"

Max grinned at his photographer. "Remember how we always wanted excitement at the fireworks? An accident of some sort? Well, we got it. Enjoy the ride, Pal."

*   *   *

"How could you be so damn stupid?" Conrad Lazare paced across the velvet carpet, pausing directly in front of his wife. "Father is on his way now. This may cost me the presidency."

Jade sulked on the couch, blonde hair flowing across her

face. "What's the big deal? The guy said he was trying to help the family."

Conrad dropped to his knees bringing his livid face close to hers. "Reporters lie. They're out for themselves, not you," he spat.

Jade pulled her legs underneath her and turned away in anger. "You're just mad because he came to me instead of you."

"What exactly did you say?"

"I just said Laura didn't like it when Marc worked late. Big deal. Who cares anyway?"

The doorbell clanged like a stroke of doom. Conrad opened the door to face Pierre Lazare, a crimson-faced, beaten man. He limped in, his blue eyes watery and bloodshot.

Conrad braced himself as he helped his father into the living room and motioned him to a chair.

"I'll stand, thank you," Pierre said with careful control, staring directly at Jade. "You've been married to Conrad for four years," he croaked.

Jade crossed her arms and frowned.

"By now you should know that in our family we support each other. I will not stand for this...this tattling on one another. Especially to the media. That Anglim fellow is obviously a vulture." Pierre struggled for a breath, his face turning ashen. "From now on, I will handle the media inquiries. You will refer all calls to me. Is that understood? And no one is to speak with the police without first contacting the family attorney."

Conrad helped him over to a chair. "Can I get you a drink, Father?"

"Water please. Just a little water." The elderly man mopped his neck with a handkerchief. "Maybe I will have a seat." He flopped onto the chair.

Jade looked away in disgust.

"I have whiskey if you prefer," Conrad said.

"No, no. I'm not used to this much exertion. I would have called you to our house, but, as I told Jade this morning, your mother is not well. I'm putting her in a facility in Arizona."

Conrad handed his father a glass of water. "A nursing home?"

Pierre sipped the drink. Coughing, he covered his mouth with his handkerchief. "No. The doctor recommended a place for her condition. It's more like a spa. I think it would do her good to get away from the murder investigation for a while. Fortunately, she didn't see that atrocity on television tonight." He glared at Jade.

"I'm all for it, if you think it would help," Conrad said. "Do you want me to make the arrangements?"

"That would help. I want her to have the best accommodations. The sooner the better. I'm insisting Teddy drive his mother across country. She refuses to fly. He finished his summer classes." Pierre floundered in his seat trying to stand up.

"Let me take you home, Father," Conrad said. "Jade and I can bring your car by tomorrow."

Conrad helped his father out to the car.

*　*　*

When Pierre was finally home, he poured whiskey into a glass and collapsed into his favorite green chair. "That Jade is a flea-brained idiot."

Pierre's heart sank. She was the least of his problems. "Luc is the oldest Lazare now. How can he deliberately kill family tradition? Life isn't supposed to work this way. A father should not outlive his children." A son is not supposed to forsake his father...an entire family for that matter.

Pierre's mind raged at the thought of handing the business over to Conrad. That malicious Jade. Imagine her blabbing our business on TV. And Conrad, always needing money. How could he manage a multi-million dollar business?

Teddy was next in line. "He's a mere pup with no experience. Teddy hates the family business. He wants to go to law school." He's forsaking the family as well.

"What choice do I have? There are other loyal employees, but they aren't family." He stared at the portrait of his father hanging over the mantel. I promised him I would preserve the Lazare name in the business.

He gulped down the drink, half the whiskey trickling down his chin. I suppose I could turn the business over to an outsider and insist on keeping the Lazare name. That would give me another option. He liked having options.

*   *   *

"I don't want to hear you complain about the spa again," Conrad shouted at his wife who lay naked on their bed.

"I'm just saying there are closer and cheaper places," she whined. "What about a psychiatrist?" Jade turned on her side pressing her breasts together into a deep cleavage.

"Don't try the sexy routine on me tonight," Conrad raged. "I'm too angry." He tore a hanger from his closet. "If I lose that presidency because of you, the house is off."

Jade sprang from the bed like an attacking cheetah. She grabbed a white satin robe, slid into it, and tied the sash tightly around her slim waist. "We'd...we'd better get that house!" she blasted. Losing control, she fought to contain herself.

"You already betrayed the family," Conrad thundered. "How will we face Laura?"

"Laura. It's always Laura. Just because her husband dies, everyone caters to Laura. She wasn't even in love with him."

Conrad whirled her around and shook her by the shoulders. "Don't ever say that again. How would you know? It's none of our business and Father will kill you if you talk to the press again."

She jerked away from him. "I have a mind of my own," Jade stomped. "Nobody tells me what I should and shouldn't do." Her body tensed. She could feel the storm erupting. With fire in her eyes she swiped her arm over the top of his dresser. A brush and assorted jewelry flung through the air. A bottle of cologne crashed against the wall, the strong scent pervading the electric air.

Aghast, Conrad stared at her. "Calm down. We can talk about this rationally."

"Rational, he wants." She stalked around the room, dragged a print off the wall and slammed it against a wooden chair. The frame splintered, glass sprinkling over the carpet. Jade ripped the curtains off the window, balling them up and tossing them on the bed.

Conrad tackled and wrestled her to the floor. "I won't let you ruin this house. Get a hold of yourself." He softened his grip when he saw her eyes fill with tears. "Crying won't do it tonight, Jade." He let go of her arms and slowly sat up. "I'm going downstairs to get the vacuum and a garbage bag," he said evenly. "I'll help you clean up."

When he left the room, Jade jumped back on the bed. "I won't let him do this to me."

CHAPTER 8

ON TUESDAY, July eighteenth, Teddy and Katherine Lazare cruised along the freeway well into Indiana. The trip to Mesa-Verde would take nearly a week, as Katherine was too fragile to travel more than a few hours at a time.

"You're such a good son to make this trip, Teddy," she said, her voice feathery. "I'm so fearful of flying. I don't think I could do it the way I'm feeling." Her pale hand trembled, prominent blue veins snaking over the top. "I was doing well helping your father until Marc—" Her voice broke and she reached for a tissue.

"You don't have to talk, Mother," Teddy soothed. "Just lie back and close your eyes. I'll play a CD of your favorite symphony. We'll stop in another hour. Conrad made reservations for us all across the country."

I could drive straight through if I were alone, he thought. Why do I always get suckered into these things? This month I wanted to send out law school applications. I envy Luc. He escaped this family. Once I get my law degree, I'm out of here too, as far away as I can get. You can't stop me, Father.

* * *

As another week passed, the summer heat raged on. On Monday evening, Webb Hannis, the room air conditioner chugging away in his apartment window, dug into the pocket of his jeans for his keys. "Damn it, I put them in here!"

Crouching on his knees, he ran his hand under the couch, then tore off the cushions. "Where the hell are they?" He fumed at Samuel.

Samuel chuckled.

Webb tossed the cushions back in place and dropped back down. "I need to get out of here. I have things to do."

He stared at the notes spread out on his coffee table.

"Well, Sam, I guess you're not gonna' tell me where the keys are. Then how about dropping a hint...as in who murdered Marc Lazare?"

"Solve the mystery." Samuel said. "It's your bag."

"Why the hell can't you just tell me? Would one damn clue kill you?"

"When you need a clue, I'll make sure you get it. It's up to you to pay attention." Samuel offered a jovial grin.

"Blast it, Sam." Webb pounded his fist on the papers. "And wipe that smirk off your face."

Webb shook his head, fingered through the papers, and grabbed for his tape recorder. "Almost a month and I have little to show for it." He glared at Samuel.

Speaking slowly into the machine Webb dictated, "The murder weapon was positively identified as a Smith and Wesson owned by Pierre Lazare. So far the family is tight-lipped. They all refuse to take lie detector tests. Without their cooperation, we're totally stymied."

Webb turned off the recorder. "What about the old guy...Pierre? Did he do it?"

"Maybe."

"So you're gonna clam up on me again."

"Bud, if you want to know everything, why don't you dump your body and join the spirit world?"

"Does it have to be so blasted frustrating in a body?"

"Lose the anger, and follow your guidance. Frustration stops it. Mistakes aren't mistakes. Accidents aren't accidents. Coincidences aren't coincidences."

"Then what the crap are they?"

"They're perfectly planned steps toward solving your problem. They're synchronicity."

"Oh yeah? What about traffic jams?"

"Could be just what you need at the time."

"They drive me crazy."

Samuel lounged back on the couch, kicking his feet onto the coffee table. "If you only understood that you're always right where the universe wants you. Always."

"In a friggin' traffic jam?"

"If that's what will see that you arrive at the exact time to meet the right person, yes. I told you this before. It's time for you to start following my advice."

Webb scratched his head. "What about this right person? Are they supposed to help me?"

"Maybe."

Webb tossed a pillow right through the spirit. "Why won't the Lazares take a polygraph? Hell, in most big cases, suspects want to take the test. Even the guilty ones think they can fool the scribbling machine. Rubel says nobody can dupe the Detroit technician. He supposedly can detect even minute changes on the polygraph and finger the guilty party every time. If the Lazares are so innocent, why don't they want to clear themselves?"

Samuel just smiled in his irritating way.

Webb, shaking his head, started the recorder again. "Pierre can't be ruled out as a suspect. He knows how to shoot the Smith and Wesson. He was definitely nervous when interviewed. But why would this father kill his son? What was his motive? He seems to dote on his kids." Webb eyed Samuel for reaction.

Samuel nodded. "Good, Bud, speak your thoughts out loud."

"Conrad Lazare is a definite possibility." Webb drummed on the table. "He's chafing to get that hefty insurance settlement to build a lavish house. That could be his motive. Pierre said Conrad always competed with Marc. He probably wants to take over Lazare Fireworks to show up his brother.

"Now I wonder if Conrad paid off Luc to split and leave him with the business? I checked every fireworks manufacturer in the country and overseas. I'm sure Luc would look for the kind of work he did best. But nobody has a record of Luc Lazare." Webb leaned back in his chair. "He probably changed his name. That would make it almost impossible to track him, especially if he joins the hundreds of gypsy pyrotechnists who roam the country looking for excitement.

"Teddy checks out. He didn't really have a motive, and he was out of town the day of the fireworks display. I pretty much discount Jade; no motive or knowledge of guns. But Laura...definitely suspicious. Her body language tells me she really isn't mourning her dead husband. This family has secrets, that's for sure. Unfortunately they aren't spilling them.

"Purp Strickland is an enigma. He had plenty of motive and possible access to the gun cabinet." He switched off the recorder again.

"I'm losing it, Sam. These games are ridiculous. Why won't the Lazares talk?"

"At the perfect time. In the perfect way."

The phone rang and he reached for it.

"Webb, this is Daisy at the station. I just took a call from Jade Lazare. She wants to talk to you."

Webb scowled at Samuel.

He was laughing.

"Thanks Daiz. I'm on my way."

Samuel tossed Webb his keys. "You'll need these."

* * *

Max Anglim stood in front of a beautiful wooded lot in the exclusive new development in Grosse Pointe Woods called Chipping Norton. "My real estate source tells me that Conrad Lazare bought this expensive tract and plans to build a whopper house," he said to Glen.

"I'm meeting Paul Weston here for an interview. He's the contractor. This hoity-toity development has all the luxuries. I'd like to live here with indoor/outdoor swimming pools, tennis courts, exercise facilities and a roaming security guard."

"Since when do you do stories on ritzy communities?" Glen laughed and kicked away the loose soil underfoot. "But then again, you do like dirt."

Huge equipment was already busy digging the basement for what appeared to be the Lazare mansion. The hole could swallow five apartments the size of Max's. Glen's camera fixated on an enormous crane, the bucket gulping dirt like a hungry dinosaur.

Max chuckled. "Bear with me. Weston should be here any minute. In fact, there he is now." Max waved as a dark green Jimmy pulled behind the news van. He grabbed the microphone and practically dragged Glen and the camera to meet the contractor. "Mr. Weston, I'm Max Anglim. Thank you for meeting us here."

Weston hopped out of the SUV and shook Max's hand. "I'm glad you guys want to do a positive story for once," he said.

"This type of development seems to be the growing trend in this area, but by the look of the houses, you need some big bucks to build here," Max said into the microphone. "How much would a lot like, lets say this one, cost?" Max gestured toward the Lazare excavation.

"They can go for up to two hundred thousand dollars depending on the size and location. This is prime land with all the trees." Paul Weston was smooth on camera, Max's favorite type of interview.

FIREWORKS   157

"That's just for the lot?" Max rolled his eyes. "I see a house is going in here now. How much will that cost?"

"Well, I've built houses in this area for more than a million dollars. Many of the owners are in their mid-thirties with successful careers and two-income families. They want the best their money can buy."

Those words sealed the interview for Max. He handed the microphone back to Glen who began to shoot cutaways of Max talking with the builder. "Thank you, Mr. Weston," Max meowed, pumping the builder's hand.

Weston droned on about the clubhouse, golf course, and other luxury frills in the unique development.

Max longed to move on to the next subject. Casually he asked, "Whose house is going in here?"

"That's one of the Lazare brothers. They put on the fireworks every Fourth of July."

"Oh? Which Lazare?"

"Conrad."

Max reached for the microphone again. "What can you tell me about the house?"

"It should be one of the premiere homes in the neighborhood. Eight thousand square feet, all brick, oak trim and six-panel doors throughout. The owner wants open spaces for entertaining and a large pool in the backyard."

Max tingled as Paul Weston produced the perfect sound bite for the six o'clock news.

*   *   *

Jade whisked Webb into her designer living room. "Do you want a soda, or maybe a beer?"

"No, thank you."

Jade sat down in the middle of the plush sofa.

Samuel motioned for Webb to sit next to her. "*Close, close gets attention.*"

"I know, I'm a cop," Webb scoffed. He plunked down onto the couch.

Jade stared at him. "What?" She moved away, her eyes flickering with uncertainty.

Webb moved closer. "Let's cut right to the meat. You didn't want to talk to me before. Why now?"

Jade sat up straight. "Pierre warned us not to talk to the police. He's trying to run the show like he always does. I'm sick of that old man."

"What can you tell me, Jade?" Webb turned on his tape recorder and placed it on the coffee table.

Samuel hung over the back of a chair across from them.

"I'm thinking Pierre wants us to keep quiet because *he* murdered Marc." She chewed the edge of her ruby fingernail.

"How do you know that?" Webb worked to keep his voice even.

"Well, I don't know for sure, but I hear you found the murder weapon in his gun cabinet."

Webb nodded.

"Well, I visited Pierre the week after the murder." Jade dropped her leg to the floor and leaned toward Webb. "I walked in on him and Purp in the study. They didn't know I was there, and they had guns out of the cabinet and were talking about shooting them."

"Is that so unusual? Pierre is a member at the Rafferty Shooting Gallery."

"Pierre has special guns for the shooting range. He never uses the collectibles in the gun cabinet," Jade said. "He told Purp, that's Harry Strickland, that he wanted to use his Smith and Wesson to shoot at the Gallery. I hear that's the gun that killed Marc."

"Why would Pierre kill his son?"

"I don't know. Pierre is nuts. Maybe he knew Marc was goofing up the business, and couldn't bear to see all his hard work go down the drain."

"Why do you say Marc was ruining the business?"

"My husband bitches about him all the time. You can check that out yourself."

"Why would you turn in your own father-in-law?"

"If he did it, he should pay."

"Won't you pay when he finds out?"

Jade tossed him a sly smile. "I'm depending on you not to tell him."

"Everything you told me is hearsay, Jade. It would never stand up in court"

Jade jumped to her feet. "You better leave. I don't want Conrad to find you here."

Webb clicked off the tape recorder and glanced at a non-committal Samuel. "Call me if you find out more about Pierre and Purp."

With that, Webb was out the door.

*   *   *

That evening, Webb — dressed in a navy blue knit shirt and khaki slacks — left the parking lot of his apartment complex. As usual, Samuel was with him. "I need a break, Sam. Have you ever been to a bar?"

"I've been hangin' out with you for a lifetime, Bud. Remember?"

"Yeah, I keep forgetting. I'm bushed. Probably shouldn't go out tonight. But a nice scotch on the rocks appeals to me right now. I'll just slip into Levi's Saloon for awhile." He pulled the car into the street and headed toward the highway. Once on I-75, Webb rolled down the window only to be blasted by the assiduous heat. "When is this summer going to end? Hell, this year Detroit is as hot and humid as Cincinnati."

He undid another button on his shirt. "Do you think Pierre Lazare killed his son?"

"Maybe."

"Did you prompt Jade Lazare to tell me that?"

"Didn't need to."

Once downtown, Webb pulled into the parking lot of Levi's Saloon. All the parking spots were taken. Some cars were double-parked. "The place must be jam packed," he grumbled. His eyes meandered across the street to a hotel. "They must have a cocktail lounge." He zipped across and found a parking spot in front, hopped out and saw an entrance with a sign reading: The Silver Slipper.

Inside, the lights were low with soft music playing in the background. Blinking silver slippers flickered above the bar. The quiet atmosphere suited his mood.

Webb slid into a booth. Samuel sat across from him, leaning against the wall, one foot on the padded bench, the other dangling onto the floor.

A shapely waitress adorned in a short black skirt and silver top approached the table.

"I'll have a scotch on the rocks," Webb said. Except for Samuel, Webb's social life was nil since arriving in Detroit. Work occupied most hours, and after his head injury, he preferred sleep to socializing.

"Now that I'm in Detroit, I regret moving. I don't know anyone in this town."

"What about Daisy Farrell?" Sam asked. "She wants you to ask her out."

"I don't like to mix with people from the department. I had nobody else to call the night of the accident. I hope she doesn't think I'm interested in a relationship."

"You could do worse. Daisy's beauty comes from within," Samuel said with a wink.

Webb looked up just in time to see Jade Lazare. A knockout dressed in a chic green A-line dress with a bright yellow pashmina draped around her shoulders, she lingered in the doorway, glancing around the room.

Webb jumped up, waving. "Mrs. Lazare!"

Jade looked his way and strode over to the booth.

Webb eyed her. "Isn't this a coincidence? Out on the town?"

"Actually, I'm meeting Conrad here for cocktails before dinner, but I'm late," she said, continuing to scan the room. "I hope he didn't leave. He's always on time."

"As long as you're here, join me for a drink," Webb said, eyeing Samuel.

Samuel nodded and moved into the corner of the booth.

Webb smiled. "What'll you have?"

"A pina colada," she said. "It makes me feel like I'm in Hawaii. So, what are you doing here?"

"I...ah...just had an urge to get away from the grind for awhile." He thought, what *am* I doing here? Was I supposed to run into her? The coincidence felt oddly planned.

The drinks were served. Jade sipped her pina colada through the straw while keeping her eye on the entrance. "Damn it. I'm not that late. Why didn't Conrad wait for me? He knows I have trouble with time."

Suddenly an idea popped into Webb's head. He eyed Samuel.

Samuel winked at him.

Webb cleared his throat. "I was wondering, Jade, how would you like to work with the police?" Now where did that idea come from?

She brightened. "You mean like a spy?"

"Something like that. I need you to get information from Pierre Lazare. "

"Hell, yes. I'll do anything to get back at that old man," she said scowling. "He treats me like dirt."

"Okay, that's fine. I'll wire you, and you can get him to talk about Marc and the business. Press him for details, but be careful he doesn't catch on to what you're doing," he said. "Come to my office tomorrow."

"Oh, that's exciting," she said gleefully, clasping her hands together. "This will be fun. Besides, both Conrad and Pierre have been harping at me lately. It would serve them right if I can help the police."

"Be at the station around nine tomorrow morning," Webb said, "I'll teach you how to use the recorder. Wear loose clothing so it won't show."

Jade's eyes opened wide. "Oh, there's Conrad!" She jumped up. "I don't want him to see me with you." With her pashmina floating from one shoulder, she rushed to the entrance.

Webb turned toward the wall.

"She's guiding him over to the other side of the room," Samuel said. "We can leave now."

Webb slid out of the booth, reached in his pocket, slapped a twenty-dollar bill onto the table, and hurried out to the hotel lobby.

He fished in his pocket for the car keys and started toward the revolving doors.

"Hannis!" A voice echoed through the lobby.

He whirled around, recognized the face, but couldn't place the fellow. Another coincidence?

"Remember me? I'm Glen Gerard, photographer for Channel Three. I met you on a couple interviews with Max Anglim."

"Yeah, I remember you."

"I saw you come into the bar," Gerard said. "My girl's a bartender here. She doesn't get off 'til midnight."

"Are you guys at Channel Three practicing tabloid journalism now?"

"Lately it seems that way. I don't know what's up with Anglim. He's off his rocker."

"You mean he's not always obnoxious?"

"He's obsessed with this Lazare murder." Glen's eyes looked glassy and he smelled of whiskey. "He worries me," Gerard said.

"Does Anglim always play dirty to get his information?"

Glen leaned toward Webb, a bit unsteady on his feet. "That's just it, Detective. No. It's just since this murder. Hell, I wouldn't be surprised if he committed it himself just so he could cover the story."

"What are you saying?"

"I'm saying I'm worried about my reporter," Glen said, grabbing onto an overstuffed chair for support. "I shouldn't be talking to a cop about this, but Max is always saying that you two are a team. He makes it sound like he knows everything about this case and thinks he's going to win an Emmy for the coverage. That's all he cares about...that damn Emmy. Well, I'm not going to get sued just so he can have a statue for his mantel."

Glen spoke in low tones. "Today he lied to a contractor and told him he was doing a story about a new neighborhood concept. I thought the same thing until I saw the story on the six o'clock news. He used the sound bite describing a big house in an expose' about Conrad Lazare and his insurance settlement. He totally embarrassed that contractor. I wouldn't be surprised if the guy isn't pounding on the door tomorrow with a lawsuit."

"My only real contact with Anglim was for his Fourth of July tapes," Webb said.

"Well, he says you two met at your apartment. What are you up to? This affects me, Hannis. I want to know what's going on."

"I don't trust Anglim anymore, Glen. Tell me everything you know. It's important to me."

"Why? Are you involved in this sordid case, too?"

"Don't be crazy," Webb said, glancing at Samuel. "Listen. I never knew Max Anglim before he came to my office after I was assigned to the Lazare case. But if you think he's involved I need to hear everything."

Glen looked away. "I don't like working with Max on these slam stories. The Lazares could ruin us. How is Anglim getting the scoops for these exposes?"

"For one thing, I'm sure he lifted information about the insurance from some papers I had in my apartment," Webb said. "He must be making up the rest."

"Well, I wouldn't trust him, that's for sure," Glen sighed. "I hope I can trust what *you* told me."

Out in the car Samuel said, "Didn't it strike you that the 'perpetually punctual Conrad' was late tonight?"

Webb sighed. "I suppose you set that up."

"You set it up, Bud. You asked how Jade could help you. Then you followed your hunch to come here," Samuel said. "Late isn't always what it seems. You're actually right on time."

CHAPTER 9

ON TUESDAY, the twenty-fifth of July, Luc Lazare puttered around his efficiency apartment above a pharmacy in downtown Louisville. The long, narrow space served as a living room, bedroom and kitchenette with a tiny attached bathroom. He rented the cramped place because it was cheap and furnished. The one nice feature in the historic building was the tall windows offering a panoramic view of the city.

Settling onto a brown wool davenport, he laid back against a tattered pillow in thought. At age thirty-seven his goal was still out of reach. In fact, his entire life seemed a waste. He had a dream, but could never quite get it together. Parts of the puzzle always eluded him.

"If I turn forty without getting my life on track, I'll always be the family failure. I won't let that happen."

Louisville was the perfect town to begin. Home of the famed *Thunder over Louisville*, the banks of the Ohio River were lined with a quarter-million people in mid-April for the biggest fireworks extravaganza in the United States.

The Lazares were well aware of *Thunder*, put on by the Zambellis, a competing company out of Pennsylvania. Almost fifty tons of fireworks exploded in dazzling, meteoric arrays. One year, three bridges were outlined by glittering plumes planted along the edges.

Luc badgered Pierre to compete with a bigger display in Detroit on the Fourth of July. His father preferred to stick with tradition. Luc longed to stand out in the industry, and he knew what he must do to attain that goal.

He planned to start his own fireworks company, specializing in unique colors that he created, especially the elusive purple. Luc knew that was the key. Long ago, Luc begged his father to actively market Harry Strickland's trademark ability to create purple. They could make millions. But old Purp hoarded the secrets. He wanted the glory. That damn secretive bunker. The accident!

"Purp, it's time to learn your secret," he vowed.

*   *   *

Inside Pierre Lazare's home, the telephone rang and he scrambled to get it. Maybe it's Katherine. But the voice on the other end was definitely male.

"Luc!"

"Hello, Father. I called to let you know I'm fine."

"Oh, I'm so glad to finally hear from you. Where are you, son?"

"It doesn't matter where I am. I just want you to know I won't be taking over Lazare Fireworks."

Pierre's heart sank. "I was counting on you, Luc. You're next in line."

"Please, Father—"

"Is it because of the accident?"

Except for heavy breathing, silence.

"Nobody blames you for what happened to Purp. We all know it was just a twist of fate. That was so long ago. It's time you let go. Purp has forgiven you."

"I don't think so, Father. Anyway, that's not why I left. I'm starting my own fireworks company."

"Why ever would you do that? You have an established company waiting for you to lead."

"Give it to Conrad." He hung up.

Pierre fumbled with the receiver, finally placing it back on the cradle. "Has he gone mad? It's his duty to take over the family business." But Pierre knew his son had won this round. Now it was important for him, the family patriarch, to think of the company. "Lazare Fireworks needs firm leadership with all that's happened. Now I'm forced to make Conrad the president."

* * *

The next morning, Conrad stood at the window in his office staring out at a summer rainstorm. With both Luc and Teddy gone, he was the only one left to deal with the police investigation. "Damn! Maybe I was wrong about wanting all this responsibility."

He returned to his desk and fiddled with Marc's nameplate. President was carved above his name in block letters. "No, I want this more than anything." He set it back on the desk.

His mind raced. The house, all that new furniture and Jade's spending sprees…he could manage.

He heard a knock on the door. Though his mind shouted *go away*, he called out, "Come in."

The door slowly opened and Purp entered, his hand stuffed in his jeans, the ubiquitous purple sweatshirt stained from fireworks chemicals.

"What's happening, Purp?"

The bushy man took a seat across the room. "I've spent years perfecting *The Purple Flame*. Your father knows all about it."

"Yes, he spoke of it. It sounds fantastic. Hell, I liked the purple one on Fourth of July," Conrad said.

"This one is better. Nothin' is better than *The Purple Flame*."

"Pull up a chair, Purp," Conrad said. "Have you done a test fire?"

Purp didn't move. "Nope. It's too big and expensive to test. I know the formula is perfect. I want to debut it during the Labor Day show."

"Great. We could make a killing with that formula."

Purp frowned. "*The Purple Flame* is mine."

Conrad's body tensed. All I need is another problem. "Purp, you've been part of this family for years. We respect your abilities. But you work for us, and we own the rights to your inventions."

"Nobody gets the formula."

"I don't think Father would ever give up the rights to that. Lazare Fireworks will market and sell the bombs."

Purp's eyes sagged. Slowly he turned. As he walked out the door, he thrust his hook into the air. "Nobody is gonna take my masterpiece."

* * *

That afternoon Jade Lazare tore off a piece of masking tape and carefully placed it over the thin microphone wire, tucking it underneath her yellow blazer. She met with Webb that morning, and he showed her how to use the mike. She stuffed the recorder into her trouser pocket. Too bulky.

She switched it to the back of her waistband. "I look fat," she moaned, checking her behind in the full-length mirror. "Who cares? I'm only going to see Pierre. It will kill me to be nice to him after the way he bullied me lately. What if he won't talk?"

The doorbell rang. Quickly she clipped the silver microphone disk to her lapel. "I'm coming!" The bell sounded again, and she whipped open the door.

Tristan sashayed in, his arms loaded with fabric samples. "Jade, Dahling, I've scads of books in the van. You'll expire when you see the leather pieces I chose for the den." He dumped the samples on the coffee table.

"I'm on my way out," Jade said. "But I'd love to see what you have. Can I help you carry anything?"

"No, dahling. The van's a sight. I just came from the VanHulle's. We're redoing the entire west wing. Gorgeous antiques." He caught his breath in ecstasy.

A catlike smile crept across Jade's face. "I'll show Conrad," she hissed when Tristan was out of hearing range. "We'll build to my taste or else."

Tristan returned, pushing several books on a wheeled cart. "Make yourself comfortable on the sofa, Jade. While I page through these books, feel the texture of this leather." He tossed her a tobacco colored sample. "It's simply buttery."

After viewing fabric samples and leafing through books of custom furniture, Tristan wrote an order for twenty thousand dollars worth of leather chairs, ottomans, and love seats.

"We must have the patterned silk draperies in this room to bring in the peach tones," Tristan said, rolling his eyes in rapture. "The downright splendor is worth the cost."

As Jade signed the order, Tristan straightened her lapel. "I love your jacket, but a gold pin suits you better. Silver clashes with yellow," he said, tapping the tiny microphone disk.

Jade jumped away from him. "You're so good with color, Tristan, but this is a family heirloom."

After he left, she gathered her purse and was out the door.

*   *   *

When Purp Strickland approached his private bunker, he could tell someone had disturbed the lock. He always left it hanging from the right side of the U-shaped hook. Now it dangled from the middle.

Clicking it open with a silver key, he rushed inside. Sure enough, one jar of chemicals was moved forward slightly on the shelf. Purp knew every inch of his bunker, each intricate detail.

Someone is trying to steal my formula! The thought galled him. He moved to his journals carefully lined on another shelf. Meticulously, Purp had marked their formation with pencil dots on the shelf so he could detect any shifts. His latest journal was a tad askew.

"Stupid ass. Do you really think I'm dumb enough to keep my formulas in this bunker?" He scratched his bushy beard.

No doubt about it. "Luc! That damn bastard. He's not going to quit until he gets that formula. Well, it's my masterpiece, Luc, and it's time I set you straight." Purp painstakingly arranged his bunker back in order.

*   *   *

Jade felt the chill in the air as she sat in Pierre's study, waiting for him to down a drink.

"I must say I'm surprised to see you here after all you did," he said with a dour face.

"That's exactly why I came, Father."

"Do you want a drink?"

"No thank you," she said smiling sweetly.

Pierre breathed laboriously and set his glass aside. "What do you want this time, Jade?"

"Oh, Father, I don't want anything. I'm here to apologize." She looked away from him in mock embarrassment. "I'm so sorry I taunted you about Conrad's job. Now I understand he needs to pay his dues. We can wait for the position...and money." She almost bit her tongue on those words.

"What about your fancy new house?"

"We'll have the insurance money from Marc's death. I mean, that's greatly appreciated even though it's a sad way to get it."

"What do you really want from me?"

Jade sat at the tip of her chair. "Believe me, Father, I'm here to offer an olive branch. Conrad was furious after I went on the news."

"How could you do such a thing?"

"That reporter tricked me. I swear. He told me I was helping the family solve the murder. You know...people would see the story and maybe call in with information. I mean it when I say I'm totally embarrassed, and I apologize to you and the family. What a dumb thing for me to do." She fingered the silver disk.

"Apology accepted." He eyed his empty glass. "This murder is tearing my family apart. I can't bear to see such dissension."

"That's just what I thought. And that's why I'm apologizing. Oh, please, say you'll forgive me."

"I said, I accept your apology. You need to have more confidence in yourself, Jade."

"I know. My therapist tells me the same thing. I get angry, blow up, then I feel guilty. It's a habit with me. I'm trying to break it. I really am. I'm totally sorry for making your life any more difficult. My God, your son died, and here I am carrying on about money."

"Fine, Jade. You're forgiven."

Jade's heartbeat quickened. "What was Marc like? I didn't know him well." She could feel the rolling tape recorder vibrating against her back.

Pierre coughed and reached for a handkerchief. "He was smart, but maybe not smart enough." With glazed eyes he peered into the gun cabinet.

"What do you mean?"

He shook himself to attention. "He was a good man. Even the doctor said—"

"I can't hear you, Father," she said.

"I said Marc was a good man."

"It's really strange that Luc ran off like that. I hope he's safe," Jade coaxed.

"Don't worry about him. He's tough. After all, he's been in the service."

"I don't know much about Luc either," Jade said, crossing her leg and leaning toward Pierre. "What was he like as a kid?"

"Oh, he was always getting into things. Marc would get so mad at Luc. He used to kick him out of his room." Pierre's look was nostalgic. "But then, all siblings fight, you know." Pierre seemed lost in his thoughts. "Those boys loved to create the fireworks colors. Of course, Marc got the red bunker when he was just a teen. Luc was jealous. He was after Purp's post. Purple is the most difficult color to create in fireworks. Luc wanted to outdo Marc. Then there was Conrad—"

"I didn't know there was so much friction between Luc and Marc," Jade said, not wanting Pierre to say anything derogatory about her husband for Hannis to hear. "How did they get along when they were grown?"

"Still sparring. Marc got on Luc a couple times for breaking into Purp's bunker, trying to learn his formulas. Luc was mad. He never did like authority. It was even worse when his biggest rival was also his boss."

"Is that why he ran away?"

Pierre's body slid lower in the chair. "Maybe. I don't understand it."

"Did you ever think Luc killed his brother?" Jade hoped the silver disk would pick up his answer.

Pierre glared at her. "It's time for my medication." He tried to stand.

"Oh wait, Father. I'll get it for you. Don't try to get up."

He sank back into the chair. "It's on the cupboard in the kitchen.

She rushed out of the room. Perfect timing. The tape was running out.

In the kitchen, Jade reached back and pulled the recorder out of her waistband. "Now how did Hannis say to do this?" Her hands began to shake as she tried to open the case. "Damn, my nails are so long. Come on, case, give me a break." She dug into the plastic and tore the edge of the nail. "Ouch!"

She stuck the nail between her teeth. Reaching back down, the case finally opened and the tiny tape was exposed. She plucked it out of the recorder. Trying to guard her broken nail, she dropped the tape onto the floor. As she bent to retrieve it, she heard footsteps.

"Jade, what is that?" Pierre stood in the doorway.

Hurriedly, she retrieved the tape and tried to slip it into her pocket.

"That's a tape," Pierre said, his voice rising. "You recorded our conversation?"

"Oh...no, Father," she stammered. "This is just a gift I bought to give to Conrad."

"Do you think I'm stupid?" he raved. "I should have known you would never come here to apologize. You don't have that much couth, you trailer park tramp."

Jade bristled. "Don't you call me names, you crazy old man." Anger burst through her brain. "Your money doesn't make you any better than me."

"I told Conrad not to marry you," Pierre raged. "All you want is his money, you free loader. No wonder he's in so much debt."

"You sonofabitch. All you ever do is try to run everybody's lives in this family. Even your own wife couldn't take it any longer."

"You're not good enough to even speak my wife's name. Thank God, she's not here to witness what's happened to this family."

"Does she know you're a drunken sot?" Jade snarled.

Pierre tottered, his color deepening. "Get out of my house."

"You hateful old crow! You're trying to break up my marriage." Jade started toward him, her fingernails poised. "I'll scratch your eyes out!"

Hands trembling, Pierre grabbed a butcher knife off the counter and aimed it toward her.

Jade screamed. "You murdered your own son, you bastard. I knew it all along. Remember I saw you with that gun the last time I was here. I'll tell the police." She ducked away from him, raced down the hall, and lit out the door.

In the car, she slammed the recorder and tape onto the passenger seat and sped away.

*   *   *

Purp Strickland's wooly hair dripped with perspiration, his body sweltering as he toiled over the workbench, locked in the protective womb of his private bunker. He didn't dare turn on an electric fan. It could spark an explosion.

Even friction or static could ignite the mixture of chemicals spread out on the bench. Nimble fingers, stained from the black powder, carefully measured the explosive compound. "Not too much." Carefully he scraped the remains back into the canister. Sweat dribbled down his forehead, and he swiped at it with his sleeve before it ran onto his creation. He loved his work more than life itself. It bore into his very soul.

His sweatshirt, rank with perspiration, stuck to his back. He pushed the sleeves above his prosthesis. Almost twenty years after the accident, the sight of the steel appendage still tortured him.

"Damn, Luc. He was always so bright." Purp remembered the tubby adolescent rolling and wrapping the paper tubes to form the shells. Hell, I encouraged him. He was damn near an expert at thirteen.

Jealousy surged through him. "I was generous, but I'm in charge of the masterpiece. I showed him how to mix purple." He smiled. "I just left out a few details."

"I should have locked the bunker. How was I to know the kid would sneak in here, mess with the chemicals, and not bother to clean up afterwards? Those compounds should have been locked up."

He remembered that horrible morning. How, after switching on the radio, the gut-wrenching boom sent his body slamming backwards against the wall. He woke up in the hospital, his arms and torso swathed in bandages.

Later they told him the radio cord must have had a short.

The explosion charred his nerve endings, but they would recover in time. The agonizing pain, especially in his left hand, still seared his memory. Even morphine couldn't blot it out. Finally, putrid with gangrene, the arm had to be amputated below the elbow.

Now his purple sweatshirt covered the scars, but the mental horrors still persisted. And the metal claw. It nagged him, reminded him of the torture, but would never defeat him.

No, the masterpiece always spurred him forward. Since childhood, his dreams were obsessed with magnificent purple flames. He could never figure out what they meant, only that he couldn't rest until those dreams became reality in the night sky.

"I am the creator of *The Purple Flame*," he raved, waving his hook in the air.

* * *

Jade Lazare flew into Webb's cubicle breathless, her blonde hair disheveled. "That old coot tried to kill me," she shouted. "He belongs in the crazy house."

Hannis looked up from his desk. "Calm down. What are you talking about, Jade?"

"I went to old man Lazare's house and recorded our conversation." She told him about going into the kitchen to change the tape. "He walked in on me and went berserk."

"What do you mean berserk?"

"He tried to stab me with a butcher knife."

"Did you get the attack on tape?"

"No. I was flipping it over when he walked in."

"I had no idea Pierre is violent. He seems so frail."

She tossed the recorder on the desk. "Well, here's what I got. I bet that bastard will tell Conrad about this, and I'll have hell to pay." She turned on her stiletto heels and spun out of the department.

Stunned, Webb turned to Samuel who remained silent in the corner while Jade was there. "Wow! That scheme sure backfired. I never should have put her in such a position. Lazare certainly likes to hide the family's personal business."

Webb picked up the tape recorder, grabbed headphones, and ran the twenty-minute conversation.

"So old Pierre thinks Marc wasn't smart enough to run the business. I've heard that enough."

Samuel smiled.

Webb ripped off the headphones. "Damn it, Sam, I suppose you think my gut feeling supposedly led me to wire Jade, but it didn't yield a damn thing!" he shouted. "This case is wacko with the family refusing to cooperate. It could end up in the dead file."

"I know, Bud. I'm here, I hear. Sometimes you refuse to hear. Other times you ignore your instincts and have to learn the same lesson all over again."

"I'm about ready to give up," Webb said wistfully.

"Just remember the universe doesn't give up. You'll be supplied with endless situations to learn each lesson. It's up to you to decide when you've had enough."

"Just tell me...can I solve this crime? If I know that much I can relax."

"Maybe."

Webb spun his chair around toward the window. "Thanks a lot, Sam. You're great inspiration."

"Think back. You met Jade, purely by coincidence. Go on from there." Samuel said.

"I thought of wiring her—" Webb pushed the rewind button, then play and strained to listen to Pierre's murmured comments. He frowned at Samuel. The tape was a bore. "What was that?" He rewound the tape and listened again. "A doctor? No one mentioned anything about Marc seeing a doctor."

Samuel nodded.

Webb scribbled a note, "His wife should know about this." He listened to the end of the tape. "The old man doesn't want to talk about the possibility that Luc killed his brother." He peeled off the headphones. "The Lazare brothers didn't like each other, and Dad defends the missing son. Interesting. But what about Pierre, the big gun of the family?"

Samuel remained silent.

* * *

That evening, Purp crouched low on the roof of the main building at Lazare Fireworks for a perfect view of his bunker, his trusty video camera beside him. He swigged coffee from a thermos and downed the last of a lemon-filled doughnut. He couldn't resist a balcony seat when Luc tried to break into the bunker again. He patted the camera. He would wait here every night until he caught Luc on video.

The outside lighting was poor around the bunker, but hopefully with the camera's new technology he would capture the bulky figure.

* * *

Later that night, Luc Lazare parked the jeep down the street from Lazare Fireworks and hopped the chain link fence. Tools and a flashlight tucked into the bagging pockets of his cargo pants, he made his way to Purp's bunker.

It was dark but he hesitated using a flashlight. Slowly, he picked the lock. When it finally gave way, he laid it carefully aside to replace later.

Once inside, Luc moved stealthily, shining the flashlight on the shelf lined with chemical jars. He moved the beam around the room until it fell on a crate of completed bombs in the corner. "Finally...Purple Flame," he declared. "All ready for Labor Day. I'll take one of these back to Louisville and analyze it."

He lifted one of the weighty shells, placed it on the table, and slit it open with a penknife to see how Purp had packed the bomb. It's probably something in the wrapping as well as the mixture. Inside, the shell was separated by paper cylinders of chemicals. He poured them out on the worktable to check the pattern, spreading it out on a sheet of plywood.

"This is it! Sorry, Purp, but I have your secret."

* * *

When Purp saw the stout shape approach the bunker, he froze, knowing it could only be Luc. He could not believe his luck. Nervously, he reached for his video camera and began recording. The lighting was too low to identify the intruder, but Purp's heart thundered as he captured the break-in on tape.

Now the wait was interminable. Minutes seemed like hours. The air was still except for crickets chirping. What's going on in there? His arm ached.

Just as he considered laying the camera aside, the night sky suddenly exploded, propelling him backwards, the camera flying from his grasp. The blast was so powerful Purp's ears gonged.

Struggling to his feet he saw flames launch toward the sky in angry purple daggers. Sonic booms hammered his body, tore at his eardrums.

Just as he tried to cover his head against falling cinders, another bomb exploded. A soft violet plume shot upwards. His heart seemed to halt as the color intensified through six different hues. Mesmerized, he studied and counted each one. Another explosion. Then another and another. Six in all. Each a work of art. Brilliant.

Perfect.

The Purple Flame.

My masterpiece.

When the display abated, he stood, brushing ash from his clothing. The show was more dazzling than he ever imagined. It was then he noticed his pants were soaked in urine.

CHAPTER 10

The next morning, investigators swarmed the scene at Lazare Fireworks, meticulously sifting through charred debris and ash. All three television stations set up their live trucks and were now beaming video of the explosion all over the Detroit metro area.

Webb Hannis shook his head as his eyes drank in the pandemonium. "What in the hell is going on with the Lazare family?"

Samuel strode beside him, comfortable in his heavy jacket despite the heat. He stopped for a moment. "Pay attention to everyone and every thing."

Off to the side Max Anglim, trying to look stern and authoritative, delivered his report to a live camera. "The fire officials got the call about three this morning. An explosion in one of the bunkers. The blaze was so intense that it spread to several nearby bunkers. They, in turn, blew up. I talked with neighbors who say they heard numerous smaller explosions after the initial whopper."

Webb bristled at the sight of Anglim. "I want no part of that bastard right now."

"Pay attention," Samuel mused.

A familiar cackle sounded behind him. He spun around to face Jake Rubel, notebook and pen poised. "So you're finally here. I interviewed several people. The fire marshal says they found body parts. Nothing so far to identify the victim." He flashed Webb a wicked grin. "What have *you* found?"

Webb turned to walk away when his ears suddenly focused on Max Anglim, "I have covered the Lazare Fireworks Fourth of July display for many years. I personally know each of the Lazare brothers, and have toured the compound," he boasted.

Samuel listened too.

"Damn ego-maniac!"

"I know the bunker that was destroyed early this morning was used by an employee named Harry Strickland. He's the mind behind the purple fireworks many of you enjoyed at the show just weeks ago."

Webb's heart quickened. "The weird guy with the hook." He's dead?

Webb turned and jolted at the sight of old Purp walking toward him, grimy in his purple sweatshirt. Webb looked at Samuel in confusion. "Now am I seeing dead people?"

"Look what he did," Purp muttered. "He was always after my secrets."

"Who are you talking about? We thought you were in that bunker."

"It was Luc Lazare. He was sneakin' around again. This time I caught him. He blasted himself to smithereens."

Webb studied Purp's sharp eyes. He seemed almost triumphant. "What are you telling me, Strickland?"

"I got it on videotape. He was tryin' to learn my secrets."

Webb's heart began to hammer. "What videotape?"

"It's at my house. Don't want any of the brothers gettin' their paws on it and destroyin' the evidence."

Webb grabbed Purp's upper arm, remembered the hook and let go. "I want to see that video."

"It's hidden at my house."

Webb ushered Purp to the squad car.

*   *   *

Webb followed Purp's rusty Impala Sedan into his driveway, spraying gravel as he ground to a stop. He could barely contain himself. "This is it, Sam. I can feel it. I'm finally gettin' somewhere."

Samuel was silent.

Webb anxiously waited while Purp worked the lock. "The place ain't that tidy," he said as he led Webb inside. The living room was a cluttered pigsty, yellowing newspapers piled against the wall, dirty dishes on the coffee table, everything layered in dust and grime.

The stench clobbered Webb's senses, a mixture of musty furniture and pungent cooking odors. As his eyes roamed the room, his nose twitched against the vile smell.

Samuel made his way through the living room into the dining area.

"I hid on the roof with my video camera. I knew the kid would try to break in and steal my secret formulas." Purp tapped his head. "I got my thinker goin'. I can prove Luc was in the bunker."

Webb's mind clicked into slow motion as the purple man headed into the dining room and went straight for a chest of drawers.

Purp yanked the top drawer. It stuck.

Webb shoved him aside and jerked the drawer open. Inside, nestled among old electronic parts, was a video camera.

Purp grabbed a stack of small tapes from the drawer. "Let me show you what I got." He inserted one into his VCR and motioned for Webb to sit. Oblivious to the filth, Webb settled onto the sagging couch and focused his attention on the television.

The tape was too dark to make out the murky figure entering the bunker, but Webb recognized Luc's portly shape.

"You got this last night before the explosion?"

"Yep. I knew Luc broke in before to steal my formulas. I decided to stake out the place." Purp's voice rose with excitement.

"You saw the explosion?"

Purp's eyes fluttered in almost euphoria. "It was magnificent."

"What?"

"The purple."

"Why did the bunker blow up?"

"Accident, I suppose. Them chemicals are volatile."

* * *

The moment Webb was back in the detective bureau, Fred Gallister summoned him to his office.

"Goddammit, Hannis, the media is hounding me and if that's not enough, the prosecutor is all over my ass about this explosion—"

"Listen, Fred, it's worse than that." Webb said. "Luc Lazare was in the bunker that blew. He's dead."

Gallister let out a long breath and leaned back in his chair. "That's all we need. Two Lazares dead. How do you know that?"

"The bunker belonged to an employee named Harry Strickland. He showed me a tape of what looks like Luc Lazare entering the bunker last night just before the explosion. The fire marshal says they found body parts, so we can assume it's Luc. Of course, we need a positive ID."

"How in the hell did this Strickland fellow get a videotape like that?"

"The guy's weird. I interviewed him after Marc's murder. He says this Luc character was trying to steal his fireworks formulas, so he hid on the top of another building and staked it out."

"Sounds like Strickland also set up a little surprise hello."

"I don't know about that," Webb said. "Harry wanted to turn the tape over to police to have Luc arrested. Why would he show it to me if he blew the guy up? Strickland thinks it was an accident…you know, fireworks chemicals are highly explosive. But I have a hunch it's more than that."

"What do you mean?"

"I don't really know yet. Give me some time."

"Dammit, Webb. I don't have time. We gotta solve this case and now!" His palm slammed against the desk.

Webb winced.

"I put you on the Marc Lazare murder because you're the only one in the department who can figure it out. Now we have two Lazares dead and if we don't break these cases soon, we may be out of our jobs."

Webb shut his eyes, trying to relieve the pressure in his head. Slowly he opened them again. "I'll solve it," he declared. "First I need to tell Pierre we suspect Luc was killed in the explosion. He can inform the rest of the family."

* * *

The next morning, Laura Lazare gathered several cucumbers and piled them carefully into a wicker basket. Summer was peaking. Soon she would enjoy her favorite month, August, with the garden harvest. After two months of weeding and watering, she relished the fresh salads with her homegrown fixings. With all the heat and humidity this year, her tomatoes were waist high, offering green fruit daily.

"Mommy, me pick 'matoes," Austin squealed as he pulled a green ball off the vine.

Laura smiled. "No, honey. The green ones aren't ripe yet. You can pick red ones in a few weeks." She tucked the green tomato into the front pocket of her bib-top jumper. "You can pick the cucumbers."

Austin began to pout. "Me wanna' pick the 'matoes." He stomped his foot and Laura braced herself for a tantrum. How she longed to be in the garden alone with her own thoughts. She had a lot to think about. She scooped up Austin. "Time for your nap."

The toddler protested with kicks and screams, but Laura carried him firmly inside, up the stairs, and tucked him into bed. "Sleep tight," she said softly. Ignoring Austin's rage, she retreated down the steps.

In the kitchen, she poured herself a tall glass of iced tea. With Austin still screaming upstairs, she took the cool drink out on the back patio. "What's happening to this family?" She sighed, hoping Austin would settle down quickly. "Why does everything have to be so difficult lately?" She thought of her husband and shuddered. Now Luc. It didn't make sense.

Her mind wandered. "I should never have—" She shook her head, refusing to wallow in guilt. "No one knows about that, except him."

Reclining in the lounge chair, she shut her eyes against the harsh sun. A week had passed since Detective Webb Hannis' visit. His arrest threat still frightened her. I've seen things like this on the news. They put innocent people in prison to manipulate them. No way is that happening to me.

Now an explosion that killed Luc. What could cause a blast like that and why was he in the bunker so early in the morning? Is someone trying to get rid of the Lazare brothers? The thought shocked her. At least the reporters weren't calling her today.

Her mind spun round and round as she dozed into a fitful slumber. A half-hour later, she awoke in panic. "Austin!"

She leaped up and ran into the kitchen. The house was quiet except for the hum of the refrigerator. Stealing up the stairs, she crept to Austin's room and saw the door was ajar. She peered into the room. Austin was draped over the bed sideways, his head bent sharply back.

She gasped and tiptoed over to him. Her son, his mouth gaping open, breathed evenly. Laura caught her breath, righted the sleeping tot on the bed, and pulled the blanket over him. Get hold of yourself girl. Of course he's fine.

Back down in the kitchen, the phone rang and Laura hurried to answer before it woke Austin.

"Hello, Laura." The man's voice was forcibly low. "Are you alone?"

She struggled to identify the caller. "Who is this?"

"I know you weren't with Marc the night of the fireworks."

Laura sank onto a barstool, clapping a hand over her heart. "Who are you?" she asked, trying to sound controlled.

"The police would love to know who was with you that night."

The words made her vision sway. She slammed down the phone, backing away in horror. She checked her Caller-ID. Unknown caller with no phone number. Stumbling into the bathroom, she splashed cold water on her face, sunburned from her siesta on the patio. Staring at her reflection in the mirror, she whimpered and broke into tears.

*   *   *

The caller set the cell phone on the floor of his car. "Shook her up a bit." He peered through the windshield at Laura's regal home, maroon shutters against sand-colored brick with coining on the corners of the towering two-story house. Parked down the street, he could safely case the place. He had seen her working in the garden, relaxing on the patio. He even saw her hurry into the house when she woke.

After several days of surveillance, he also knew she took her son somewhere at three o'clock, stayed for an hour and returned at ten past four. He also knew today was the maid's day off. Perfect. He glanced at the clock on the dash. Two-fifty. *I hope I didn't scare her into staying home.*

To his relief, at four minutes until three, the garage door went up and Laura's navy blue BMW backed out of the driveway. "A bit late today," he said. "I'll have to work fast." He glanced at the neighbor's houses. Garage doors were shut tight. "Everybody seems to be at work in this neighborhood."

As soon as Laura was out of sight for five minutes, the man casually got out of his car, walked around to the back of a neighboring house and stole through the yard. Fortunately nobody was sunbathing on the tiered deck. He watched windows carefully. *All I need is for someone to see me now.*

At Laura's house he moseyed about the patio. A tall glass, a lemon rind still floating in the bottom, sat next to the lounge chair. He reached in his pocket, pulled out a pair of gloves, and drew them onto his hands. Quickly he moved to the French doors and tried them. Locked. With deft fingers he fished out his credit card and ran it up and down between the door and the frame. The lock clicked.

He entered the house, scanned the kitchen quickly, and moved into the living room. The room was immaculate except for the newspaper tossed on the coffee table. He pulled open the drawer on a chair-side table. Inside were silver coasters and cocktail napkins. He shut the drawer carefully.

Next he inspected an antique roll top secretaire, gingerly sliding open the cover. Nothing. The bottom drawer was locked, and he picked it with a pin. It was filled with stationery, postage stamps, and an address book. He was tempted to steal the address book, but decided against it. *Too risky. She would notice it missing.*

Stealthy like a cat, the man moved through the first floor, mindfully covering his invasion. He looked at his watch. Three-thirty. Panic gripped him. *He hadn't planned to take this long.*

He dashed up the stairs and entered the master suite. His mind swam with the possibility of being caught, and he had no time to waste. Under the bed? In a drawer? The closet?

A careful search of the master bedroom turned up nothing. His watch glared three-forty. He hurried into the child's room and noticed the open closet door. Small outfits hung neatly on hangers. The built-in shelves and cubbies were laden with toys and books. Up high, he saw what he wanted. Without hesitation, he gathered it in his arms, stepped out of the closet and turned to leave.

He froze at the sound of the garage door raising.

She was home early! How could he escape? The second story was too high to try a window. There was no way to reach any of the doors without being seen. With perspiration dripping down his forehead, he stepped back into the child's closet and quietly closed the door.

* * *

"I've had it with you today, Austin," Laura scolded as she dragged the boy into the kitchen. "You go straight to your room this minute. And you might as well know that any time you act up at the stable, I'm taking you home immediately. I simply won't put up with these tantrums in public."

Yelling and stamping his foot, the child started to climb the stairs, turning every few steps to see if his mother was still at the bottom. "I don't wanna go to my room. I wanna ride my pony!"

Laura glared at him, and the boy scampered into his room, slamming the door.

Laura sighed deeply and shook her head. "He must learn. It's up to me now."

As she started toward the kitchen, she saw the iced tea glass on the patio. Reaching for the doorknob to go outside she realized the French door was slightly ajar. "Wait a minute...I swear I locked this before we left."

Terror seized her.

"Oh my God. Someone broke in." She felt faint. "That strange call. Maybe he's still—"

She dashed for the stairs. "Austin! Come on, Honey. Mommy forgot something at the stable. We have to go back."

Silence.

She raced to the child's room. The door was locked.

"Austin, open this door immediately!"

No answer.

"Austin, do as I say or we'll never go back to the stable again," she said in near panic.

The lock clicked. Laura's heart staggered as the door slowly opened.

Austin jumped at her from behind the door, shrieked, and dove under the covers in his bed.

In a daze, she flew over and wrestled the child from under the blanket. "Please, Austin, don't do this to me. For once be my good boy."

Gathering him in her arms, she was about to leave the room when something seemed strange. She eyed the closet door. It was closed. She always left it open so Austin could get his toys. She stopped and breathed deeply. That cologne. Her mind raged. Oh, dear God, no!

With a vice grip on Austin, she stumbled from the room. Plowing down the stairs, she felt as though she was wading through chest high water, each step slow and labored no matter how she tried to hurry. Invisible hands reached out to grab her as she landed on the first floor and struggled out to the garage.

* * *

The intruder heard the electronic door grind open and the sound of the car motor. Did she know I was here? How could she? Thank God she didn't open the closet door.

Hurriedly, he left the room with his stolen treasure, slipped out the patio door, and retraced his steps through the neighbor's yard. Back in his car, he breathed a sigh of relief.

*   *   *

"Austin, don't play with the window," Laura snapped at her young son. In her haste, she had tossed Austin in the back seat without strapping him in. Now he was free and pressing the window up and down.

Laura was lightheaded, her arms and legs feeling bloodless, as she mechanically steered the car out of her neighborhood. She wanted to get as far from her house as possible. She reached for her purse to retrieve the cell phone before realizing she had left it in the kitchen. Turning toward the police station, she stepped on the gas. I don't want him to get away.

Through her hysteria, Laura tried to imagine who would break into her house. And, that scent. Someone was playing with her mind. She gripped the steering wheel, breathing short, shallow breaths.

Austin jiggled the door handle. "Mommy, what's this for?"

"Get away from that door!" Laura screamed.

The little boy began to cry and suddenly hugged her around the neck with his arms. Startled, she slapped his hands away. "Austin, please climb into the front seat." She helped him across with one hand and stretched to fasten the seatbelt. "Mommy needs you to be very good now, honey. Please sit and don't say a thing."

"I want my car seat," he whined.

Turning onto Jefferson, she drove frantically until she reached the police station. Unsnapping Austin from the seatbelt, she half dragged him inside.

"Please help me!" she screamed as she entered the lobby. "Someone is in my house!"

An officer beeped her through the locked door and ushered her to a chair.

Austin began to wail. "Who's in my house?"

"Please," Laura gasped for breath. "He'll get away. I live at 1422 Harrison. I...I came home and somebody broke in...he was still—"

The officer leaped up. "Still in the house?" He flipped on the two-way radio and dispatched a patrol car to the address. "Ma'am, I want you to return to your home. An officer will meet you there."

"Thank you," Laura said in almost a whisper. Picking up Austin, she hurried to her car and drove back toward the house. As she turned onto her street, she began to quake.

Two police cars were parked in the driveway. An officer hurried Laura and Austin into a police cruiser. After fifteen minutes, another officer knocked on the window.

"Whoever was inside is gone now." He looked at Laura. "The French doors to your patio were open."

Laura climbed out of the car. "I know, but I locked them before I left. When I got home, I noticed the patio door was ajar. It frightened me, and I thought he could still be in the house." She told about rushing upstairs to get her child and the closed closet door. Fighting back tears, she said, "My husband—"

"Do you think your husband broke in? Are you estranged?"

Now the tears began to flow. Laura sniffled. "Do you have a tissue?" The officer offered her a box of Kleenex and she blew her nose. After a moment she composed herself and wiped her eyes.

"My husband was murdered last month. I'm Laura Lazare. My husband Marc was president of Lazare Fireworks."

The officers looked at each other. "Please come inside, Mrs. Lazare, so we can write a report."

*   *   *

Captain Fred Gallister, his tall frame hunched a bit at the shoulders, peered into Daisy's cubicle. "Where's Hannis?"

"He stepped out about two o'clock and I haven't seen him since," she said. "Probably doing something with the explosion. What's up?"

Gallister threw his hands into the air. "Rubel's gone, too. Someone broke into Laura Lazare's house."

"No kidding." It was Webb, suddenly behind him, breathless and disheveled. He dropped his suit coat onto the desk in his neighboring cubicle.

"I just heard from the Grosse Pointe Police Department," Gallister said. "It happened less than an hour ago. See me in my office, Hannis." He walked away.

"You look like you just finished boxing the champ," Daisy said.

He wiped his forehead. "I know. It's still so damn hot out there." He sucked in a big breath. "Actually, Daiz, I could use your help. Laura Lazare doesn't like me right now. I think I scared her. I've been thinking about this. She needs a woman's touch. Maybe you can get something out of her."

Daisy brightened. "Sure. Just tell me what you need to know, and I'll do my best."

* * *

Inside Gallister's office, Fred drummed his fingers on the desk. "We have a crisis situation on our hands." He stared at Webb over the top of his glasses. "God! Somebody is out to get that fireworks family. You better find out who it is before another Lazare turns up dead."

"I want these crimes solved as much as you do, Fred, but nobody in the damn family will cooperate."

"To hell with the family, I'm talking about you and your instincts. C'mon, Webb, we both know you have something special in that big head. Use it now!"

Out in his unmarked squad car, Webb's mind buzzed like a hornet's nest.

Samuel lounged in the seat beside him.

"Listen, Sam. I still haven't figured you out. I don't know where you came from or why you showed up at this point in my life, but if you really are a spirit guide here to help me, the time is now." Webb glanced toward Samuel. "You heard Fred, my ass is on the line and so is his. Stop this bullshit and tell me what I need to know."

"What *do you* know?"

Webb shook the steering wheel with both hands. "God, I hate you!"

"You hate God?"

Webb ground his foot into the accelerator.

"You know everything you need to know at this point," Samuel said. "Think it over."

"I don't get you, Pal." He shook his head in frustration.

Suddenly he had an idea and made a U-turn in the middle of the road.

*   *   *

Daisy was on the highway headed toward Grosse Pointe. When she pulled up to Laura's house, a police car was still in the driveway. She let herself in the open front door and found Laura in the living room with an officer.

She pulled out her badge. "Mrs. Lazare, I'm Daisy Farrell, a detective with the Detroit Police Department."

"The Grosse Pointe Police are handling this," Laura said firmly.

Daisy took a seat across from Laura. "They're handling the break in, but we're investigating your husband's murder and the explosion at Lazare Fireworks. We want to determine if the two crimes are related."

The other police officer stood. "My report is complete. We'll be in touch, Mrs. Lazare. Here's my card if you have any questions." The cop nodded to Daisy and left the house.

"That must have been quite a scare," Daisy hurried to say. "I can't imagine coming home and finding a stranger in my house."

Laura shook her head. "It was awful." She dabbed at her eyes with a tissue.

"There's nothing worse, especially for women. Are you okay to stay here tonight?"

"I don't know quite how I feel at this point."

"You're still in shock. That's normal. But you may fall apart once the police leave. If you need someone to stay with you—"

Laura rose, straightened her blouse, and began pacing through the thick carpet. "I have Conrad. I'll call him. I just feel so damn violated. Someone was in here touching my things."

"Was anything taken?"

"Not that I can determine."

"Any ideas who did this?" Daisy coaxed.

"I never saw the intruder."

"Is it possible someone you know broke in?"

Laura sank onto the couch again and shoot her head. "I don't know. I just can't figure out what's going on here."

"What do you mean?"

Pulling her thick curls away from her face, she looked directly into Daisy's eyes. "I know you'll think I'm crazy, but I knew the intruder was in the closet because I smelled a man's cologne." Laura looked spooked. "It was the scent my husband wore."

"What are you saying?"

Laura let go of her hair, allowing it to spring over her shoulders, and looked away from Daisy. "Are you certain the man you found over the mortar tube on the Fourth of July was my husband?"

"I believe they identified him through dental records and that's a reliable method. Are you saying your husband is still alive?"

"Maybe. Unless it was his ghost."

"The Grosse Pointe Police found signs of a break in," Daisy said. "I doubt a ghost would have to tamper with a lock." She leaned forward and offered a sympathetic look. "I understand your concern and fear. Hopefully you can stay with Conrad tonight."

"It bothers me to take Austin out of familiar surroundings. He still thinks Marc is coming home. Maybe he has."

Daisy got up. "Mrs. Lazare, please know the police are actively working on your case. If I can assist you in any way, please call me. I know it's sometimes easier to talk with a woman."

Laura led Daisy to the door, thanking her for her sympathy.

On the drive back to the station, Daisy played with the idea that Marc's ghost was back. "Or does someone want her to believe that?"

* * *

Webb parked in the driveway, and hoping nobody saw him, hurried to the front door and rang the bell. Minutes ticked loudly in his mind before the door opened.

Samuel beamed beside him, his khaki trousers sweeping the porch.

"Detective Hannis, I've been waiting for you to come back." Dressed in a royal purple robe, Phoebe Farrell ushered him into her ethereal abode.

Webb brushed past her and took a seat on the living room couch. "What do you mean you were waiting?"

Phoebe smiled warmly and sat down close to Webb on the sofa. She patted his knee. "You left way too fast last time."

Webb, shifting uncomfortably, looked at the floor. "I need help. I mean...I'm assigned to Marc Lazare's murder case, which is a bitch. The family simply refuses to cooperate. And now Marc's brother Luc blows up in an explosion at the plant. I'm feeling the heat to solve these crimes."

"What has Samuel told you?"

"Squat! I mean, why can't he just tell me who murdered these guys? I'm sure Sam knows."

Phoebe chuckled. "I'm afraid it doesn't work that way, big fella. You are in a discovery process, learning your own lessons as you solve this case."

"Then why do I have this damn Samuel? What in the hell good is he to me if he can't even give me information?"

"Samuel offers information all the time." Phoebe waved her hands in the air. "But spirit guides are just assistants."

"I'm a living soul just like you, Bud," Samuel said. "I just don't have a human body right now. But I have access to more information in spirit form. I can pop around from place to place at will and gather facts quickly."

"Why don't you share them with me?"

"He does all the time," Phoebe said. "You would recognize it if you paid attention. Ideas that pop into your head. That sense that something is wrong even before you get a phone call with bad news.

"Everyone has psychic abilities. They're perfectly normal. Unfortunately most people fail to develop them anymore, because our culture has made them sinister or scary. It's so sad. People let this imposed fear rule their lives."

"Then why didn't someone warn me before that accident after the fireworks?"

Samuel did a handstand, and walked on his palms across the carpet. "It was a great way for you to meet me," he gibed.

"There are no accidents, Webb," Phoebe said. "Just new opportunities to learn."

"They don't teach this stuff in school," Webb said.

"Oh, dear, unfortunately many of us are taught early that we're too unworthy to expect anything from God. We're told he's a vengeful deity up there who's out to get us for the slightest mistakes, when the truth is that God, or whatever name you call Him, only loves us."

She smiled, her eyes glowing. "Before we're born, we all choose what we want to accomplish in this incarnation, and we select loving guides to help us," she said. "Unfortunately we forget all that at birth. Many people never awaken to their true mission on earth and can't figure out why they're so unhappy."

"Everybody has talents. Use 'em or lose 'em," Samuel interjected.

"That's right," Phoebe said, her ruby hair glaring. "Do you follow Samuel's guidance, Webb?"

"He's always harping at me to think of a question and expect an answer. Then wait for it to show up. That's too easy."

Phoebe laughed, her full belly bouncing beneath the caftan. "Have you tried it?"

"Yeah. I guess you could say it worked, but I know Sam. He pulls tricks just to make things seem simple. Come on, it can't be that easy."

"Actually, it is that simple. It's we humans who make it so difficult with negative or fearful thinking. Then when things appear to go wrong, we get angry. Anger and fear stop synchronicity in its tracks."

Samuel sat up, nodding. "The more you trust, the more answers you get."

"The secret is to remain positive no matter how things appear," Phoebe said. "If you can do this, you'll get the right answer. The synchronicity is always perfect."

"Yeah, Sam used that word synchronicity too."

"It means the universe sets up brilliant coincidences to put you exactly where you need to be at all times."

"Pay attention to everything that happens to you," Samuel said. "Then ask yourself why it happened."

"Trust synchronicity," Phoebe added. "It works magic."

*   *   *

Laura reluctantly called Conrad, but declined his invitation to stay in his home. Later, her nerves flared again. Alone in the house with Austin, she felt vulnerable. Every tiny sound made her flinch. She didn't dare enter Austin's bedroom again, and so she kept her son by her side. The noise of the banging air conditioner frightened her, so she turned it off despite the heat.

The phone rang, jangling her nerves further. It was Detective Hannis.

"Mrs. Lazare, was your husband seeing a doctor?"

Puzzled, Laura paused.

"Mrs. Lazare? We need the name."

"I have no idea. As far as I know he was in good health."

"Do you have records of bills he paid or insurance claims?"

She hesitated, then realized she better cooperate. Hannis was already out to get her. "I suppose so. If you can hold on I'll check his papers."

"I'll wait."

She went into the den and opened Marc's file cabinet. Paging through insurance claims, she spotted one from a doctor Dunn. Returning to the phone, she told Hannis what she found.

"That's what I need."

"What does this mean?"

"Probably nothing. It's just something I want to check. How well did you know your brother-in-law Luc?"

"Not well," she hesitated. "He was always kind of the oddball in the family. Kept pretty much to himself."

"Surely you saw him at family functions."

"Really, Mr. Hannis. I don't know anything about Luc's death. I need to hang up now. My son needs me." She hung up quickly.

By nightfall she was ready to jump out of her skin. *Maybe I can take Austin to a motel*, she thought.

Then without warning the doorbell rang, its resounding clang hurling her from the chair.

Shaking, she crept to the door and peeked through the sheer

curtains on the side window. Conrad stood on the porch. Relieved to see him, she tore the door open.

"Laura, I wanted to check on you," he said, a concerned look on his face. "Are you sure I can't take you to our house?"

Laura preferred distance from Jade, but staying alone in a motel room frightened her even more. "Come in, Conrad. Thank you for thinking of us. I'll pack a few things if you'll wait in the living room."

Austin rushed into Conrad's arms and clung to him. "Police came here, Unca Conrad. We got robbed."

"Everything is okay now, Austin. You and Mommy will go home with me."

Laura gathered things in the kitchen, then rushed upstairs and returned in record time with a suitcase and some toys for Austin. "I hope Jade doesn't mind this intrusion. We won't stay long. I'd stay with your father, but he's so distraught over Marc…now, with the explosion and Luc's death, I'm afraid Austin would be too much for him."

"You're welcome at our place, Laura. I'm sure Jade will enjoy the company. She's usually alone during the day."

* * *

At ten o'clock Jade heard the kitchen door from the garage open. She was curled up in an overstuffed chair wearing one of Conrad's T-shirts with only panties underneath. The television blared.

"Jade," Conrad called. "I brought Laura and Austin here. Someone broke into their house this afternoon."

"Damn it!" Jade hissed under her breath. Loopy Laura is always trying to get the attention. She grabbed the cotton afghan off the back of the couch and covered her legs.

He has some nerve bringing her and that kid here. Jade's fists clenched as the trio entered the room.

"I'll take your bags upstairs, Laura," Conrad said.

"I'm so sorry to put you out like this, Jade," Laura offered over the television racket. "I know you have a lot on your mind with Luc and all."

"Mommy, I watch cartoons." Austin lunged toward the wide-screen TV.

Jade gasped. "I'm in the middle of a good movie. Sit down on the couch...sweetie."

Laura pulled the boy onto her lap, sitting at the edge of the seat. "Really, Jade. I know we're spoiling your evening. I was just so...afraid. Someone was in our home, touching—" She bit her lip, hugging Austin close to her.

Why do I have to rescue her? Jade thought bitterly. "Did they take anything?"

"Austin, why don't you go upstairs with Uncle Conrad?" Laura patted him on the bottom. "Go now."

As soon as he scooted up the stairs, Laura leaned toward Jade. "I don't want to scare him. He doesn't really understand what happened."

Jade made no attempt to turn down the volume on the television and continued to glance back and forth from the screen to her sister-in-law.

"I know my house," Laura said. "I can tell the intruder was in every room, opening drawers and cupboards, digging through closets."

"Oh, my God!" Jade howled.

Laura looked startled.

"That woman is cheating on her husband," Jade snickered, slapping her knee and pointing at the TV. "The one in the movie, I mean."

Laura sighed and sat back on the couch.

I don't have to entertain you, Jade thought. You barged in on me.

Conrad returned with Austin by the hand. "Can I fix you two something to eat, Austin? Are you thirsty?"

"I like juice."

"I brought apple juice," Laura said, and went to the kitchen. Jade could hear Austin screech the barstool away from the counter. "I want cookies," he shouted.

Shut up, kid! Jade was livid. You and your needy mother are ruining my movie.

"No sugar before bed," Laura said.

Conrad called to Jade. "Honey, do we have any crackers? Come and help us out here."

Jade jerked off the afghan and slowly rose from the chair, pulling the shirt over her thighs. "Good grief, Conrad. You know where the crackers are." She padded into the kitchen, found the Saltines and slid them in front of Laura.

"I'm turning off the TV, Jade," Conrad said. "Laura needs us now."

Jade slumped at the table next to her sister-in-law.

Laura told about her terrifying ordeal in simple terms so Austin wouldn't be upset.

Conrad shook his head. "God, after Luc, then this...what next?"

"Detective Hannis was asking about Luc and how well I knew him."

"Do you know something?"

"No, but be careful around Hannis. He has a way of squeezing you 'til you croak."

When the child was finished, Laura wiped off his face and hands, took him upstairs and tucked him into the double bed in one of the guest rooms.

Reluctantly Jade gathered extra towels and blankets and took them to Laura.

Conrad helped Laura pull down the comforter in the second guestroom. "How did you know someone was in the closet?"

"That's the frightening part, Conrad. I smelled Red cologne."

Conrad frowned. "Isn't that what Marc wore?"

Laura trembled and sat on the bed. "Yes. But he's dead...isn't he?"

* * *

The next morning, Jade was awakened by a loud shriek. That damn kid again. She groaned and rolled over to check the clock. Seven-thirty. Laura was scolding Austin in the hall. Then she heard them ascend the stairs.

Though Jade longed to return to slumber, she tossed aside the covers and stepped into a steamy shower. Let her get her own breakfast. Jade took her time dressing in a pair of black twill pants and a plum silk blouse. She set her hair and applied make-up too elaborate for daywear. Anything to take time away from that bratty kid. At nine-thirty, she finally entered the kitchen.

Laura was finishing up the breakfast dishes. "Jade, I know we're imposing. I'm sorry if Austin woke you. He's so full of energy in the morning."

"You just do your thing," Jade said, half-smiling. "I don't have any toys or kiddy foods in the house."

"I brought some along." Laura walked to the breakfast nook, decorated in a taupe and cream stripe with swag valances over the bay window. She glanced outside. "It looks like rain."

Oh, goody. I get the monster indoors all day. Jade carried a slice of jellied toast into the living room and sat in her favorite puffy chair.

Austin dragged a metal car across the wooden edge of the glass-topped side table, sputtering car noises.

"Don't do that, dearie. You'll damage the wood." Jade glared at the child.

"This is like my daddy's car." Austin thrust the toy within inches of Jade's eyes. "Vroom—" He shot the car through the air, screeching a loud crashing sound as it slammed into the granite fireplace.

Jade almost choked on her toast.

Laura rushed into the room. "Austin!"

The phone rang and Jade reached for it. "Hello," she said over the ruckus.

"Jade? This is Max Anglim with Action Three News. You really looked terrific on that story I did with you. Your blonde hair is great for television."

Jade pepped at the compliment. "Don't think you can sweet talk me into doing that again," she teased and carried the cell phone into the kitchen.

"I read on the police blotter that someone broke into your sister-in-law's house yesterday."

"Yeah, she's living with us right now. That's her kid you hear whining in the background."

"Is she okay? I mean, does she want to talk to us? We could help her find the intruder."

"No way, Max. You got me in enough trouble. But good luck on your story."

"What about Luc Lazare? Do you have any photographs of him?"

Jade hung up before Max could talk her into going on television again.

*   *   *

Max heard the phone click in his ear. "Thanks, Jade. I have you well trained." He clapped his photographer on the back. "Let's get going. We'll take my car. It's unmarked and we need to stake out Conrad Lazare's house."

As they headed down the highway, Glen asked, "How long will we be there? Should we pick up fast food?"

"Who knows? Jade told me Laura Lazare is staying with her. I need video of her coming out of the house. Everyone will have the police bite and video of Laura's house. We'll have an exclusive angle, saying Laura fled to her in-laws in fear."

Glen parked the car a few houses down from Jade's. "Do we really need to upset this woman any more than she already is? I swear, Anglim, you're so heartless lately."

"Hell, if we can't get anything new on Luc Lazare blowing up right on the family property, this is the next best thing. We gotta work every angle. I changed my tune. No more Max Anglim the cordial reporter. I'll be displaying my Emmy next May." He flashed his white teeth at Glen. "I'm through playing it safe."

That evening, Anglim's story aired on the six o'clock news. He smiled smugly as he watched a close-up shot of Laura carrying her son out to the car in Conrad's driveway, oblivious to the recording camera. "If you appear in public, you're fair game," he laughed.

*   *   *

Webb Hannis, search warrant in hand, waded through the plush carpeting in the office of Doctor Clement Dunn, the psychiatrist. The reception area was inviting with its soft lighting and a round table splashed with popular magazines.

With one leap, Samuel planted his posterior on the reception desk and crossed his legs.

A stout woman, deep cleavage peeking through the gaps in her colorful uniform, turned from a computer. She smiled at Webb. "May I help you?"

"I need to speak with the doctor."

"I'm sorry," the woman said. "He just left. He has a meeting across town. He couldn't see you today anyway." She turned to her computer. "In fact I have nothing for the next two weeks."

Webb flashed his badge.

The woman's smile faded.

Samuel fell off the desk and collapsed in giggles on the floor.

Webb shook his head at the spirit guide. Why is he laughing? Webb was confused.

At that moment, a short, rotund man with a full head of blonde hair rushed through the door. He wore a powder blue blazer with a silver tie carefully knotted around his thick neck. "I forgot my notes for the meeting, Shirley," he said struggling for breath.

"Oh, Doctor, this man is from the police—"

Before the woman had a chance to finish her sentence, Webb bolted to the doctor's side and held up the search warrant.

Dunn adjusted his glasses and reached for the document.

Webb stuffed it into his hand.

"Oh, right now? I'm already late for my meeting," the doctor said.

"Now," Webb said. "Where do you keep the files?"

The doctor sighed and led the way down the hall.

Webb strode into the posh office and plunked into a chair across from the desk.

Doctor Dunn slowly took a seat. He didn't say a word while he perused the search warrant. Then, clearing his throat he looked over the top of his glasses at the detective. "My records are confidential."

"The doctor/patient privilege is null and void upon the patient's death," Webb explained. "I need Marc Lazare's files dating back to his first visit with you."

Doctor Dunn called the receptionist on the speakerphone. "Shirley, please get me Marc Lazare's file," he asked blandly.

The receptionist, her hosiery loudly chafing between chubby thighs, scurried in with a thick file, her face a fusion of excitement and concern. She rounded the desk and carefully handed the folder to the doctor. Webb sensed she was alive with curiosity.

Doctor Dunn opened the file. "Thank you, Shirley. Please cancel my meeting. Then you're free to leave."

"I have a few things to finish before I can go," she said. "I'll be right out here if you need me." She left the office.

Dunn sifted through the report. Slowly he pushed the folder across the table. "I'm uncomfortable sharing a patient's records.

I want my clients to know their personal business stays in this office."

"These files can't hurt Marc Lazare," Webb said as he began to study the notes. "But they may help solve his murder."

Webb scanned through the handwritten notations on the first ten pages of Marc Lazare's file. His eyes searched for three key words, Pierre, Luc and Conrad.

Meanwhile, Samuel did his usual tour of the office, poking among the books on a wall of shelves behind the doctor's desk. He let out a sigh when he spotted a picture of Doctor Dunn on a beach with a plump blonde woman and two young men.

Webb immediately took notice and pointed to the picture. "Is that your family?"

Dunn turned toward the shelf and handed the picture to Webb.

"My wife and I flew to Aruba last Christmas with our sons," the doctor said. "It was a real family reunion I have a great family."

Webb watched Samuel carefully, then the detective studied the picture. Okay, so there's something about family. "What did Marc Lazare say about his family?"

"Oh, he had problems being the oldest son." The doctor seemed to relax a bit. "He felt that burden, especially when he had to take over the family business after his father's stroke."

"Did he have problems with the father?"

"Deep respect. And that scared him. He didn't want to let the old man down."

"Was he afraid of Pierre? Could Pierre be violent?"

"He never spoke of anything like that."

"What about the brothers? Luc?"

"Normal sibling rivalries."

Webb set the folder aside and leaned back in his chair. "So why were you treating Marc Lazare?"

Doctor Dunn removed his glasses and shifted in his seat. "Oh, he suffered from anxiety which led to depression. He refused medication."

"Did he seem to improve with the therapy sessions?"

"Actually, I think his anxiety escalated in recent months. He had business pressures, and he was concerned about his wife and their marriage."

Webb, suddenly alert, leaned forward in his chair. "What about his wife?"

"He thought she was pulling away from him over the past year. Marc said she avoided intimacy and would often toss cruel and cutting remarks his way. He was worried she would leave him. He felt like a failure."

"Did she seem threatening in any way?"

"She had a temper," the doctor said. "Marc was really concerned after she threw a glass bowl at him in a fit of rage."

Webb gathered the file and stood. "That's what I need. You may be subpoenaed. I'll be in touch if I have more questions."

Webb left Dunn sitting at his desk and returned to the reception area.

Shirley looked up from the computer and smiled at him. Glancing toward the doctor's office she motioned the detective closer. In a near whisper, she said, "Marc Lazare called our answering service early in the afternoon on July fourth. It was a holiday but Mr. Lazare said he had to talk to the doctor...something about his wife."

Webb's eyes lit.

"Did Doctor Dunn talk to him?"

The doctor came into the reception area. "Shirley, it's time for you to go home."

The woman blanched, gathered up her purse, and quickly left the office.

Webb confronted the doctor. "So Marc Lazare called here on the Fourth of July. What did he tell you?"

Doctor Dunn leaned against the counter. "I tried to reach him that day, but nobody knew where he was. The next morning, I heard about his murder on the news."

CHAPTER 11

ON SATURDAY morning, Webb Hannis woke to a sun-filled bedroom and a chipper Samuel sitting at the foot of his bed. Webb ignored him. Pleasurably groggy from an elaborate dream, he squinted at the clock. Nine-fourteen, the longest he'd slept in awhile. The phone rang, shocking him from the dream-state. "Hannis here," he croaked.

"Did I wake you? I thought police never sleep." Webb recognized Max Anglim's disc jockey delivery.

"What's up, Anglim?"

"That's what I'm asking you, chum. You still owe me that promised scoop."

Why in the hell did I give this guy my home number? "You'll be the first to know if there's something I can release."

"Did they ID the body from the explosion yet? C'mon, everyone knows it's Luc Lazare."

"Probably won't get anything until next week."

"I think you're holding out on me, man, and I don't like it. We have a pact to share. I held up my end of the contract, now drop some dirt."

"Listen, Anglim. I don't like the way you handle *scoops*. I've seen your coverage on television and it's reckless."

"Just because I'm a step ahead of you," Anglim sneered. "Continue watching my stories if you want to solve those crimes." Max hung up abruptly.

Webb slammed the phone down and rolled on his back. Tucking his hands behind his head, he stared at the ceiling fan. "What a goddamn asshole." Webb kicked off the covers, sat up and grabbed the phone.

*   *   *

The phone rang at Daisy's house across town . She turned down the sound on a weekend talk show and answered.

"Anglim is a complete jerk."

She recognized Webb's voice. "Well, what a lovely morning."

"I'm pissed at Sam, too. I should tell you, Daiz, I went to see your Aunt about him."

Daisy stood up, smoothing her long hair. "Really? Did it help?"

"I guess so, but why Sam can't just tell me the truth about these crimes bugs the hell out of me."

"I think you need a break, Webb. Get away from the investigation for awhile so you can think."

"Can't, Daiz. Gallister's all over my ass to solve these Lazare cases."

"Well, you can't do much without the lab reports."

"Come on, Daiz, you know there's always something I can do. I just wish the hell Samuel would fess up."

Daisy smiled. "Why don't we get out of town for at least today. See some pretty scenery beyond Detroit."

"Like where? I don't know much about Michigan."

"We could go straight to Hell."

"Huh?"

"Hell, as in Hell, Michigan." She laughed.

"I'm surprised they didn't name Detroit 'Hell.' So there really is a Hell?"

"Yup, and it freezes over in the winter."

"I need some good humor this morning," Webb said. "I'm already in Hell. Is there somewhere we can hide from Rubel and Anglim? A place to relax for awhile?"

"Well, there's Tawas, but the traffic going up there is *murder* on the weekend. Especially this late in the summer."

"Forget anything to do with murder."

"Ann Arbor is interesting if you like artsy shops and bookstores."

"What about water? Take me to one of the Lakes."

"How about Grand Haven? My cousins lived there, and we visited every summer. They have a beautiful beach, and a fantastic boardwalk along Lake Michigan that leads to an old lighthouse."

"Now you're talking. I'll pick you up at ten-thirty."

*   *   *

Tired of rambling around Conrad's house, Laura decided to go to the stables. She would need to arrange for a time when her favorite horse was available. "I really should memorize that phone number," she said. "That's the trouble when you install those numbers in the phone memory." She looked around the kitchen. "Where does Jade keep the phone book?"

Rummaging through drawers, she spotted the directory. A pile of bills lay on top. She picked up the envelopes and tossed them on the counter. Thumbing through the phone book, she finally found the stable number and dialed. Her horse was reserved for the entire day. Disappointed, she tossed the book back in the drawer and went to check on Austin.

In the family room, the child was engrossed in a cartoon on TV.

Grateful he wasn't messing up Jade's decorator-perfect room, Laura crept back into the kitchen and got juice out of the refrigerator.

Conrad came downstairs dressed in light tan pants and a white Polo shirt. "Good morning, Laura. Did you sleep well?" "The room was very comfortable, Conrad, but my mind refuses to rest. All I see is that creature pawing through my personal belongings."

"I'm sure the police will find the punk," he said, and poured juice into a small glass. "I'm going into the office this morning. If you need me—"

Jade appeared in a colorful nightgown and peignoir, her blonde hair swept back and tied loosely with a matching scarf. "Save some juice for me, Conrad," she huffed. "I didn't plan on company. That's the bottom of the carton."

Conrad reddened and ambled over to the counter. "What are these?" He leafed through the collection of bills and opened one of the envelopes.

Laura recognized a Visa credit card statement.

Conrad gasped. "Jade, we need to talk." He motioned upward.

A moment later Laura heard voices from upstairs. The volume escalated.

"How do you think we can pay this off?" Conrad bellowed.

"Just pay the minimum," Jade screamed. "What's the big deal?"

"The Lazares don't have credit card debt," he raved. "Do you know how much interest we'd pay on a bill like this?"

"I don't give a damn," Jade wailed. "I need those things and I'm keeping everything I bought."

"Keep your voice down," Conrad seethed.

Laura felt like a voyeur and went into the family room to be with Austin.

The quarrel continued though the words were muffled by the television. We can't stay, Laura thought. We have to get out of here. Maybe our house will seem safer in the daylight. "Austin, pick up your toys, honey. We're going home."

"I wanna watch tooneys," he whined.

"It will be over in five minutes. After that I want you to help me pack."

Laura heard someone hurry down the stairs, and Jade flew into the family room dressed in jeans and a T-shirt, braless, her nipples clearly visible. "I know you purposely left those bills on the counter, Laura," she shrieked. "You're just jealous of me, you bitch!"

Laura's mouth fell open in shock.

Jade grabbed her car keys and shot out the door to the garage.

A moment later Conrad came downstairs, his face a study in anger and embarrassment. "Laura, I'm so sorry. Jade loses control. She flips out and says things she doesn't mean."

"Please, Conrad, you don't have to explain anything to me. I'm much better this morning and we're going back home. Austin needs his familiar surroundings."

"Are you sure?"

"I have to face it sometime. We'll be packed in a few minutes," she said. "You were kind to let us stay last night."

The TV cartoon ended and she left the room.

*   *   *

Daisy's hair flapped in the warm breeze that streamed in through Webb's sunroof as they cruised along I-96 toward Grand Haven. The four hour ride that bored her as a child now energized her as she and Webb chatted amicably.

"This was a good idea," he said, cocking his head toward her. "It's about time I explore this state. Everyone raves about going up north every weekend. I only see concrete buildings and the grungy Detroit River."

"You need to open your eyes and your mind," Daisy said. "Detroit is a great city. It has everything."

"Including traffic jams, plus everybody driving on your tail."

"Is Samuel with us today?"

Webb looked in the rearview mirror. "He doesn't miss anything."

Daisy patted Webb's arm. "Speaking of spirits...remember I told you Laura Lazare thought she smelled cologne when she was in her little boy's room? Well, it was her husband's cologne. He always wore Red."

"Lots of guys do. It's a common cologne. I even have some." He smiled, his white teeth gleaming at her.

"I'm telling you she thinks the intruder might be Marc Lazare's ghost."

Webb exited at 104 in Spring Lake. "C'mon, Daisy. That's crazy. The guy's dead and I doubt his spirit is lurking around, doused in Red cologne." He glanced in the rearview mirror. "Then again, I've been living with a spirit myself."

"It's a fun idea."

"Yeah, real fun." He glared at Samuel in the back seat.

She pointed to a road sign. "Grand Haven is just ahead. Follow the signs down to the State Park. This county has about thirty miles of beach. You'll love it."

*   *   *

Relieved to be away from Conrad and Jade, Laura drove toward home. "Maybe now that it's light I'll feel braver." Anything was better than living with her warring in-laws.

When she pulled into the driveway, her fears rushed back.

Austin cringed. "Mommy, is somebody still in our house?"

"Oh, no, honey. Our house is just fine," she soothed, "but I think we'll go stay with Grandpa for a while. He's lonely with Grandma in Arizona."

Laura needed more clothes for both her and Austin. She even forgot her toothbrush in the rush to reach the safety of

Conrad's home. Pressing the button to open the garage, she watched, hypnotized, as the door chugged up. Slowly she pulled her car in.

This is crazy! I'm usually so in control. Nobody is in this house. It was probably a neighbor kid.

With renewed determination, Laura got out of the car. "You stay here, sweetie. I'll only be a minute."

As soon as she opened the door to the kitchen, her heart began to race. That phone call! Someone is out to get me.

She slammed the door shut and hurried back to the car. Trying to act cool in front of Austin, she started the motor and quickly backed down the driveway.

"I wanna sleep in my bed," Austin wailed.

"Honey, we're going to Grandpa's house. He'll be glad to see us."

As she drove to Pierre's, she thought of her garden. Without water, the tomato plants might die, and the cucumbers would grow too big to enjoy. What a waste. She considered calling Rosa to come by and water the plants. "I'll think about that when I get to Father's house."

Pierre had no idea she was barging in. He didn't answer when she rang the bell. Laura tried the door. It opened. "Father?" She stepped into the foyer. "Father, it's Laura."

She heard movement in the back of the house and Pierre, his Einstein hair erratic from neglect, shuffled from the study. Laura was shocked at his gaunt appearance, trousers hanging from bony hips. Her heart almost burst for him. After all, he knew it had to be Luc who was killed in the explosion. To lose two sons—

"Oh, Laura. You gave me a fright. You sounded like Katherine."

Laura hugged the elderly man. He felt fragile, breakable beneath her embrace. "It must be so difficult for you without Katherine. How is she doing?"

"She's coping nicely." His face clouded over with sadness.

"Of course, I haven't told her about Luc yet. Come in." He motioned her toward the study.

"Father," she said, hesitating as Pierre turned to her, his eyes heavy and bloodshot. "Austin is in the car."

"Bring him in."

"We need a place to stay," she blurted out, wishing she didn't have to spill the entire story. "We had a little problem at home." Pierre froze.

"Everything is okay, but someone broke in yesterday afternoon. Nothing was taken. Probably a teen pulling a prank."

Pierre's shoulders slumped in relief. "Damn kids. Where are the parents? Is the place a wreck?"

"No. It really is fine, but I was afraid to stay there alone," Laura said. "Would you mind if Austin and I spend a few days with you? I thought, with Katherine gone and all, I'd help you cook, and I could get Rosa to clean the house."

"Oh, I eat very little these days, but you're welcome to stay. The bedrooms are probably dusty." He started for the study. "Bring the boy in."

Laura gathered Austin and the suitcases from the car and carried them up the winding staircase.

Austin flipped one leg over the banister and started to slide down. "Look at me, look at me," he squealed.

Laura caught him by the seat of his pants and pulled him off. Stooping to his level, she stared him straight in the eye. "Austin, you absolutely must mind while we're at Grandpa's. Do you hear me? Grandpa is ill and can't take your antics."

Austin nodded his head.

She shook him by the shoulders. "I mean it. We need Grandpa right now. I won't be this nice again."

Austin hung his head and dragged up the stairs behind her. At the top, he tore past his mother and flung open the first door on the right. "Let's stay in Daddy's room."

Laura's heart pounded.

* * *

Jade careened down the streets of Grosse Pointe at dizzying speed. "That bitch! She really must hate me. Leaving those bills where she knew Conrad would see them. She's probably laughing now." She shook her fist in the air. "She can't do this to me." She drove up one street and down another trying to regain control, but her temper flared at the thought of Laura's snobbish airs.

"Just because she was born into money, she thinks she's better than me. She thinks I'm trash. Well, I'll show you, Lady Snootface. We're building the biggest house in this lousy town, and Tristan is my decorator. You'll be the jealous one when it's finished. That is, if I let you in the place after what you did to me."

She screeched to a stop at a red light, drumming on the wheel waiting for the light to change. "That's what I'll do. I'll go see my new house. I can visualize just what it will look like when it's finished." As the light turned green, she made a U-turn in the middle of the street and raced toward the new subdivision.

When she arrived, several homes were in the framing stage. Jade drew up to her lot and sprang from the car. She raised her head and breathed deeply.

Sunlight danced through the towering old trees she insisted be spared in the backyard. So far, only the footings were in place for the poured basement walls. These other houses will be finished before us. I wanted to move in first. She stood tall and smiled. Oh well, ours will definitely be the biggest house in the neighborhood.

She felt her feet sink into the loose soil, dirt coating her pristine tennis shoes. "Yikes! I've got to get out of here." Turning, she dashed to her car.

Back inside, thoughts of Laura returned. "So you went to a fancy college. What did you learn? To smoke and drink gracefully? How to ride those stupid horses? You don't know anything, you prissy prude. I learned more in a trailer park, where neighbors heard every move and word...and my mother said plenty...more than any school could teach me."

Jade burst into tears, covered her face and leaned against the steering wheel. "I worked hard to get away from that hell. No one is going to stop me now. No one."

*   *   *

Conrad Lazare stared out the window of his office, his eyes transfixed on the charred remains of bunker number fourteen. Much of the rubble was removed, but the explosion left the grass scarred and nearby bunkers destroyed Now he would have to deal with the insurance companies. A nightmare since the company was already hairy about Marc's policy. Now, would it handle Luc's?

He returned to his desk. Piled high with paperwork he ignored after the explosion, he sighed and reached for the phone to check his voice mail. The red light blinked with twelve calls. He punched the speakerphone button.

"Mr. Lazare, I'm calling from the city of Saginaw. We want to order some fireworks for our sesquicentennial celebration in September—" The caller left a phone number.

Conrad, bored with the phone messages, picked up some mail and began opening an envelope.

The phone messages droned on. "I need to speak with some-one about your fireworks. We had two duds on Fourth of July and we want a refund—"

Conrad sighed. My secretary can handle these phone calls Monday. It's enough just dealing with the mail.

"Beep!" the voice mail jumped to the sixth message.

"Mr. Lazare, I know what happened to Marc on the barge—" The voice sounded electronically altered. Conrad jerked to attention.

"I saw everything!"

Quaking, Conrad listened as the odd voice reverberated, "Wouldn't the police love to know what I saw?"

Conrad's heart pounded in his chest. His hands trembled. "Now that Luc is dead I know we can work out a deal between the two of us. I could easily keep quiet for . . . oh, say ten-grand a month? I'll be in touch."

The line went dead.

Conrad stood abruptly. He listened, hoping nobody was in the building on Saturday.

Feeling lightheaded, he collapsed back into his chair.

*　　*　　*

Laura hesitated outside Marc's boyhood bedroom. After a moment she took a deep breath and went into the room. It was decorated for a teenager, Detroit Tiger posters still tacked to the blue walls. The red corduroy bedspread and matching pleated curtains looked faded, dusty. The entire room needed a good cleaning.

"Daddy won this," Austin shouted, holding up a small trophy of a Little League slugger.

"Daddy was a good baseball player," Laura said, gazing at a framed picture of ten year old Marc in a dark green baseball cap and white uniform, body cocked with a bat, poised to hit a home run. So young and innocent.

Scanning the room, she studied book titles. The Hardy Boys mysteries lined one shelf along with high school textbooks, still covered in paper grocery sacks.

Austin started to climb on the bed, but one glare from Laura sent him sliding off. "I be good, Mommy."

She moved to the desk where Marc had lined up several coffee mugs and filled them with pens, pencils and paper clips. Always so organized. Marc's young life, frozen in time, coated with a layer of dust.

His dresser held several pictures. She picked up one that showed a row of grinning men in front of the Lazare Fireworks' sign. Each wore a different colored sweatshirt. She recognized Harry Strickland in a purple shirt that aptly said Purp in black letters across the front. The next man wore a pink shirt with Pinky emblazed on his chest. Another fellow's cobalt shirt read Blue Boy. Marc stood tall in a scarlet shirt labeled Red.

Laura began to shake. Marc often expressed his fondness for the name Red, his favorite fireworks color. After that, people bought him everything red from his bedspread to clothing and socks.

One year, Teddy gave him Red cologne by Giorgio as a Christmas gift. It became his signature scent. Laura spotted a dusty old bottle of Red on the dresser. She picked it up and sniffed the aroma. Her shaking hand dropped the bottle, sending it crashing against the side of the dresser.

Get hold of yourself. Lots of men wear Red cologne. It's a popular scent. She picked up the bottle and put it back on the dresser. "Let's take Uncle Conrad's room. We don't want to mess up Daddy's."

At five-thirty, Laura looked through the cupboards in the kitchen and checked the refrigerator. She found only a large bucket of take-out chicken. Good thing I came over here. He doesn't have any decent food. I suppose we can use this for dinner. "I'll have to grocery shop. I need shampoo, soap and a toothbrush." She could hear Austin in the study talking with Grandpa.

She brought in a platter of chicken.

Pierre sat in his green leather chair, smiling at his young grandson. "He looks so much like my boys when they were young. So full of life."

Pierre looked brighter than Laura had seen him in months. Maybe it will be good for him to have Austin underfoot.

"I thought we'd have a picnic supper," she said, placing the platter on the ottoman. Laura noticed a half-empty glass on the table next to Pierre and wondered what he was drinking. He seemed alert. He was enjoying Austin. "Father, we need some groceries. Would you mind watching Austin while I run to the store after dinner? If he would be too much, I can take him with me."

"Oh, no. I'd enjoy that. After all, I raised four of my own. I need a diversion."

Austin devoured the chicken with gusto, while Pierre only picked at a drumstick.

After dinner, Laura washed the platter and made out a shopping list. When she returned to the study, Austin was curled in his Grandpa's lap. She felt secure in leaving that Norman Rockwell scene.

When she returned from the grocery store, the clock in her car glared seven-thirty. "Was I really gone that long?" She felt an odd chill. Maybe I shouldn't have left Austin with Pierre. He's so frail, and Austin can be a handful.

Laura pulled into the driveway, hauled two heavy bags from the trunk, and managed to open the front door.

Inside, the house was silent.

She set the bags down in the front hall, and heart pounding, tiptoed to the study.

She gasped in horror.

Pierre was slumped in the chair, his shriveled head collapsed against his chest, eyes shut, arms dangling over the sides of the chair.

Austin stood in front of him, a gun pointed at the old man's head.

*   *   *

The weather was ideal on Lake Michigan's shore. After a stroll down the wooden boardwalk at Grand Haven State Park, Daisy and Webb leisurely walked the long concrete pier out to the lighthouse.

"I thought we could go inside," Webb said as he gazed up at the aged structure.

"It looks pretty old, been closed for years," Daisy said.

On the way back, Samuel jumped up on one of the mammoth rocks that were piled along the pier. Hopping along from one boulder to another, he grabbed onto Daisy's sweater. She was unaware of his assistance as she leaped up on the rock next to him.

"This is how we walked the pier as kids," she said. "It's much more fun." She latched onto Webb's shoulder as she bounded from boulder to boulder. "Try it, Webb."

Samuel began to cartwheel between rocks. Then, without warning, he dove into the lake with a giant splash.

Webb grabbed Daisy around the waist and swung her down to the ground. "I don't want to lose you to Lake Michigan." He shook his head at Samuel who was just surfacing.

"Okay, Sam, I get your drift. You're right, the view is great here." Webb gazed over the expansive lake. He turned to Daisy. "This was a good idea to get away. I hope I'm not missing something back at the station."

"Forget about work for one weekend," she said. "Samuel will let you know if you need to get back in a hurry."

The sun reflected off the water, casting Samuel in a golden glow as he casually backstroked toward shore.

Webb smiled slightly. "Do you know a good place to eat?"

"Gosh, I haven't been in this town for years. I wonder if the Bil-Mar Restaurant is still on Harbor Drive."

Webb hesitated. "Can we see the lake from there?"

"Of course. We can even eat on the deck."

"I'm in the mood for seafood."

Samuel was instantly out of the water and now, bone dry, hopped the boulders back to land.

Inside the Bil-Mar Restaurant, the hostess seated them by the deck rail.

Samuel strolled about the patio eyeing other patrons.

Scanning the menu Webb said, "They have escargot. Are you game?"

"I've never eaten a snail." Daisy wrinkled her nose. "Okay. I'm adventurous."

She ordered the broiled whitefish with basil pesto.

Webb ordered the escargot in garlic butter as an appetizer, and selected the seafood platter. "I'm starving," he said. Hair windblown and face pink from the sun, he felt relaxed for the first time in weeks.

Looking out over the sandy beach, they saw a young couple snuggled together on a blanket enjoying the postcard view.

Suddenly Daisy blurted out, "Were you ever married, Webb?"

"Long ago." Webb stared out the window. "Didn't work out. We were too young. The pressure of police work gets in the way of a good marriage. That's why the divorce rate is so high."

Her question marred the comfortable mood, and Webb was glad when the waitress served the escargot.

"I don't know about those," Daisy said grimacing. "They look awfully slimy."

"The garlic overrides the chewy texture," Webb teased and popped one in his mouth. "They're great. You said you'd try one."

"You'll have to feed it to me." Daisy leaned toward him, shut her eyes, and opened her mouth.

Webb grinned.

She took the snail on her tongue and opened her eyes. Chewing lightly, her face contorted, she said, "It's so...squishy." Hurriedly she swallowed it. "Okay, I've eaten a snail. Do I look any different?"

Webb laughed, his entire body feeling the glow.

The two chatted easily and Webb had to admit, Daisy was a great companion. In casual attire, with her hair hanging free, he forgot for the moment she was a fellow detective.

Forty minutes later the dinner still hadn't been served. Webb looked at his watch. "Damn, this is taking a long time. Where is our waitress?"

"*Patience,*" Samuel said. "*You're always exactly where you should be.*"

Back on the boardwalk at seven-forty, the sun was a blazing orange ball. "We should probably round up a place to stay tonight," Webb said.

Daisy's head turned toward a large gray house with bright pink shutters. "That's the Harbor House Inn. It's a bed and breakfast built in the late eighties, and I hear it's very charming. I bet the view is beautiful from that upstairs balcony."

Webb looked up and saw Samuel on the balcony gazing over Lake Michigan.

Webb shook his head. "I was thinking along the lines of a Holiday Inn. Didn't we pass one coming into town?"

Daisy nodded. "That's fine." She tugged on Webb's arm.

Now Samuel was tugging on Daisy's other sleeve, whispering something in her ear.

"Let's go look for my cousin's old house," She said. "I know it's in the older section of downtown."

"It's getting late," Webb protested.

"C'mon, where's your sense of adventure?"

Samuel draped his arm over Daisy's shoulder, leading her.

They returned to the car, drove to the downtown area, and parked on the street. Strolling a tree-lined neighborhood they came upon a huge white Victorian house.

"This place looks haunted," Webb gibed, pointing to a sign in the front yard. It read, *Madame Minerva — Medium: Join our summer seances and talk with the departed.*

"Look, Webb, her seances are on Saturday nights at eight." She glanced at her watch.

"Don't tell me," Webb sighed. "Perfect timing."

Samuel grinned gleefully. "*Now do you think the waitress was a slow-poke?*"

"Let's go in," Daisy urged. "It'll be fun."

"Oh, no." He backed away.

"Come on. Maybe we can contact Marc Lazare. Is Samuel with us?"

"God, Sam, get lost for a while."

"I bet Samuel would love this. He probably led us here," Daisy said.

"Well, the spook in my life seems to think I'll learn something," Webb said. "Okay, Sam, but you know I hate this stuff."

*   *   *

"Austin!" Laura ran to the child. "What did you do?" She snatched the gun from his hands, and he collapsed in tears. Laura checked Pierre for a pulse. His chest heaved, and she could smell alcohol.

"Oh, my God. He's drunk." Her eyes darted around the room and rested on the open gun cabinet. "How did you get in there, Austin?"

The child looked terrified. "It was open, Mama. Grandpa has a gun like mine."

"Your gun is a toy. These are real. Don't ever go in this cabinet again!" Laura was shaking as she replaced the gun and snapped the cabinet shut. "I thought this cabinet was always locked."

Laura heard someone enter the front door. "Who's there?"

Now she heard footsteps and pulled Austin into her grip.

Teddy appeared in the doorway. "Laura? What's going on here?"

She let go of the child and fell into Teddy's arms.

He hugged her in confusion.

"Oh, Teddy, someone broke into my house, and now I'm afraid to go home."

"Looks like Father's been drinking again." Teddy's face fell. "Help me get him into bed."

* * *

A clammy aura saturated the eerie room at Madame Minerva's house of horrors. "Maybe she murders people in here," Webb whispered playfully to Daisy. A man dressed in a faded tuxedo collected the ten dollar fee and ushered them to chairs surrounding a table. Engrossed in murky darkness, muted faces and heavy breathing revealed the presence of other clients.

"The session will begin shortly," the man said.

Webb squirmed.

Daisy took his hand in hers and squeezed it.

Reluctantly, he settled down. How did I get myself into this? I hope I leave here with my wallet intact. Slowly, his eyes adjusted to the darkness.

A moment later, rattling beads and the scent of herbal oils announced the entrance of Madame Minerva. A slender woman, deluged in a sea of gauzy red material, she floated to the chair at the head of the table next to Webb.

Overhead a tiny beam of light appeared, surrounding the medium in a mystic glow. Heavy make-up failed to hide an aging face. A thin white veil, held in place by a silver band, covered her long, black hair.

Webb wanted to laugh and hoped nobody recognized him in this loony place.

The clients remained faceless in the surrounding darkness. Yet Samuel was illuminated by a heavenly glow as he moved behind the chairs.

I wonder if the marvelous Madame can see Samuel.

Madame Minerva spoke in a near whisper. "Let us all...relax and shut our eyes. Let the spirits know we welcome them," she said. Her head began rolling around as if in spasm. "Let us join together."

Webb stiffened as he felt her bony fingers grasp his hand.

He didn't dare close his eyes. Instead, he studied the Madame, her pointed nose twitching.

"Someone in the room is giving off negative energy," Madame moaned. Her throat gurgled and Webb was certain she was about to belch. He stifled a smile.

She opened one eye, looking around at the attentive audience. When she came to Webb she scowled. "The entities will not come under these circumstances. Everyone's eyes must be closed."

"Webb," Daisy whispered. "Chill out."

I hate this stuff, Webb thought. I'm leaving.

Samuel shook his head at Webb.

He hesitated. Well maybe I'll stay, just to show Daiz this dame is a fraud. He took a deep breath and forced himself to settle down.

"Ah...that is better," Madame said in her ethereal voice. "Now they're coming in. I feel the spirits surrounding us."

Webb felt a blast of cold air.

"A spirit is here who wishes to speak to David," she crooned in a breathy voice.

"Oh, that's my Jenny!" an excited fellow shouted from across the table. "Jenny, are you all right? I miss you so much."

Suddenly Madame's voice assumed a higher pitch. "I'm so happy, David," she said. "You must come here often so we can be together." Madame's hand on Webb's started to tremble. Her normal voice returned. "I'm sorry, David. Jenny is gone."

David sighed.

Madame dropped Webb's hand and began to writhe, her head falling back, mouth gaping open. Frantically, she waved her arms in the air, gasping and moaning.

Webb wondered in amusement if this creature was having a seizure or an orgasm. He folded his arms and watched the act.

Now the medium's voice lowered into a masculine range. "There are negative forces here that must be expelled," the voice shouted.

"Who is it?" Madame droned, continuing her frantic movements. "Show us who is giving off negative energy."

The chill in the air grew more intense.

Webb caught his breath. Across the table, Samuel stood behind one of the clients. He waved at Webb, pointed at Madame Minerva and shook his head.

Webb shuffled in his chair, clearing his throat. He nudged Daisy and nodded across the table.

Madame's frenzy increased. She grabbed her head, tore at her veil.

Webb saw Samuel round the table and drop a silver charm directly in front of the medium.

Madame Minerva gasped and jumped from her chair.

"Who threw that?" She glared at Webb. "It was you. You're filled with negative energy."

Samuel chuckled behind her. He tugged on Minerva's black tresses. She grabbed the veil, but her wig fell to the floor revealing gray hair pinned close to her head.

An ear-piercing scream split the air. Minerva covered her head and fled from the room.

Webb doubled over in laughter. "Where can we get our refund?"

A low murmur spread throughout the room. David wept. "What happened?"

"She's a fraud," Webb said. "Let's go, Daiz." He grabbed Daisy's arm and hustled her outside.

Back in the car, Webb told Daisy about Samuel's antics. "So why did you want us to see that?" He asked his spirit guide.

"*Many people think spirits are spooks. You don't need all that ceremony to talk with us. Thoughts, Bud. You clear it, we hear it.*"

Down the road Webb pulled into the Holiday Inn and asked for separate rooms.

Samuel approached the computer monitor.

Studying the screen, the clerk narrowed his brow. "I'm sorry sir, we don't seem to have any vacancies," he said with a look of puzzlement. "Would you like me to check with the Harbor House Inn? I think you'll find it very attractive."

CHAPTER 12

LAURA STEPPED onto her patio. A sunny Sunday, she was relieved to be home. Teddy moved in for her protection. He was still sleeping. She felt safe with Teddy.

Austin was busy in the sandbox. "I dig a cave, Momma."

Gathering a basket laden with, cucumbers and peppers and fresh herbs from her garden, Laura checked Austin before going inside to the kitchen. "I'll make a big salad for lunch," she decided and began peeling the cucumbers. While she worked, her mind raced.

Nothing registered on her Caller-ID or the answering machine while she was away. Whoever called her and broke in was lying low. It still frightened her to think the intruder could be watching the house.

Thank God for Teddy. He arrived just in time. She thought of calling Pierre. The incident with Austin and the gun continued to haunt her. She left a note the night before explaining that Teddy would stay with her. At least Father's refrigerator is stocked with healthy foods. I'll still shop for him.

She looked out the window for Austin who had moved from the sandbox to his swing set. He constantly explored his world. She felt a wave of love for her small son. It devastated her to think how much he missed his daddy.

I really should set up a trust fund for Austin. If something happens to me— "No! Don't think that way. You're paranoid again." Laura had her own trust fund from her family. "I'll call about that tomorrow."

Teddy sauntered in yawning. "Do you have orange juice?"

"Help yourself. I can make waffles."

"Sounds great," he said and stretched his arms toward the ceiling. "How did you sleep last night?"

Laura walked over to him and hugged him warmly. "You're a lifesaver, Teddy. I don't know what I'd do without you."

He pushed her away. "Listen. I was glad to stay last night, but you know this is a risky arrangement."

Laura's heart fell. "I need you Teddy. Please stay."

*   *   *

Before Webb left for work on Monday morning, he answered a call from Jake Rubel. "I hear you took Farrell on a little rendezvous over the weekend. Are you two having an affair?"

Webb leaned against the bedroom wall. "What's up, Rubel?"

"You should have worked on this case over the weekend. Instead you goofed off with that dame while I discovered new evidence." Rubel's voice rose. He sounded almost giddy. "I finally tracked down Teddy Lazare's roommate from Purdue. He told me Teddy went home on the Fourth of July. He was away all weekend."

Webb jumped to attention, but kept cool. "Is that true?"

"I lined up more interviews with people who knew Teddy at school."

"Just keep working those interviews," Webb said. "Wow, you're really moving." He hung up before the elf could annoy him further.

"Damn it. I knew I should have stuck around over the weekend."

Samuel lolled on the bed. "No, you needed that visit to Madame Minerva."

Webb tossed a towel at the spirit guide. "Why would Teddy lie about where he was that night?"

Samuel remained mum.

"Did he kill Marc, then set up Luc's death? But what was his motive?"

Samuel strolled over to the window. "Good questions."

Webb eyed him, then an idea popped into his mind. "If he did kill his brothers, maybe he broke into Laura's house too." Webb grabbed the phone. "God, Sam. If that's true—"

*   *   *

While Teddy showered, Laura set an extra set of towels on the bed in the spare room including a small bag of toiletries. She wiped the headboard with a dust cloth, running it quickly over the top of the pictures on the wall and along the baseboard.

Just seeing Teddy's duffel bag open on the floor comforted her. Laura was glad to be away from Pierre and his gun collection. A dangerous place for little boys. It was my fault Austin got into that gun cabinet. I knew Pierre was drinking.

She moved to the dresser and polished the mirror. Teddy's watch and a class ring were on the dresser along with a silver chain strung through a medallion. She picked it up and held it to the light...a sunburst.

"Oh, my God! That detective mentioned a sunburst medallion." She racked her brain. Why was the medallion important? What did Hannis say about it? Her mind was a blank. Laura studied the unique piece. She never saw Teddy wear it before. What did the medallion have to do with Marc's murder?

Teddy emerged from the bathroom wrapped in a towel, his hair dripping.

Laura held up the necklace. "Where did you get this?"

"I've had that for years." He snatched it away from her and clipped it around his neck. "I wear it under my shirt because some people think medallions are for witchcraft."

Laura's body tensed. She felt threatened but didn't know why. Suddenly she had the urge to flee the room, but Teddy loomed like a fortress between her and the open door.

The phone jangled, and she grabbed it off the bedside table. "Hello."

"Webb Hannis."

"Yes," she said, surprised she had a voice.

"We have new information about your brother-in-law Teddy. I need you to help me find out if he broke into your house."

Laura, her body inert, stared at Teddy whose image began to pulsate before her.

He gave her a puzzled look. "Who is that?" he mouthed.

Laura looked away, backing against the wall.

Austin bounded into the room. "Unca' Teddy." The little boy leaped into his uncle's arms.

"Austin! Go downstairs," Laura shouted. "I'll have to call you back," she said and hung up.

"Austin, Teddy is trying to dress," Laura said, her voice shaking. "Let's go downstairs." She stumbled out of the room and floated down the stairs with her child. "I have some errands to run, Austin." Grabbing her purse in the kitchen, she picked up the boy and fled the house. Stabbing the key in the ignition, she sped out of the driveway.

Her mind raged as she careened onto the highway heading downtown. God, don't let it be Teddy! To think I invited him to stay with us last night. She shuddered. Why in heaven's name would he break into the house? And that call. She was so confused. Minutes later she pulled into the parking lot at the Detroit Police Department.

Webb Hannis was not in. "He just called me," Laura ranted to the desk officer.

"He didn't call from here. Let me see if anyone is in the detective office."

Laura paced in the lobby while Austin slid along the floor on his hands and knees.

"Ma'am, I just spoke with Detective Farrell. She'll be right out."

A moment later Daisy appeared. "Hi, Laura," she said. "Let's go back to the conference room. Webb is on his way over. Can I get you a cup of coffee?"

"Yes, that would be wonderful." Laura collapsed into a chair, wearily lifting Austin onto her lap.

He kicked away from her. "I wanna go home," he pouted and sat on the floor.

My poor baby, Laura lamented as she ran her fingers through his tangled hair. He's been through so much. She longed to live a normal life again where Austin's tantrums were her biggest problem.

Daisy returned with the coffee and a bottle of punch for Austin. She flipped open a notepad. "What brought you here?"

"Detective Hannis called me at home about a half hour ago. He said he has new information about my brother-in-law, Teddy. What exactly does he know?"

"You look shaken. Did something else happen?"

"I really need to talk with Hannis."

Daisy left the room and five minutes later returned with Webb.

Laura jumped up and demanded, "What do you know about Teddy?"

Webb took a seat and looked intently at Laura. "He wasn't at school the weekend of July fourth. He was here in Detroit."

Laura bubbled over in tears.

Daisy put her arm around her shoulder. "You're under tremendous pressure. We can help if you let us."

Austin gazed at his mother in confusion.

Daisy took Austin by the hand. "How would you like to see the police department? I know an officer who'd love to give you the grand tour. You can even try on the handcuffs."

Laura was grateful to talk without Austin hearing. She sniffled and covered her face with her hands.

Hannis offered her a box of tissues.

"I do need your help, Detective," Laura said suddenly. "I'll tell you what I know."

Webb's eyes lit up and he reached for Daisy's notebook. "Who was in the car with you the night of July fourth?"

Laura shook her head and hesitated. "I didn't want to get him in trouble. The family doesn't know."

Daisy returned and exchanged glances with Hannis.

"Is it okay for detective Farrell to sit in on this?" Hannis asked.

"Yes. It doesn't matter now."

"Who was in that car?"

"He was having problems with the family. They wanted him in the business, but he was pulling away."

"Who?" Hannis pressed.

Laura began to cry again. "Oh, Detective, it's really not that big a deal. I was with Teddy. I was always sort of a sounding board for him. Marc was away a lot and we would discuss our problems."

"Why did you lie and say your husband was in the car that night?"

"Tell me about the medallion," Laura said. "You asked me about a sunburst medallion. How does that fit in with all this?"

Webb perked to attention. "You tell *me* about it."

"Is it some kind of evidence in the murder investigation?"

"Who does it belong to, Mrs. Lazare?"

At that moment, Jake Rubel stuck his head in the door. "Finally getting a little work done, eh, Hannis?" He looked at

Laura. "Oh, interviewing Marc Lazare's wife without contacting me." Rubel pulled out a seat and sat down.

"Who is he?" Laura asked.

"This is a private meeting, Rubel." Hannis stood up. "I need
to speak with you outside."

The two men left, and Laura could hear bickering through
the closed door.

"Don't worry. Hannis will get rid of him," Daisy said and
patted Laura's arm. "You're doing fine. Do you need a break?
Are you hungry?"

"I don't think I'll ever eat again. My stomach is in knots."

Hannis returned without Rubel and took his seat again.
"Let's get back to the Fourth of July. Why did you tell us your
husband was with you in the car?"

"Marc and I were fighting. That much is true." She mopped
her face with a tissue. "Teddy came home to inform his father he
was definitely going to law school. Pierre refused to pay for 'this
ridiculous venture' and told Teddy he expected him to join the
family business. Teddy was livid and walked out on his father. He
called me and wanted to talk. We decided to go to the fireworks."

"Why didn't you tell us this before?"

"I didn't want Pierre to know Teddy came to me right after
their argument. Father's been so paranoid lately. I was afraid he
might think we were plotting against him. I had no idea Teddy
was involved."

Webb stared at her. "Involved in what?"

"I don't know. That stupid medallion. It belongs to Teddy."

"What do you know about it?"

"I don't know anything. Teddy says he's had it for years.
Why do you think he broke into my house?"

"We have no evidence it was Teddy," Hannis said. "After I
heard he was in Detroit over the Fourth of July, my mind started
spinning."

Laura felt completely drained, like someone had pulled the
plug on her energy and sucked it out of her body.

"You look exhausted," Daisy said. "Do you want me to drive you home?"

Laura's eyes brimmed with tears again. "I can't go home. Teddy's there."

* * *

Outside the conference room, away from Laura, Webb beamed at Daisy. "I guess my dream was true. Sam, what's the significance of the medallion?"

"*You asked to know who was in the car with Laura.*"

"Do you think Teddy murdered his brothers?" Daisy asked.

"He's a strong suspect, that's for damn sure." Webb paced the hallway. He headed back to his cubby, dropped into his chair and propped his feet on the desk. An idea popped into his head. "I've gotta' talk to Teddy." He picked up the phone and dialed Laura Lazare's number.

No answer.

He dialed Pierre Lazare.

Teddy answered.

"This is Detective Webb Hannis with the Detroit Police Department."

"My father is sleeping, Detective."

"I want to talk to you, Teddy." He smiled at Daisy. "I'll stop over in a half hour."

"I don't know anything about Marc's murder or the accident at Lazare Fireworks."

"You're not a suspect. Just routine questions."

"I'll be here." He hung up.

"If he agreed to an interview, he must not realize he's a suspect," Daisy said. "I hope that dog Rubel left. All you need is that jerk tagging along."

"Daiz, would you mind staying with Laura tonight? She needs protection, and I want you to get her permission and set up a phone tap to record all calls. If she doesn't have Caller-ID, install that too. I'll be in touch." With that, Webb was out the door.

In the car he turned to Samuel. "Things are heating up. My instincts are starting to pay off."

"Instincts?"

"Okay, I admit I treated you like shit. It's just so damn frustrating to wait for information. If Teddy messes up and I catch him in a lie, I could make an arrest soon."

It took him just twenty minutes to drive to Grosse Pointe and rap on Pierre Lazare's door. Teddy answered and offered a handshake.

Once seated in the living room, Webb plunged into his questions. "Where were you last Thursday?"

"Driving back from Arizona. I took my mother to a spa. She's been nervous and depressed since Marc's death. She doesn't even know about Luc."

"Do you have any proof of where you were? Restaurant receipts from that day?"

Teddy pulled out his billfold and flipped through a stack of receipts. "Here's one dated Thursday from a gas station in Missouri." He handed it to Webb.

Webb studied the receipt and his heart sank. "This one's good. I'll keep it." He frowned at Samuel.

"How else can I help you, Detective?"

Following Samuel's eyes, Webb noticed a necklace dangling around Teddy's neck, the end buried under his shirt. "What's that chain around your neck?"

Teddy pulled off the medallion and handed it to Webb.

Webb studied the sunburst. It was the same as in his dream. "Nice," he said.

Pierre Lazare stood in the doorway. "What are you doing here, Hannis? Did you get a positive ID on Luc?"

"Not yet. We expect lab results this week."

"Then you have no business here. I told you to go through my attorney."

Webb rose. "Your son and I are having a nice chat. I have all the information I need at this time." Webb tossed the medallion back to Teddy.

In the car, Webb's blood boiled. "Why are you leading me on this crazy chase?" he shouted at Samuel. "You knew damn well that Teddy didn't break into Laura's house. For God's sake, I'm sick of these dead ends."

"Anger stops the flow of universal energy," Samuel said calmly. "But you can change your thoughts in an instant."

Webb mulled that over in his mind. He let out a long breath. "So what if I flip out over other people always messing me up?"

"It's never about other people. It's how we *think* about those people."

"I don't get it."

"When you get all uptight and frustrated, put on the skids, Bud. Stop and ask God what you need to learn from this situation. You gotta let go of the negativity if you want help solving the problem."

Webb tried to relax his tense shoulders. "This is gonna' take practice."

Samuel nodded his head. "The answers to your questions aren't necessarily what you *want*, but what you *need*. Trust."

*   *   *

That evening, Laura lay on the couch in her living room covered with a quilt. Overwhelmed with fatigue, she longed to sink into a deep slumber, but sleep evaded her. Why would Teddy murder Marc? She was afraid she knew the answer. What about that explosion at the plant? Will Teddy try to kill me too? Laura was grateful the detective was in the house with her.

Daisy brought Austin into the living room. "Do you want to go upstairs and rest, Laura? I can entertain Austin." She mussed the child's hair. "Right, Buddy?"

"Thanks, Daisy, but he had a long day. I'll give him a bath and put him in bed." She dragged herself up from the couch.

Upstairs in the bathroom, Laura gazed into the mirror as Austin splashed in the tub. Her eyes were swollen and blood-shot, ringed in red. With no make-up, her skin was blotchy and pale. She hadn't washed her hair in days. Coiling it into a bun, she pinned it high on her head.

She bent over the tub and shampooed Austin's hair, glad to be alone with him. He giggled when she blew bubbles in his face. How she longed for happy times like this again.

After Austin was tucked in bed, Laura returned to the living room where Daisy flipped through a magazine. "Go to bed, Laura," Daisy urged.

"I'm so restless."

"What about some food? I made tuna salad for Austin."

Laura followed Daisy into the kitchen. Tuna salad sounded good to her. "On toast with a thick slice of tomato."

*   *   *

By ten o'clock, Laura was finally asleep, and Daisy called Webb at home.

He sounded tired.

"How is Laura?" he asked.

"She's asleep."

"Do you think Teddy and Luc worked together to kill Marc?"

"It's possible, but why?"

"Neither wanted the business," Webb said. "I really need to talk with Teddy again, away from his father's house. Pierre won't even put him through on the phone."

"I'll have Laura ring him tomorrow," Daisy said. "She can tell him to meet you at the station."

"Tell him I have interesting information."

"Things are moving right along," Daisy said. "You sound tired."

"Try stumped. I hit one roadblock after another, and Sam refuses to set me straight. Teddy has an alibi for the day of Laura's break-in. I was so certain—"

"Do you still trust Samuel?"

"I have to trust him. What else can I do? But whenever I think I'm on the right trail, I get shot down and he leads me someplace else." Webb groaned.

*   *   *

The next morning, Laura woke at nine-thirty. She felt much better with almost twelve hours sleep. After her shower she held a cold washcloth over her eyes to reduce the puffiness. Austin must be down with Daisy. With coveted time to herself, she sat at her dressing table, applied a bit of make-up, and fixed her strawberry ringlets. Finally she dressed in a cream colored knit top and an olive green jumper.

Downstairs, Austin was sitting on the counter helping Daisy add blueberries to pancake batter. "Me cooking, Mommy."

"It smells great in here."

"You look much better this morning, Laura."

"I feel more like my old self again." She poured orange juice in a glass and sat on a barstool at the counter. "I really appreciate everything you've done for me, Daisy. I'm sorry for the way I acted in the beginning. Pierre insisted we avoid the police. I think everyone should start talking if we're going to solve Marc's murder."

Daisy flipped a pancake onto the plate and handed it to Austin. "Oh, Laura, we need you to call Teddy at Pierre's and have him meet Detective Hannis at the police station downtown. Tell him Webb has some interesting information."

Laura bit her lip. "What is the penalty for breaking and entering?"

"Teddy didn't break into your house. He has an out-of-town

receipt for the time of the burglary. We just want to question him about Luc."

"Then who did break into the house?"

"We may never know," Daisy said. "Especially if nothing was taken."

Laura dialed Pierre's house. "Father? This is Laura, is Teddy there?"

Daisy flipped four pancakes onto a plate and turned off the griddle.

"Okay, thank you, Father." She hung up and Daisy noted the time in her notebook.

"Father says when he got up this morning, Teddy was gone."

CHAPTER 13

JADE STAYED away a couple nights.

Conrad, beside himself, paced the floor until almost four in the morning the second night. As if he didn't have enough burden on his shoulders. At least the anonymous caller at the office hadn't tried to reach him again. No way could I afford to pay off some blackmailer, he thought. But what choice did he have? He tossed and turned before falling into an exhausted sleep on the family room couch.

He woke with a start at eight when he heard the kitchen door open.

"Jade! Is that you?"

She ambled in, her face in despair. The moment she saw him, she burst into tears. "Oh, Conrad, I'm so sorry. I don't know what makes me act so crazy."

He caught her and shook her to attention. "Why do you get so angry?"

"I don't know why I do anything anymore," she cried. "Maybe I'm insane. I just get ticked off and once I start, I can't stop."

"That's no excuse for not calling for two days," Conrad bellowed.

She tore away from him, collapsed onto the couch and broke into tears.

Sliding next to her on the couch, he smoothed her hair. "Jade, you must get hold of yourself."

She bent forward wailing pitifully. "Help me, Conrad. Please help me."

"Maybe you should change therapists."

She sat up straight and threw her arms around Conrad's neck. "I'll do anything you say, Conrad, but please don't be angry with me."

He patted her head. "Where have you been? I was worried sick."

"I went to a motel. I should have called, but that damn anger—"

Jade looked into Conrad's eyes. "Darling, I promise, I'll make it up to you. I know I try your patience on the new house when you're still mourning your brothers. It's just that it means so much to me."

He smiled and took her in his arms. "When this is all over, you and I will get away by ourselves for a second honeymoon."

*   *   *

Laura drove onto the gravel lot at the stable, kicking up a fog of gray dust. Continuing her watchful vigil at the house, Daisy offered to stay with Austin so Laura could get away on her own for the afternoon. Laura felt self-indulgent as she tugged on her black rubber riding boots. "Darn, the clouds are moving in." The weather forecast called for afternoon thunderstorms. "I hope they hold off long enough for me to get an hour on the trails."

Inside the wooden building, Laura inhaled the mellowing aroma of sweet hay and oats. She chose this stable because of the impeccable facility, cleaned regularly by a crew of care-takers.

"It looks like the rain may move in early. I better get mov-ing." She smiled and strolled to stall number twelve. Mocha, her favorite horse, poked his nose over the gate as if to greet her, his swarthy coloring the exact shade of a chocolate latté.

"Hi, baby," she cooed, patting Mocha's neck. *I really am lucky to have Austin safe at home with Daisy and Teddy out of my hair.*

Inside the stall she busied herself, brushing the horse's coat and mane until it glistened. Her mind wandered. *Where in the hell is Teddy? Pierre said he left early this morning.*

"How you doin', Mrs. Lazare?"

Laura whirled around to see the head stable-hand. Always mysterious with green cat eyes against leathery skin and matted, straw-like hair, he had a way of sneaking up on people, silently moving about the grounds. Laura usually avoided him.

"Fine. I'm in a bit of a hurry." She tossed her hair over her shoulder and reached for her riding tack.

"Storm's movin' in. You sure you wanna' go out?"

Placing the bit in Mocha's toothy mouth, she pulled the reins over his head. "I'll watch it. The rain should hold off at least another hour. Anyway, I've ridden in rain before."

She glared at him over the top of her streamlined saddle.

The stable hand swaggered away on skinny, wishbone legs.

Laura relished her solitude. She led Mocha out of the stable and donned a domed riding hat. With experienced agility, she mounted her beloved horse and left the stable.

The trails were breathtaking, wild flowers scattered every-where, blossoms tilted upwards, basking in the sun. To the north, the sky was a smoky gray, not really threatening, but enough to mottle the green summer palette. "I look forward to a cool down and the autumn colors this year."

Following a trodden path through the woods, Laura prac-ticed her riding skills. Long ago privately instructed in English posting, she still preferred the pompous technique to holding onto a saddlehorn. Relieved to be without Austin, she cantered into the open meadow, her ringlets flapping against her back in perfect rhythm.

Across the clearing she chose a narrow trail and slowed as she maneuvered Mocha between tall weeds and branches.

She heard a stick break behind her and whipped around. "Who's there?" she called, pulling the reins taut. Except for leaves rustling, there was silence. You're paranoid again, she berated herself.

Then she remembered the time Teddy helped Austin with his riding lesson and afterward, followed her and the boy on the trails. He's not here now! She chided herself. "God, Teddy. Don't tell me you killed Marc." The idea made her heart thud.

*   *   *

Daisy and Webb relaxed on the patio at Laura's home while Austin tumbled on the grass. Samuel basked in a lounger.

"Austin's a cute kid," Webb said. "Looks just like a Lazare." Webb picked up a magazine and thumbed through the pages.

"He's a feisty little guy," Daisy said. "But I enjoy children. I told Laura to go to the stable for a few hours. She needed to get away. She trusts me with Austin."

"You're great with her, Daiz."

Daisy sat up. "Could you help me set up the outside sur- veillance cameras?"

"I can do that," he said, laying the magazine aside. "Then I'm on my way to interview Conrad. Hopefully I can get him to talk."

Daisy lifted a video camera out of a large box.

Samuel was immediately at her side, patting the camera ten- derly.

Webb jumped up from his chair and grabbed the camera. Holding it high, he studied all angles. A Panasonic, he noted mentally. "So, why did you drag my sorry ass over to this camera?"

"It's for surveillance," Daisy said. "You asked me to bring it."

"I'm talking to Sam, Daiz."

Samuel was back in the lounger with his irritating smile.

"That's what drives me crazy with this guy. He gives me a clue, but when I run it down, like I did with Teddy, I'm still confused." Webb looked off into the distance. "I have to admit when I follow his lead, I actually end up finding a piece of the puzzle." He stared at Samuel. "But now I have to figure out what this video camera means besides surveillance."

"Maybe Pierre Lazare has a camera like this," Daisy suggested.

"Sam?"

"*Maybe.*"

Daisy pulled on Webb's shirtsleeve. "What did he say?"

Webb sighed heavily. "He's not telling. God, that bugs me. I definitely have to get in that house again. Damn it, why do you have to make it so tough, Sam?"

"I'm just glad you finally realize you have a special gift," Daisy said.

"I still don't get it. Why me?"

"Remember, Phoebe said you're not the only one. We all have guides. You guys are just lucky you can actually see them."

"Yeah. Lucky me." He shook his head and carefully placed the camera back in the box. Then, staring into Samuel's eyes he declared, "Okay, God, show me why the video camera is important."

Samuel collapsed onto the ground in a mock faint.

*   *   *

Mocha trotted along the path, but every sound frightened Laura. With the sky darkening overhead, she decided to turn back.

FIREWORKS 247

Soon, large raindrops pattered against her helmet. She slapped
Mocha on the hip with her riding crop.

The narrow path muddied quickly, and Mocha lost his foot-
ing several times, jarring Laura forward. Now she wished she
had a saddlehorn. Pulling back on the reins, she slowly steered
the horse down the sodden trail.

She had ridden many times in the rain. Yet this time her
heart raced and her arms felt leaden. An ungodly image blasted
through her mind. Teddy, hidden behind a tree, shooting her off
the horse with a rifle.

When she reached the meadow, she dug in her heels and gal-
loped across the open field, her hair and clothing soaked from
the torrential downpour. Mocha was wobbly on the slippery
grass. Laura blinked wildly through the slashing rain.

She felt disoriented. Where is the path?

Panic mounted.

"Where do we go, Mocha? You always know the way
home." She slowed to a trot, heart thundering, and jerked the
reins back and forth in search of the trail that led to the barn. The
relentless storm battered her face. She shuddered from the
sudden chill, her teeth chattering from nerves as much as the
temperature. A wet clump of hair clung to her cheek. Why did I
ride when I saw the dark clouds? I'm an open target out here in
the meadow. The pummeling rain blurred her vision. She cow-
ered forward in despair.

Slowly she maneuvered Mocha along the edge of the
woods, commanding herself to stay calm until she found the
path. A half hour passed and she was still lost.

The rain finally stopped. Soaked, tired and cold, Laura was
near tears. "Daisy will wonder where I am in this storm."

She heard movement in the woods. She stopped the horse
and held her breath. "Who's there?"

A raccoon scurried from under the brush.

Laura burst into tears and bit down on her lip. "You must get
hold of yourself. Panic can kill you."

After an interminable time, she finally found the trail, and her energy surged. "We're almost home, Mocha." She leaned down and hugged the horse's neck. "You've been a trooper through all this, now just get us back to the stable."

Suddenly Mocha shifted sideways, slipping on fresh mud.

Laura screamed.

Lurching to the right, Mocha toppled over, her massive body crushing Laura's leg. The animal spooked, jumped up and headed home without its rider.

Riddled with pain, Laura lost consciousness, her face nestled in the muddy soil.

*   *   *

Inside Conrad's office, Webb looked around at the pictures and momentos. "I see you're the official president of Lazare Fireworks," he said, ignoring Samuel who was standing beside Conrad.

"It's about time." Conrad sat back in his chair. He looked weathered since Webb first met him at Pierre's house. The skin beneath his eyes billowed, circled in dark lines.

"What can I do for you, Mr. Hannis? My secretary said you have new information."

"Does your father own a video camera?"

"He has an old movie camera and boxes of family films. But he never caught on to the modern ages. We had to force him to computerize the business."

"What about other family members? Anyone own a video camera?"

"I think Marc and Laura bought one when Austin was born. Why?"

"Is it a Panasonic?"

"I have no idea. Is that part of the new information?"

"Not exactly. Were you aware Marc was seeing a psychiatrist?"

Conrad's face registered surprise. "No. Who told you that?"

"Your father said something. I thought you might know more."

"I said I don't know anything. It's time for you to leave, Detective."

* * *

Jade tossed and turned in her bed, glad for the rainy afternoon. Bored and battling remorse, she longed for sleep to obliterate her problems. Instead, her head pounded and her arms and legs twitched helplessly.

She jumped a foot when the telephone rang.

"Jade, this is Gillian. Get your buns down to Fario's at four o'clock. I know the owner. He's having a private showing of collectible Persian carpets. I thought with your new house and all—"

Jade sat up and fluffed her hair. "How much are they?"

"Oh, honey, I know Fario. I bought my dining room rug from him. He'll give you a deal at this special showing. If Tristan is doing your house, you should have him go with you."

She was infused with new vitality. This was just the thing she needed to lift her out of the doldrums. She called Tristan and hopped out of bed to shower and dress.

* * *

Laura fought to wake up, glimmering into consciousness for a moment before darkness claimed her again. She winced in pain. My leg! Where's Mocha? She tried to move, but her leg felt as if it were encased in cement. "Help me," she whispered.

"I'm here, Laura."

"Teddy?" She forced her eyelids apart. A distorted figure bent over her. She struggled to focus her eyes. "Teddy!" she screamed clawing at the face. "Get away from me." She tried to kick him, but her leg wouldn't budge.

Her wrists were wrestled down to her sides. "Listen to me, Laura. You're okay. It's me, Conrad."

"No," she wailed remembering her fall from the horse. "Don't kill me Teddy," she wailed, yet couldn't muster the energy to fight him.

A shadowy figure in white appeared. "Be gentle with Mrs. Lazare. She suffered quite a trauma."

The man reached out and patted her forehead. "Try to relax, Laura," he said. "Your horse threw you in the woods. Your leg is badly broken, and you had surgery to pin it."

Laura heard the words, but her mind was a jumble. Slowly, her blurry vision sharpened. She stared intently at the man beside her bed. "Teddy, why are you trying to hurt me?"

"She's hallucinating," the woman in white said. "It's common after surgery."

"Teddy isn't here, Laura," the man said. "The stable hand found you in the woods after your horse returned alone. He summoned help. What's all this about Teddy?"

"I'm afraid of him. He's dangerous."

*　*　*

Just before four, Jade put in a call to Conrad. I better tell him what I'm doing or he'll have a fit. Gillian says I'll get a good deal.

"I'm sorry, Mrs. Lazare," his secretary said. "He left about a half hour ago. Laura was in an accident."

Jade clenched her teeth. "Of course, he must help Laura. If you see him again, please tell him I'm out." She slammed down the phone.

"Goddamn Laura. She's always more important than me." Then Jade remembered Conrad's tenderness after her tirades and felt a stab of guilt. Yet a moment later she boiled with outrage.

"I can buy that friggin' rug. I have an opinion in this family."
Anger always overpowered any other emotion.

Twenty minutes later she was inside the Fario showroom,
perusing the magnificent carpets with Tristan and Gillian.
Exquisite rugs draped the walls, illuminated by strategically
placed can lights.

"Oh, Jade love, stand next to this apricot wonder," Tristan
oozed. "I want to see how it goes with your complexion."

Jade fingered the fine nap. "I do like the subtle greens in the
pattern." She posed like a fashion model, pirouetting in front of
the spotlight.

"Red goes with my personality," Gillian said. "That's what
I used in my dining room. You've seen it. Isn't it dynamite?"

"Red is definitely your color, Gillian," Jade said, though she
barely remembered Gillian's dining room decor.

"Gillian's color scheme is simply delicious," Tristan
drooled. "It was my design. But I like the softer, cozier colors
for you, Jade darling."

"The apricot is striking," said the merchant, an Iranian with
a thick accent.

"No, I've changed my mind. It's too...apricoty." Tristan
scowled. "I want peach, the shade of a freshly plucked blossom."

Fario showed them a twenty by thirty foot carpet bordered
in a taupe and ivory design. The center, a Dhurrie pattern, was
predominantly peach and included subtle shades of sage and
Wedgwood blue.

Tristan, his face flushed, rhapsodied into a near coma. "You
simply must have this for the living room," he said. "Look at my
hands, Jade. They're quaking. This happens when I find the perfect piece." He slumped onto a nearby chair.

"Oh, definitely," beamed Gillian. "If you're doing peaches,
this is beautiful, yet subtle enough for patterned upholstery."

"I love it," Jade said, examining the wool weave. "How
much is it?"

Tristan sucked in a long breath, jumped up and pulled Jade

aside. "It's tacky-tacky to mention price in an exclusive place like this," he hissed under his breath. "Let me handle the bargaining, darling." Tristan jotted something on a sheet of paper from his planner and handed it to the merchant.

The paper passed back and forth between the two, both scribbling something each time. Finally Mr. Fario nodded and smiled. Hurriedly he swept out of the showroom.

"The rug will set the tone in the living room. Consider it the very backdrop, the canvas for everything else in the house," Tristan declared, sweeping his arms through the air like a hawk preparing for flight. "I'd like to bring out the sage in the dining room. I'll commission a custom area rug for under the dining room table and inlay it with the marble."

"Tristan, you are the best," Gillian bubbled. "You're worth every penny."

Jade was led to a private room decorated in expensive antiques and soft lighting. The Iranian handed her a leather bound box. Slowly, she opened it and glanced at the bill. Sixty thousand dollars. She felt faint and grabbed onto Tristan.

"Your house will be the most sumptuous in town," he whispered.

Jade swallowed hard. Oh well, what's sixty thousand when we'll soon have a million? She accepted a pen from Mr. Fario and signed the order.

CHAPTER 14

CONRAD SAT in his office contemplating the last couple weeks. *If I let myself think too long, I'll lose my mind. The damn police are zeroing in.* Conrad laid his head down on the desk. *Marc and Luc are dead, Father's drowning in booze, and Mother is in a rest home. Laura's all upset in the hospital, and Jade...well, she's getting worse with her spending and tantrums. And that anonymous caller?* "God, what next?"

He raised his head and gazed around the room. "I can't deal with all this. I have to get out of here now."

He grabbed his suit coat and lit out the door. Leaping into his car, he sped onto the street and drove toward downtown Detroit. His heart hammered so loudly it frightened him, but he zoomed on.

A sign for the tunnel to Canada caught his eye. He followed it. Within minutes, he was under the river on his way to Windsor, Ontario.

At the border, he gave his place of birth and told the guard he was in the country to shop.

He drove around until he spied a coffee shop, parked and

went in. At eleven in the morning, the place was empty except for the plump waitress, busy at the counter filling a metal rack with sugar packets.

With her mousy brown hair piled on top of her head, sagging jowls and double chin, Conrad envied her. She's so ordinary. She probably worries about grandchildren. Maybe her bathroom faucet drips or her cholesterol's too high. Mundane problems.

He sank down at the counter, ordered coffee, and slowly sipped the steaming brew.

The waitress looked his way and smiled at him.

He smiled back and stirred his drink. He welcomed the quiet and safety of this prosaic little coffee shop. I could meld into obscurity in this city, he thought. Maybe even find some happiness in a bourgeois existence.

Thoughts of Jade's tirades destroyed his tranquil fantasy. Conrad laughed out loud. If she only knew how deep we're buried in debt.

He ordered more coffee. It burned his tongue. He winced and tears filled his eyes.

Embarrassed, Conrad glanced at the waitress.

She looked away, polishing the plastic doughnut dome.

"Check, please," he said.

After paying the tab, he left a tip and returned to his car. It was nice to escape the madness, in fact, the country.

* * *

Laura poked at the tray of food. Pushing the hamburger aside, she stirred a scoop of mashed potatoes and watery gravy. "Heavens. Don't they have any fresh vegetables in this place? You'd think they would be into health in a hospital."

Daisy, on guard in a vinyl chair next to the bed, grinned. "At least they're serving you lunch. When you're finished, I'll run down to the cafeteria and grab a sandwich."

Laura tried to sit up straight, but couldn't get comfortable with her bandaged leg.

"Here, let me help," Daisy said. She placed pillows behind Laura's back and adjusted the electric bed. "How is that?"

"Miserable. I don't think I can bear this position much longer."

A nurse whisked in, flipping open a patient chart in a silver case. With a pen she tapped the pole next to Laura's bed. "Remember, you're delivering your own pain medication with this pump. If you're suffering any discomfort, just press the button. The machine won't let you overdose." The nurse checked the readings on the pain pump. "You haven't used much." She wrote on the chart.

Laura groaned "How long will I have to be in the hospital?"

"Your doctor can answer that question. He'll make rounds again tomorrow morning." The nurse offered a sympathetic smile and breezed out of the room.

"If you're finished eating, I'll get this tray out of your way and head downstairs for lunch," Daisy said.

Laura nodded. "I don't know how to thank you for your kindness. I'm sorry I'm so irritable."

"I'd be cranky too if my leg was broken. I'll be back in about a half hour." Daisy lifted the untouched tray and placed it on the dresser.

Alone in the room, Laura felt suddenly vulnerable. With the door open, and strangers milling down the halls, it would be so easy for someone to—

She pushed the thought away and closed her eyes, but her frightened mind envisioned Teddy sneaking into the room and tampering with the IV line.

Her eyes flew open, wildly searching the dreary room. Concentrate on something else, she commanded her mind. Thank God for Rosa. She loves Austin. He's in good hands.

Laura switched on the television. She flipped through the channels. Home improvement and game shows claimed the airwaves. The mindless racket grated on her nerves. She clicked it off.

Solitude alarmed her. What if Teddy shows up? Fingering the pain pump, she pressed the button, surging the narcotic through her vein. She squeezed a second time, a third, and a fourth. The nurse said I can't overdose. In staccato rhythm, she pressed the button until she sank into oblivion.

* * *

About eight o'clock, Conrad slipped into Sparky's, a female strip bar in downtown Windsor, Canada. His pals dragged him there for a stag party the week before he married Jade. It's time to live again, he thought as he handed over the cover charge.

At the bar he ordered his traditional highball and carried it to a table flanking the dance floor. The club was only dotted with customers at this early hour, strobe lights pulsating on the stage in time with classic rock numbers.

It was nice to be away. Nobody breathing down his neck. No decisions to make other than ordering the next drink. The thought of buxom beauties gyrating in his face aroused him. He swilled the whiskey and soda, coughing at the effervescence.

An hour later, the place was bristling with people. Mellow from the spirits, Conrad's eyes transfixed on a curvy blonde onstage, undulating her long body in time with the erotic music.

Half-crocked, Conrad's loins heated to attention.

A few highballs later, he left the joint. As he tottered toward his car, a blonde woman stepped out of the shadows.

"Need some help, doll?" Dressed in a mini skirt encasing her rear like a sausage skin, she slinked over to Conrad.

He leaned against the hood of his car. "I'm okay," he slurred.

"Better let me drive that dishy car, handsome."

He protested, shoving her away from him.

The woman shrieked. "I'll call the cops on you—" She tidied

her top over deep cleavage. "Have you arrested for assault." She stomped away, continuing her tirade.

Through his alcoholic stupor, Conrad thrust the key into the ignition, woozily managing the car out of the parking lot. Turning right, he crept down the street, slouching over the steering wheel so his bleary eyes were closer to the windshield.

He turned into the first parking lot and killed the motor. Quickly, he let the seat back and shut his eyes.

It was the last thing he remembered.

*   *   *

Awake again, Laura found a dinner of dry chicken and another scoop of mashed potatoes sitting on the tray table. It was eleven o'clock, and the food was cold. She switched on the late news and turned to the relief guard, who was munching on a bag of potato chips. "Maybe you could smuggle in some decent food for me."

Laura's ears perked at the mention of the Lazare name on the news. "Oh, God, Anglim's at it again." She turned up the volume.

Max Anglim was live in front of her illuminated house.

"I don't believe this. How dare he stir up the neighbors. Rosa will be worried."

Laura watched as Anglim outlined the hierarchy in the "Lazare Dynasty." A moment later she gasped, clapped her hand over her mouth, and pointed toward the television. "Those...those are my pictures."

The guard stood up.

"They're...from my photo album. Did Teddy steal them during the break-in?" He was hiding in Austin's closet where she kept the album, she remembered. Tears welled in her eyes. "It had to be Teddy. But why?" I must ask Rosa to check for the album.

The guard laid the chips aside.

She shook when a picture of her pushing Austin on a swing at the park appeared on the screen. "Teddy took that picture."

Next there was a shot of Laura and Marc posing with one year old Austin. Finally, the camera switched back to Max Anglim. "Laura Lazare is in the hospital recovering from a suspicious accident yesterday. Hospital officials list her in stable condition."

"Suspicious accident? My horse fell on me. Should we arrest the animal?"

Laura switched off the set, slid down in the bed, and wept.

*   *   *

Once the tally light went off, Max Anglim leaped into the air. Another scoop.

"Great work," the news director relayed over the two-way radio. "I don't know how you did it, but those pictures were fantastic."

"How *did* you do it?" Glen asked as he shut down the camera. "Where did you get those photos?"

Max extended his chest. "I told you, man, I have my ways. I received an envelope full of pictures. No return address, no explanation. Someone wants this case solved and hopes the media will press the issue."

Glen shook his head. "You worry me, Anglim."

Back at the television station, alone in his cubby, Max pulled a photo album out of a bottom drawer. Leafing through it, he studied a picture of Laura. That Emmy is mine.

*   *   *

The next morning, Conrad woke up, the left side of his face stuck to the leather seat. Squinting against the sunrise, head pounding, he brought the car seat back into position. It was then he noticed he was parked in a supermarket lot.

A worker was gathering carts, clanging the heavy metal.

Conrad winced, started the car, and pulled out of the parking lot.

"Jesus, I'm like a street person." Woozy and bloated, he sped down the empty street, crossed the Canadian border, and headed for home. He had enough of life in the fast lane. He called the office on his cell phone and told them he would be late.

When he pulled into the garage at home, Jade's car was gone. He was relieved to avoid another scene. I'll have time to shower, maybe even take a little nap.

In the kitchen, the refrigerator was almost empty except for a couple tubs of fat free yogurt and orange juice. He guzzled the juice from the pitcher. Tossing his crumpled tie on the table, he checked Jade's calendar. Today's date was empty.

"Then where in the hell is she?"

CHAPTER 15

Laura awakened from an agitated sleep to find Daisy seated beside the hospital bed. Achy from lying in one position all night, Laura felt ornery.

She switched on the television, quickly flipping through the channels before turning it off in disgust. "What's going on with your investigation?"

"Which one? The deaths or the explosion?"

"The explosion," Laura said dully.

"The ATF and the fire marshal are working on that one. It takes awhile to get the lab work back."

Laura fell back on her pillows. "What if Teddy set up that blast to kill Luc?"

"Why would he do that?"

"C'mon, Daisy. I know Teddy is one of your suspects in Marc's death. Then Luc dies, and someone breaks into my house and takes a photo album. I feel vulnerable here." Her eyes darted around the room.

"Teddy'll have to get past me," Daisy smiled warmly. "I'm not moving from this spot."

"Now it makes sense," Laura said, nodding. "Teddy was in that closet to get the pictures. That's why the door was closed. He probably didn't expect us home so early."

"I told you, Teddy has an alibi for the time of the break-in." Daisy shook her head. "Try to rest, Laura."

"Rest? I am so sick of resting in this position, I'm going stark-raving mad."

*   *   *

Quietly, Teddy let himself in the front door of his father's home. Silence as usual.

He headed toward the study to find Pierre.

Sure enough, the old man was swagged in his green chair, a glass of bourbon within reach. Without looking up he said, "None of this was supposed to happen."

"Get a hold of yourself, Father," Teddy said. "You're totally wasted!" He grabbed the drink off the table and dumped it into the bar sink.

"Damn it, Teddy!" Pierre waved his weakened arms at Teddy. "Where have you been?"

"Do you really care? You're drinking yourself to death. Haven't you done enough?"

Pierre struggled to focus on his youngest son. "What do you mean, boy?"

"It's your fault, Father. You always want the control. Was this your plan? Two sons dead?" Teddy slammed his hand down on a side table.

Pierre shrank back, his hands covering his face.

"Why don't you shoot me too, Father? You try to make the major decisions for all of us. Look what you've done."

Tears coursed down the old man's wrinkled face. "How did my sons get so far off track? All I wanted was family loyalty. Please, Teddy, try to see my side. We need unity in this investigation." He floundered in his chair, trying to gain the strength to stand.

"You lost me a long time ago. Now you can wallow in your alcohol...Father." Teddy stormed out the door.

*   *   *

Frustrated, Webb ground his foot into the accelerator as he headed to the station. "The only person I specifically know who has a video camera is Purp Strickland," he said to Samuel. "And he already played me the damn tape."

Slowing the car, he changed course and started toward the Detroit River. The heavy traffic hindered his pace. Finally, he turned into a parking area by the river and stopped the car.

"So, you pointed out the damn camera and now I know that Luc Lazare was blasted into a zillion pieces and splattered all over Lazare Fireworks. What does that have to do with Marc's murder?"

"Watch the fury."

Webb let out a long breath. "Why are you making this so damn hard?" He pounded the steering wheel. "I don't care who broke into Purp's bunker...unless, unless you're trying to tell me Luc killed Marc."

He leaned back in the seat breathing deeply. "God, Sam, I don't know how much more shit I can take. I'm really bushed." He closed his eyes, trying to relax his body and mind. Soon he slipped into oblivion. Within seconds he was asleep.

His body was a feather floating on a breeze, hovering here and there, devoid of all concerns. All outer racket ceased. Only a gentle presence surrounded him, cradling him in invisible arms. Slowly he sank deeper into trance.

He was on the fireworks launch barge. His eyes panned the length of the deck. Tubes were planted like crops in plywood boxes filled with sand. He checked the intricate wires. They looked fine. He backed away, drinking in a wider view. "Where's Sam?"

Instinctively, he turned around. Samuel was crouched near the railing twirling a videotape on top of one finger. Webb floated to Samuel's side and grabbed the tape. Violet sparks began to flicker from the cassette. He felt tranquil as he beheld the spectacular sight. Suddenly the tape erupted in brilliant purple fire, lapping up his arms, down his legs, engrossing his entire body in purple euphoria. The flames, though painless, seemed to burn into his very soul.

Webb jerked back to reality. Sitting upright, he examined his arms that moments ago were aglow with purple fire. He leaned his head against the car seat and shut his eyes, longing to relive the beauty of the dream. The outside traffic noises returned, nagging his efforts.

Eyelids squeezed tight, he took a deep breath. "Okay, Sam. Thanks for the fireworks. Purp is in charge of the color purple." Webb sat up suddenly. "There's another videotape in that house. Is that what you're trying to tell me?" He gunned the motor and headed to the courthouse for a warrant to search Harry Strickland's home.

* * *

Inside his office, Conrad, his hangover clanging in his head, stared at the cluttered desk before him. He dialed the house, but the answering machine picked it up. "Jade, call me at work when you get in," he said. "God, where is she?"

Without bothering to knock, Teddy burst into the office. "When is this nightmare going to end? I just left Father, and he's a mess. I told him it's all his fault."

Conrad winced. "God, Teddy, I have a huge headache. Sit down."

Teddy slumped into a chair, tears springing into his eyes.

"Don't be so hard on Father. This is no time for blame," Conrad said. "He did his best. You don't know all the details."

"What details?"

"Teddy!" Conrad ordered. "Chill out for now."

"Quit ordering me around, big brother." With that he was out the door.

Not bothering to grab his suit coat, Conrad, still a bit woozy, left the building and headed for his father's home. This could put him over the edge, he thought, and picked up speed.

Inside the house, Conrad hurried straight to the study. A bizarre scene greeted him.

Pierre was prostrated on the worn carpet, a shattered whiskey glass just beyond his palm.

"Father!" Conrad rushed to Pierre's side and felt his pulse. "Thank God, he's alive." He grabbed for the phone on the side table, but was overcome by a wave of nausea. Swallowing hard, he dialed for help.

The paramedics arrived quickly.

Numb, Conrad followed the stretcher to the ambulance.

* * *

Teddy's car screeched into the driveway at Laura's house. He bounded up the front steps and sounded the doorbell.

Rosa answered. Her eyes widened when she saw him. "Mr. Lazare? What are you doing here?" She clutched the edge of the door.

"Where is Laura?"

"She's in the hospital. Her horse threw her and she broke her leg."

"What's going on with this family?"

Rosa didn't answer.

Teddy said. "I need to talk to Laura."

"She's not taking visitors," Rosa said, fingering her collar nervously. "She's very upset."

Teddy turned to leave. "Aren't we all," he said. "Aren't we all."

* * *

The phone rang in Laura's hospital room. Daisy answered. "Detective Farrell? This is Rosa Perez. Teddy Lazare just left here. Without thinking, I told him Mrs. Lazare is in the hospital. He may be on his way there. I thought I should warn you."

"That's all we need," Daisy sighed

Laura looked up from her magazine.

"Oh, by the way, tell Mrs. Lazare I think I found her photo album," Rosa said.

"She'll be glad to hear that."

"After Austin's nap, I'll bring him over along with the album. Bye now."

Laura tossed the magazine aside. "Who was that?"

"Rosa found your photo album." Daisy pressed the nurse-call button. "I think it might be safer for you at home."

"I'd like that."

A nurse clipped into the room.

Daisy approached her. "Would you please contact the doctor and tell him Mrs. Lazare is going home?"

"The doctor is seeing patients at his office today, so it may take awhile for him to release her." She scooted out the door.

Daisy's mind began to race. I get the feeling Laura is afraid of Teddy for more than the break-in. Maybe I'm wrong, but for her peace of mind, we better keep him out of here.

"I'll be back in a few minutes," she said, and hurried to the nurse's station to call hospital security. "I want all doors manned, everyone required to show identification. If Teddy Lazare shows up, detain him and contact me in Laura Lazare's room."

* * *

By late afternoon, Conrad dragged into the kitchen at home. With his father stabilized in the hospital, he wanted to crash for a few hours. He flipped through the mail on the counter.

"Conrad, is that you?" Jade appeared from the family room. "Where have you been, darling?"

She ran her fingers over the stubble on his chin. "Out with Gillian."

Conrad pulled away. "I'm bushed."

She threw her arms around his neck, and whispered in his ear, "I've been thinking. Does Luc's death mean we'll split another five million dollar settlement?"

Conrad stiffened. "Is that all you think about? Two of my brothers are dead, Jade, and Father is in the hospital. He's drinking himself to death. I found him passed out this afternoon."

"I'm not surprised," Jade scoffed. "When you didn't come home last night I thought—"

"I'm overwhelmed at work. I was trying to...catch up."

"I called your office."

He grabbed his forehead. "I'm beat, Jade. I need to sleep."

She helped him up to their bedroom and went to draw a bath.

He undressed. His trousers slipped out of his weary hand onto the closet floor. He bent to retrieve them and saw several shopping bags stuffed under the shoe rack.

He seized the bags, tossed them onto the bed, and rummaged through the contents. There were clothes that added up to thousands of dollars.

His face crimson with anger, he grabbed the bags, charged into the bathroom and bellowed, "When did you buy all these clothes, Jade? Are you trying to ruin me?"

Jade jumped a foot. "Oh, honey," she cooed. "Don't get mad. I...I was gathering those things up to...to return them. You said I was spending too much money, and I was trying to do the right thing." She patted his cheek. "Come, love, get in the tub and I'll rub your shoulders." She turned on the jets. The water swirled and frothed.

"You better be telling the truth, Jade. I'm ready to crack. This stress is killing me." He dropped the bags beside the sink and gingerly stepped into the tub.

She placed scented candles around the edge of the Jacuzzi and lit each one, the spicy fragrance suffusing the room.

Conrad sank into the swirling bath. Jade began gently massaging his neck and shoulders. Yet he couldn't relax.

* * *

Webb pounded on the door at Purp's house. "Strickland! Open up."

The scraggly man appeared at the door, a sandwich in his grubby hand. "Did you show them investigators my tape?"

Webb pushed his way into the house. "I have a warrant to search these premises."

Purp's mouth fell open. "What for? I ain't done nothin' wrong."

"Then you have nothing to worry about. Did you forget to show me something last time I was here?"

Strickland glared at him.

"It's up to you, Purp. You can give it up and save everyone a lot of trouble. Otherwise, I'll search 'til I find it." He held up a warrant.

"You ain't goin' through my personal stuff," Purp raved and swung his hook at Webb's head.

Webb ducked, grabbed the prosthesis with both hands, and shoved the man out onto the porch. "This is a police investigation, Strickland," he yelled, breathing hard. "I'm not a Lazare brother."

Purp struggled, but Webb overpowered him. He forced the man against the porch railing, jumped back into the house, slammed and bolted the door.

Inside, Webb took a deep breath and glared at Samuel. He stalked the living room, unsure where to start. "Where in the hell is it?"

Samuel moved to the dining room, motioning for Webb to follow. The detective ignored him.

Webb's mind exploded. "Just show me the damn evidence!" He kicked a ceramic lamp off a table, inspecting the inside. Then he pulled out his army knife and plunged it through the worn fabric on a chair, slashing a large X. Clawing at the stuffing, he tore it apart, checking every detail.

Within fifteen minutes, the living room was destroyed, even the electric sockets pried off and inspected. Puffing from the exertion, Webb moved to the dining room.

Samuel slipped down a hall, waving to get Webb's attention.

The detective paused at the chest of drawers. He ripped out the top drawer, examining junk wire and electronic equipment. "What is it?" he shouted.

He leaned against the chest to catch his breath and looked around the room. It would take him hours to comb through the house. Undaunted, he plunged onward, tearing the kitchen apart, never pausing to check on Samuel.

As he began toppling cans from the cupboard, something strange happened. He felt a loving force embrace him. After a moment, he realized it was Samuel. Tears sprang to his eyes, and he slumped onto a kitchen chair.

"Come with me," Samuel said.

Slowly, Webb rose and followed the spirit guide down the dimly lit hallway, his heart hammering in his ears. Light-blocking shades darkened the bedroom. He yanked one up and saw Purp Strickland's face pressed against the window. He gasped. "Get back on the front porch," Webb shouted. "That's a police order."

Webb gazed around the unsightly room. The bed sheets were gray with neglect, probably not washed in months. The fetid odor sickened him. He gagged. Other than the bed and a rickety nightstand, the room was empty. He poked in the tiny closet but found only a few shabby clothes hanging from hooks.

Suddenly, Samuel guided his face to the window. Puzzled, Webb stared out at the yard. His eyes were drawn downward, below the windowsill. The plastic baseboard was loose. At that moment he knew instinctively something was hidden under that baseboard.

* * *

At the hospital, Laura picked at her lunch. She had lost ten pounds since Marc's murder. Food sickened her. She opened a cup of vanilla ice cream, but the sweetness turned her stomach. Daisy was busy at the bedside phone working on Laura's release.

Rosa bounded into the room carrying a bubbly Austin. "I smuggled him in."

"I want ice cream," Austin squealed.

Rosa plunked him down on the bed next to Laura, and the child dipped into the frozen treat. "Thank you for bringing him, Rosa. I missed my sweet boy." She nuzzled her nose in his soft hair.

"How is your leg, Mrs. Lazare?"

"Better. Daisy's trying to get me out of here."

"I'm sure you'll be much more comfortable in your own house. Austin will keep up your spirits."

Laura cuddled her child, wiping ice cream off his cheek.

Rosa brought out a photo album. "Is this the one you thought was missing?"

Laura's heart leaped when she saw the brown leather book "Where did you get this?"

"I found it in the basement when I was getting fruit jars. Thought I'd can some of those tomatoes. They're starting to turn red."

Laura's hands began to shake. She snatched the album from the housekeeper and thrust it under the covers. This was not the album that was missing. It was a special one nobody was supposed to see.

"Mommy, me see the book."

"Later, sweetie. Mommy wants to hold you. Are you being a good boy for your Rosa?"

He nodded and took another spoonful of ice cream.

Laura leaned back on the pillows. "I took some pain medication just before you came, and I'm feeling a bit woozy."

"We'll leave, Mrs. Lazare," Rosa said. "Shall I take the album back home?"

"No!" Laura splayed her fingers over the book. "I want to look through it. Thank you for coming and bringing Austin. Hopefully I can get out of here today."

Rosa lifted Austin off the bed. Laura blew him a kiss. "I love you, sweetheart. Mommy will be home real soon."

*   *   *

Webb dove to the floor, pulled the glued baseboard away from the crumbling plaster wall, and sure enough, he found a small hole. Gingerly, he poked his finger inside, feeling for hidden treasure.

Nothing.

He kicked at the wall with his heavy boots, plaster dust flying.

Leaving the bedroom, he went into the kitchen looking for something to break up the wall, and spotted a basement door. Creaking down the steps he switched on the lone light bulb. The place was cluttered with boxes and canisters, some marked *explosives*. On a messy workbench he found a heavy sledgehammer.

Back upstairs in the bedroom, he slammed the hammer against the hard plaster again and again. Finally the wall gave way.

He pushed his hand down through the powdery plaster, and pulled out a plastic box. Brushing it off, he whistled. "A videotape."

He fell back, leaning against the bed, trying to catch his breath.

*   *   *

After Rosa left, Laura grabbed the photo album from under the covers. How could she find this, of all things? I never should have saved it. She sank into the pillow.

Laura eyed Daisy across the room and drew in a long breath, wishing sleep would take over. She fumbled for the pain pump, but knew she had used the maximum.

Her heart began to pound. "Daisy, I need more pain medication."

"I'll get the nurse," Daisy said. "I just saw her out in the hall. If you ring, it'll take all day."

The moment Daisy left the room, panic seized Laura. Frustrated, she broke into tears and glued her eyes shut, trying to gain control.

A rustling sound startled her. Her eyes flew open.

Teddy stood at the door.

CHAPTER 16

WEBB BRUSHED plaster out of the hair on his arms, his heart a staccato drum beat in his chest. Surveying the wreckage, he looked at the gaping hole in the wall and debris strewn about on the floor. "God, Sam, look what I did. For once you actually tried to help me. Instead, I went berserk."

Clutching the cassette and breathing heavily, he stumbled from the bedroom, returned to the kitchen, and eyed the mess. He picked cans of vegetables off the floor and placed them on the table. Tucking the tape under his arm, he grabbed a broom and tried to sweep some of the mess into a corner.

Back in the living room he let out a long sigh and held up the plastic box. "The answer to this case must be on this tape." He felt it in his heart. Wading through the littered room, he opened the front door and found Purp slumped on the step, his head bowed.

"I found this," Webb said.

Purp looked up. His eyes widened when he saw the tape, but he said nothing.

Webb felt the man's eyes on him as he rushed to his car. The moment he backed out of the driveway, Webb saw Purp dash into the house.

* * *

At the hospital, Laura screamed. With her leg encased in elastic bandages, she was trapped in the bed.

A nurse and two aides rushed into the room.

Laura sputtered, pointing to the man standing at the foot of her bed. "He's trying to kill me!" she cried.

Laura's nurse said, "Sir, you're upsetting the patient. You'll have to leave."

Teddy protested. "What did I do? I'm here to visit."

Just then Daisy rushed into the room. She grabbed Teddy by the arm and pulled him toward the door.

Teddy shouted, "What are you doing? I have a right to know what's going on."

"Come with me, Mr. Lazare," Daisy said, and yanked him into the hall.

Laura collapsed onto the pillows in a torrent of tears.

When Daisy returned, she said, "Teddy promises to keep his distance, Laura. I told him if he comes near you again, I'll get a restraining order."

"I can't take this anymore," Laura wailed. "I'm having a nervous breakdown."

"You're going home," Daisy said. "To hell with the doctor."

The nurse stepped forward. "I can't allow this. You're breaking hospital rules if you leave without a release."

"Sorry about that," Daisy said. "The police rule now." She went to the closet and began gathering Laura's clothes. "Get a wheelchair," she ordered. "I have a car outside."

Once they reached home, Laura fretted. "Why can't you just arrest Teddy? He scared me to death."

Daisy shook her head and looked Laura straight in the eye. "I'm as frustrated as you are, but we have nothing on Teddy to tie him to the break-in at your house. Are you sure you told us everything you know about the Lazare family? I still feel like I'm missing something, especially about Teddy."

Laura turned away, avoiding Daisy's gaze. "I told you the truth. I don't know anything about Marc's murder. I admit I wasn't the best wife to him, but I certainly didn't want him dead."

Austin rushed into the room and hopped on his mother's lap. "Mommy, Mommy," he shouted with delight.

"Watch Mommy's leg, honey," Laura said. Moving him onto her good knee, she squeezed him close to her. Thank God for you, Austin. You're my only island in this sea of misery.

*   *   *

Webb was relieved Fred Gallister was out of the office so he could use his VCR. He stole into the room, closed the blinds on the glass wall, and locked the door. He wanted to view this tape alone. Solving a murder was like putting the finishing touches on a fine painting. He intended to savor it.

With shaking hands he placed the tape in the machine and pressed play. A field with a large gully dug in the middle flashed on the screen. Nothing happened for fifteen seconds. Then a fiery missile launched into the air and exploded with violet brilliance.

Purp's voice rang out. "Goddamn! Needs more red."

Webb leaned forward. "Purple fireworks! That was in my dream." He moved closer to the television screen and watched in awe as another plume of purple burst against the darkening sky. It was the same enchantment he felt at the Fourth of July show during the segment with *Purple Rain.*

"Okay, Sam," Webb said, gritting his teeth. "I know you led me to this tape for a reason. That looks like the field behind Purp's house. It's illegal to launch fireworks in a residential area."

Webb pressed fast forward through twenty different purple explosions until he reached the end of the tape.

He clicked it off, staring straight ahead. "That's it?" Webb kicked the desk in frustration. "This tape isn't worth shit! Why the hell did he hide it? The guy must be nuts."

He looked at the clock. "All this time wasted on a bunch of crap." He pounded on the desk and kicked over the wastebasket. Jumping up, he closed in on Samuel. "What do you want from me? I've done everything you asked. I followed every lead and hunch and I have NOTHING!"

In a fit of fury, Webb punched at Samuel's face. His fist whisked through the air and slammed against the window, shattering it in an avalanche of falling glass. He jerked his hand away, blood oozing from a cut on his palm. "Good God! I want you out of my life." He grabbed a handkerchief from his pocket and held it to the bleeding wound. "I mean it, Sam. I don't believe in you anymore. Your so-called guidance led me to another big fat dead end." He felt totally drained and longed to head for the nearest bar and drown in booze.

Someone rattled the doorknob, then pounded on the door.

Webb released the lock and Jake Rubel bounded in. "What's going on in here? I heard breaking glass." Rubel eyed the broken window.

"It's all a bunch of bullshit," Webb spat. "Everything about this case is frigging worthless."

"What got a burr up your butt?"

"I just ripped apart Purp Strickland's house for nothing."

Rubel spotted the glowing television. "So, you're looking at secret videotapes again. What's on this one?"

"Not a damn thing," Webb expounded. "Listen, Rubel. You always wanted this case. Well, it's yours." He slammed his fist against a file cabinet. "I'm sick of the whole thing."

"What does the tape have to do with the case?"

Webb tossed it to him. "See for yourself if you're interested in fireworks."

Rubel shoved the tape back in the machine, rewound it, and pressed play.

An unfamiliar scene appeared. Webb shook his head. "What's going on here?" He looked at Samuel in confusion. "This looks like the fireworks barge Max Anglim had in his video." God, don't tell me I started in the middle of the tape.

Rubel pulled up a chair. "Who is that pacing back and forth in front of those bombs?"

Webb jumped to attention. "Looks like Marc Lazare." He moved closer.

On the tape, Marc, obviously upset, went to the rail and gazed out over the river. When he turned around, facing the camera, his expression was desperate. He reached for the rail and clung to it, shaking his head. Tears coursed down his cheeks. His chin trembled.

"That guy's hurtin'," Rubel said.

"Sure looks like it," Webb agreed.

Marc floundered back and forth for another minute. Then he fumbled in the pocket of his jeans and shakily pulled out a pistol.

"Christ, he's got a gun," Rubel declared.

"The Smith and Wesson," Webb said, his voice escalating.

Slowly, his hand trembling so badly the picture appeared distorted, Marc brought the gun up under his chin.

Rubel leaped in the air. "He's gonna' shoot himself!"

Webb froze to the spot.

Both Webb and Rubel jumped when the gun went off with a deafening bang.

Rubel shouted, "He committed suicide!" As the body fell, the camera clicked off, and Rubel pressed pause.

"I solved the case. It's right here on the tape," Rubel sneered. "Or were you trying to hide it from me so you'd get all the credit?"

Webb ignored him. "Keep going. There could be more."

As the pause button released, someone else entered the scene. Conrad Lazare. He caught sight of the body and gasped.

Rushing over to his brother, he declared, "My God, Marc. What have you done?" He bent down and the camera switched off. When he stood up, it clicked on again. Conrad held the gun in his hand. He burst into tears.

A moment later, Luc Lazare showed up. He took one look at Conrad with the gun and Marc lying at his feet. "You bastard! You shot your own brother?"

Conrad whirled around, trying to hide the gun behind his back. "I...I didn't do it," Conrad protested. "He killed himself."

"Like hell he did," Luc raged and lunged at his brother, knocking the gun out of his hand. The two men scuffled and fell to the ground. The camera clicked off again.

When it came back on, both brothers were on their feet, Conrad's shirt torn, Luc's hair mussed.

Without a word, they took hold of Marc's arms, laboriously dragged his body and draped it over one of the bombs.

"That bullet will blow with his brains," Luc said sardonically. "Nobody should notice the body way out here before the launch. Come on, let's split."

As they hurried away, the camera clicked off.

Gallister burst into the office. "Mind if I enter my own territory? My God, what happened to the window?"

"The murder is solved," Rubel gushed. "I found the evidence."

"What?"

"Marc Lazare committed suicide," Rubel announced, glowing with pride. "And his brothers, Conrad and Luc, put the body over the mortar tubes to make it look like an accident."

Webb sucked in a deep breath and leaned back in the chair.

"Holy shit!" Gallister declared, turning to Webb. "Where did you find this tape?"

"Hidden in Harry Strickland's house," Webb replied. "I knew he had a video camera. He used it to catch Luc at his bunker."

"How did you know he taped the crime scene?"

Webb cleared his throat. "Just a hunch. Call it cop intuition," he said, and winked at Gallister.

Samuel pointed to the VCR.

"What? Roll the tape again Rubel. I think there's more."

Gallister moved close to the set and all three watched as the camera switched on again, this time inside a dark room. In dim light, Webb recognized Purp busy at a work table.

"This must be inside Purp's bunker," Webb said.

"Welcome to my special bunker," Purp narrated to the camera. "Home of the magnificent Purple Flame." He shook a chemical from a jar onto the work surface. "Not too much." Carefully he scraped the remains back into the canister. Sweat drippled down his forehead, and he swiped at it with his sleeve before it ran onto his creation.

Next he pulled out two sheets of paper-thin copper.

"Looks like some kind of wire hanging off each of those sheets," Webb said, leaning toward the television.

Purp attached the two wires to separate terminals on top of a six-volt battery.

"Perfect!" he declared with a sinister smile to the camera.

With white glue, he stuck a small piece of sponge to the middle of one copper sheet, then sandwiched the second sheet on top.

Holding it up to the camera lens, he carefully showed all angles. "The sponge holds the copper sheets apart just a smidge. But a simple human touch will connect the sheets, completing an electric circuit."

"Zap!" he shouted with diabolical delight.

"I'm usin' liquid solder here to attach another wire to one of the copper sheets. It leads to this small bunch of steel wool." He held up the tiny mass for the camera. "From the steel wool, just gotta connect a second wire to the negative terminal of the battery." He let out a laugh.

"Ignition!" Purp yelled. "When the circuit is completed, it'll send an electric current down the wire and heat the steel wool red hot." Purp set a thin piece of plywood on top of the copper sheeting. "This will cover my handiwork. He won't even notice it. And when he leans on the board—Poof! The chemicals explode and Luc is history. I picked my best purple for your delight, you bastard."

Gallister clicked off the VCR. "Damn!"

"I discovered it, Chief," Rubel chattered. "Hannis gave up and turned the case over to me."

Webb's mouth curled into a vague smile as he stared at the dark television screen.

"Looks like we need to make some arrests," Gallister said.

Webb headed to Lazare Fireworks. Rubel followed in a squad car.

Webb gave Samuel a sheepish smile "I made a real ass of myself, didn't I, Sam?"

"You're here to learn."

"Purp sure did like his Panasonic video camera. It looks like he set it on motion detector and hid it on the barge to spy on the brothers. He was probably paranoid Luc would purposely mess up his purple segment in the show. This is better than an eye-witness account. That was damn stupid of him to tape himself setting up that booby trap for Luc. Why in the hell would he do that?"

"Purp's ego is way out of control. In fact, he's only a step away from madness." Samuel said. "He played that tape over and over, basking in his own brilliant scheme before he hid it."

"Why did I have to go through hell when you knew I would eventually find the tape and see what really happened? It would have been so much simpler for you to tell me in the first place. We could have made the arrests weeks ago."

"God works things out in his own time, Webb. Your ego wanted the case solved earlier. God had the ultimate plan."

"Why now?"

"If you had arrested Harry Strickland before this, he never would have perfected his purple flames."

"So what?"

"Harry was guided by Saint Germain, an ascended master. Saint Germain is the keeper of the purple flame."

"Now you're getting into that kooky stuff again."

"Do you think God is kooky?"

"You know what I mean. Purple flames?"

"It's a high frequency spiritual energy. Saint Germain is an alchemist and anyone can tap into his purple flames for healing, relaxation, or enlightenment. God wanted the world to see Saint Germain's masterful purple flames. It will, now that the formula belongs to the Lazares. If you had arrested Purp sooner, Bud, he couldn't have completed his work. Harry listens well. He was guided to perfect his creation. Unfortunately, he couldn't resist following his ego as well. It will get you into trouble every time."

Webb remembered the adrenaline flow he felt as violet sparks ignited the sky on the Fourth of July to the tune of Prince's *Purple Rain.*

A car in front of Webb slowed to turn right, his signal flashing. The detective jammed his foot on the brakes. "Asshole!" he shouted. He started to zoom around the offending vehicle.

Samuel cleared his throat.

Abruptly Webb let up on the pedal. "Sorry." The other driver eyed him in the rearview mirror. Webb waved, smiling. "I guess I'm right where I'm supposed to be."

*   *   *

Revived by the Jacuzzi session, Conrad went into work. "I hope Jade was telling the truth about returning those clothes. If not, I'll do it myself. This senseless spending must stop." He slumped at his desk, reluctant to listen to his voice mail. What if that maniac called again? The thought of paying that bastard every month was too much to bear.

He fingered the papers in front of him. This property damage is going to set us back plenty. By the time we get the money from Marc's insurance, if we ever get it, we'll need to plow it back into Lazare Fireworks to save the business. Of course Luc's insurance will kick in too. Another violent death, another five million dollars. He swiveled around and finally peered out the window at the blackened earth. His head began to pound, and he reached in a drawer for aspirin.

* * *

Within the half-hour, Webb and Rubel pulled up to Lazare Fireworks and barged into Conrad's office.

"We have a warrant for your arrest, Lazare," Rubel bellowed, smiling slyly.

Conrad's mouth fell open. "For what? Surely you don't think I blew up my own business."

"We have Marc's suicide on videotape," Rubel said. "You and Luc covered it up by dumping the body over a mortar tube."

Webb sighed. "Just read him his rights, Rubel."

Conrad leapt up and leaned against the desk. "How—"

"You have the right to remain silent," Rubel began.

"I know my rights," Conrad raged. "I want to know where you got a tape."

"Anything you say may be used against you."

Conrad slipped around the desk and came forward. "I demand to know where you got that tape!"

Webb stepped in front of him. "If you come along calmly, we won't cuff you," he said. "We'll explain everything at the station."

Conrad shrank back and stood silently while Rubel droned out the Mirandas. Afterwards the two detectives led him through the reception area.

His secretary looked up from her computer. "Is anything wrong, Mr. Lazare?"

Conrad shook his head. "I'll be out for the rest of the day," he said in a near whisper.

* * *

Back at the station, Webb and Rubel sat Conrad at a table in one of the interrogation rooms.

Samuel lolled in the background.

Rubel glared at Lazare. "Was the insurance money too enticing?"

"We did it for the business. I swear. My father took out that policy about fifteen months ago. The policy is void in case of suicide during the first two years." Conrad's face was flushed. He loosened his tie. "The company was in bad straits under Marc's management. We needed that money to save the business."

"Well, I have news for you, Lazare," Rubel cackled, his mouth twisted into a wicked smile. "There won't be any money...from either death. I made a few inquiries, and it seems the old man canceled the policy on Luc after he refused to take over the company."

Conrad paled.

Rubel continued, a gleeful glint in his eye, "Looks like your little scheme backfired. The body obviously shifted. What did you do with the gun?"

Conrad covered his face with his hands.

"Answer the question, Mr. Lazare," Rubel demanded.

Slowly Conrad looked up, his chin trembling. "I need a glass of water."

Webb turned to Rubel. "Get the man a soda."

"Why don't you? I'm conducting this case now," Rubel sneered.

Webb grabbed Jake by the collar, dragged him out of the room, and pulled the elf's face up to his. "Get Lazare a soda, Rubel, or I'll kick your butt up through your navel."

Samuel shook his head at Webb.

Rubel jerked away and adjusted his collar. "Watch it, Hannis. You better not question him any further without me." He trotted away.

Back inside the room Webb said, "So, you picked up the gun when you found Marc's body?"

"I was so shocked, I wasn't thinking. Luc caught me with it in my hand. I guess I can't blame him for thinking I killed Marc. We fought...I mean with fists. Hadn't done that since we were kids."

"Well, on the tape, it seems you made up pretty quickly," Webb said. "He helped you put the body over the tubes."

"I explained the situation about the insurance. Luc wanted to start his own business and get away from the family. He needed that money, too. What did we have to lose? Marc was dead either way."

Rubel returned and plunked the pop can in front of Conrad.

Lazare opened it and gulped down half of the drink. He rubbed his eyes.

"Why did Luc leave town?" Webb asked.

"I think he panicked when you found that bullet in Marc's brain. Taking over Lazare Fireworks was too much pressure with father always looking over his shoulder. Luc wanted his own business."

Webb rubbed his chin. "Do you know why Marc committed suicide?"

"Father insisted he run the company. Marc was a poor man-ager. He just wanted to work with the chemicals. He was proud of his red bunker."

Rubel scribbled furiously on a legal pad. "You're going too fast for me to take notes."

Webb patted his recorder. "I'm taping it, Rubel. You can relax." He turned back to Conrad. "Go on, Mr. Lazare."

"Marc hated running the business," Conrad said. "Within a short time the books were messed up. All he needed to do was ask me for help. It certainly wasn't a reason to kill himself." Conrad cursed under his breath. "I had those books in order within a month."

"Where did Marc get the gun?"

"From Father's collection. I cleaned it up and sneaked it back into his gun case, but somehow Father discovered it had been fired. I know he was sick wondering if one of his own sons killed Marc. I'm sure that's why he was drinking so heavily."

"What about Teddy? Why was Laura afraid of him?"

"I have no idea. Teddy is a kid. He didn't have anything to do with Marc's death."

Webb clicked off the recorder and stood up.

"Wait," Conrad said. "There's more." He told the detectives about the phone call demanding blackmail money. "I guess it was Purp. He's the only other person who saw what really happened. The tape from the answering machine is in my bottom desk drawer."

"We have a lot on old Purp," Webb said. "He rigged the explosion that killed Luc."

Conrad's face fell. He looked away.

"That's all I need for now," Webb said and headed for the door.

"Wait a minute. I have more questions," Rubel said, waving his pen in the air.

Webb turned and left.

* * *

At Laura Lazare's house, Webb jumped out of the car, dashed up to the porch, and walked in the front door without knocking.

"Webb?" Daisy called from the living room.

Webb strolled in and saw Laura sitting with her leg propped on pillows. He nodded to her and pulled up a chair.

Samuel was content to sit still and listen.

"The case is solved," Webb said. "We know what happened to your husband, Mrs. Lazare." He told them about the tape and what it revealed.

Laura looked ashen when Webb described Marc's suicide.

"You told us you had words that day," Webb said. "But Conrad says Marc was having trouble with the business, too." Tears streamed down Laura's face. "No, it was all my fault," she cried. "I'm sick and tired of secrets. They're eating me alive." Daisy stroked Laura's arm. "You'll feel better when you tell us everything."

"Marc was so sensitive. I never should have told him."

Webb leaned forward. "Told him what?"

"He was overwrought with the Fourth of July show, fearful something would go wrong. I was so damn sick of everything. Tired of his weak ways, his complaining, his lack of attention to me." She buried her head in her hands.

"I should have realized how much Austin meant to him." She grabbed a tissue. "Daisy, can you get me that photo album we brought home from the hospital?"

Daisy fetched the book.

"I loved Marc when we first met. He was so kind and honest. But after we married, he worked all the time. His father walked all over him and that really griped me. When Pierre decided to retire and insisted Marc take over, things got worse. Marc lived in hell, fearing his poor management would bankrupt the company." Laura looked from Webb to Daisy.

"I'm so ashamed, but I was bored. Teddy was filled with youthful vitality. We began riding horses together, playing tennis, swimming. Teddy had everything Marc lacked. By the time Teddy was eighteen, we were having an affair."

The tears flowed. "When I got pregnant, Marc was ecstatic. I knew it wasn't his child. I was thankful the brothers looked so much alike. Austin is definitely a Lazare, but he's Teddy's son, not Marc's."

Webb and Daisy exchanged glances.

"We carried on the affair for four wondrous years. I kept this album so I could show Austin one day." She leafed through the book filled with pictures of Laura and Teddy. There were a few of the two with baby Austin.

"I was going to ask for a divorce when Teddy graduated from college. I planned to tell him Austin was his son at that time. But during his last year at school, Teddy cooled. He was enjoying the single party life at Purdue while I was back in Detroit with all the responsibilities. I was afraid he was losing interest.

"On the Fourth of July, I was mad at the world. My grand plans for the future seemed to be falling apart. I told Marc I wasn't going to the fireworks. He was such a weakling, he didn't protest. It ticked me off. I wanted to hurt him and force him to show some emotion. Any emotion." Laura hung her head.

"In a rage I bragged about my affair with his brother, and out of sheer spite, told him that Teddy was Austin's father." Laura began to sob. "He...he broke down and cried," she wailed. "I saw emotion all right. Devastation. I might as well have pulled the trigger on that gun," she sobbed.

"I was consumed with guilt. Then Teddy showed up after Marc stormed out of the house." She looked down at her hands, examining her nails.

Daisy took a deep breath. "What happened next?"

"Teddy talked me into attending the show. Said he had something to tell me. On the way to the river, he announced he was breaking off the affair for good. Said his conscience bothered him about duping his brother. By the time we got to the parking lot at the fireworks, I was furious. I stormed out of the car. Teddy still doesn't know he has a son."

Daisy shifted in her chair and smoothed her slacks.

"After Marc died, I expected Teddy would come back to me," Laura said, her voice breaking. "Oh, he was cordial. But he suddenly acted like the loyal little brother. He had a case of the guilts and was taking it out on me. Then the explosion at Lazare Fireworks and Luc's death. I freaked out when I got that strange phone call, and someone broke into the house. I was paranoid. I thought Teddy was after me. I even feared he might have murdered Marc and Luc. My mind blew everything out of proportion." She breathed a sigh. "I'm really relieved to know he's not involved in either death. But if Teddy didn't break into my house, who did?"

"We're still investigating," Webb said. "At this point we're clueless."

Austin bolted into the room. "Mommy, when can I go ride my pony?"

Laura wiped her nose with the tissue. "Not for a while, precious. But when Mommy's leg is healed, we'll have lots of special time together."

Webb and Daisy rose to leave.

"We're going now, Mrs. Lazare," Webb said. "I suggest you get some rest. The media is merciless. They'll hound you."

"Perhaps before you go, Detective Hannis, you can help me get upstairs to my bedroom," Laura said. "I'm very tired."

Webb picked up the slender woman in his arms, and, without effort, climbed the stairs.

Austin giggled and hopped ahead of them.

Rosa met them at the top. "I have your room ready, Mrs. Lazare. Take a nap, and I'll tend to Austin."

Webb carried Laura to her bed and set her down gently, careful to mind the injured leg.

Daisy motioned to him. "I'm through here. Let me get my things together."

He followed her into the guest bedroom.

She slid a suitcase out from under the bed and started to pack.

"What a family," Webb whispered.

"Laura seems genuinely sorry for what she did," Daisy said as she folded a nightie. "I wonder how 'spoiled brat Teddy' will take the news that he's a father?"

"Who knows how these people would react to anything? They're from another planet...a world where things blow up." He winked at Daisy.

"So Samuel came through for you after all." Daisy snapped the suitcase closed and dragged it off the bed. "I wish I could talk to my spirit guide."

Webb winked over her shoulder at Samuel and grabbed Daisy's suitcase. "Your Aunt Phoebe says all of us can talk with our guides. Remember?"

"I guess both of us need to learn more about listening," Daisy said. She swatted his arm. "Want to grab some dinner?"

"Maybe later. I'd better get back to the station and make out a report on what Laura told us before Rubel gets on me again. I still feel like hell about ruining Purp's house. Now we have to arrest the old guy for murder."

They left the room and started downstairs.

"Why did Purp hide that tape? He could have deleted his murder plot and nailed the brothers early on."

"That's true. But remember he made that threatening call to Conrad. I think he was trying to extort money from the company as well as have control over his latest creation."

"Don't tell me," Daisy teased. "Something in purple."

"Something spectacular in purple," Webb replied. "According to Sam, God's masterpiece."

When Daisy and Webb stepped onto the front porch, the sidewalk swarmed with curious neighbors. The Channel Three news van was parked across the street.

In the middle of the yard, Max Anglim stood center stage, aiming his microphone at Jake Rubel's babbling mouth. "Tell us about the big break in the Lazare Case," Max said, grinning.

Rubel beamed into the camera. "I discovered the evidence on a videotape—"

"On second thought, I think I'm in the mood for that dinner after all," Webb said.

He took Daisy by the arm and led her out to the car.

EPILOGUE SIX MONTHS LATER

MAX ANGLIM and Glen Gerard sat at a round table in the historic Ford Theater. A giant Emmy statuette gleamed from the stage. Max tapped his foot on the carpet, irritated as a longwinded reporter gushed out her acceptance speech. "Our category is next," he whispered to Glen. I know I won, he thought. Nobody had more information on the Lazare cases. I even beat the newspaper.

Suddenly, the announcer's voice on stage claimed his attention. "The second nominee for Best Spot News Coverage is Max Anglim of Channel Three News—"

Max puffed out his chest. He thought back to that day at Marc Lazare's house when he stole Laura's album and was forced to hide in Austin's closet when she came home early. Sorry. I didn't mean to scare you, but the Emmy is mine.

"And the Emmy goes to," the announcer slowly opened the envelope. "Max Anglim—"

Max floated up onstage.

* * *

Webb sat at his desk hunched over the morning paper when Daisy poked her head in. "Want to grab some lunch?"

"I'm gonna order a carry out," he said. "I have work to do."

"Okay, catch you later."

Perched on the windowsill, Samuel twirled the Venetian blind cord around in circles.

"I see here in the news the chic Conrad Lazare will be wearing an orange jumpsuit for a few years," Webb said. "He pleaded guilty to avoid a jury trial.

"Harry Strickland won't be so lucky. His own videotape will hang him." Webb laid the paper aside. "Tell me, Sam, if he was guided by this spirit Saint Germain, why did he plan a murder?"

"If he had just stuck with the original plan he would have reaped the rewards of his Purple Flame. Instead, he fell for the ego's plan, and tried to force things for his sole benefit."

"So now he rots in prison?"

"It's a chance for him to understand where he went wrong. The universe is always in balance, Bud." Samuel shook his head. "Everyone has a chance to make amends. If they don't realize their mistake in this lifetime, God will offer endless opportunities later. It's amazing how long it takes some souls to learn."

Webb eyed the guide. "Okay, Sam. This is it. My headaches are gone, and I'm back on track now. You're free to leave. Maybe then I can have a little privacy again."

"Oh, I can't leave until we finish with this." Samuel patted the black book, Webb's name in golden letters gleaming in the sunlight. "We have a contract, Bud. I'm here, you steer."

Webb groaned.

Samuel smiled.

AFTERWORD

Since Jill and I began living the exciting concepts explained in this book, our lives have changed dramatically. The former worry and moments of despair have been replaced with tranquility and joy. Now we know it's as simple as changing our thoughts.

Of course, this didn't happen over night. It took six long years to live, learn and write the concepts in this novel. Now Fred and Daisy are like our best friends. It's a joy to use our natural psychic gifts. I only wish I knew this years earlier when I was raising my five children. Unfortunately, in the past, our society frightened people away from using their innate spirituality. Now that Jill and I no longer need societal approval for how we think or act, we know from within why we are on the earth and what is right for us.

Jill introduced her children to their spirit guides at a young age, and they speak freely about their guidance. She is raising them to know this is normal and fun.

Mystery writing is an exciting adventure and I am blessed to share it with my talented daughter, Jill. The integrity of the mystery is crucial to us; thus we research our books carefully.

But the spiritual messages now take center stage. Through daily journaling with Fred and Daisy, plus a clever writing guide named Carlos, we are told *Fireworks* is the first in a series of five books utilizing the Webb Hannis character in teaching spiritual truths.

At present we are completing books two and three, with Jill dreaming the endings. We still struggle with the spiritual messages. Jill's own impatience and frustration was forged upon poor Webb Hannis. Many of the synchronicities that happen to our detective happened to us.

Learning to live and utilize the concepts is an ongoing process. Jill dreamed the title for book four, but we have no idea what the plot line or spiritual concept will be. However, we trust it will be delivered in God's perfect time and way.

Now it is time for you to begin your own journey of discovery. Start by talking to your guide as though you already know him or her. Don't be afraid; this is normal stuff. Just like Samuel told Webb, "Ask a question, let it go and expect an answer." Just don't try to figure out what that answer will be. God and your guides can always figure out something much more magical.

The first time you notice a synchronicity, you will rejoice and feel special and blessed. Always look for the coincidences no matter how tiny they seem to be. The more you notice, the more synchronicity multiplies. This will bring enchantment into your life every day. Jill and I hope, through these books, to offer this same magic to the world.

Do write and share your amazing synchronicities with us. We plan to write a book using these examples in the future.

Edna Mae Holm

Please write to Jill at:

Stargate Press
P.O. Box 6535
Saginaw, MI 48608-6535

Or E-mail her at: Jill@stargatepress.com

Photograph by Todd Joyce, Cincinnati

ABOUT THE AUTHORS

JILL WELLINGTON was a journalist for more than eighteen years, starting in radio and eventually reporting television news for fourteen years. The recipient of two Michigan Emmy nominations and numerous reporting awards, she also wrote a weekly humor column for two local newspapers.

An avid photography, computer junkie and scrapbooker, Jill is also an accomplished seamstress and drapery maker.

Born in South Bend, Indiana, she moved with her family to Detroit and eventually Cincinnati, Ohio. Jill now resides in Saginaw, Michigan with her husband Mark and children Lindsay and Mark.

EDNA MAE HOLM was a professional singer for twenty-five years. She taught modeling for eight years before opening a women's specialty clothing shop. While a successful business owner for twenty years, she also wrote a humorous newspaper column for three local newspapers.

Born and raised in Kenosha, Wisconsin, Edna Mae and her husband Bob moved to Cincinnati, Ohio thirty-six years ago and raised five children.

Edna Mae and Jill are also Reiki facilitators.